Beautiful, talented, glamorous—why did Elspeth Esker, when her famous husband died, go into such a tailspin of bitterness and withdrawal? Why did she reject her gifted and worldly brother and sister, when they had always been a trio against the world—ahead of it, laughing at it, leading it on? What was there so far beyond normal grief in this death one winter afternoon? This was the problem that confronted Sebastian, the dead man's brother, when he was summoned back from his studies in Europe. His search, and the struggle to recapture Elspeth's spirit, leads him in pursuit of his brother's character through a rich gallery of personal encounters. Among these the good people of a small New England town, of the kind so familiar to Mrs. White's readers already, contribute most warmth and shed the final light.

But meanwhile, in a city world where the author has not taken us before, and where she shows herself to be equally at home, the brother and sister of Elspeth lead their own cosmopolitan lives, surrounded by a circle of lively friends engaged in the arts and professions. This is a happy bringing together of two worlds, in each of which Mrs. White's instinct for human relationships has full play. This story, charged with deep emotions that are revealed through those telling touches of character she is so adept at portraying, will satisfy her large and devoted audience, which has grown with each of the books produced by this novelist of increasing stature.

THE THORN TREE

ALSO BY NELIA GARDNER WHITE

DAUGHTER OF TIME

BROOK WILLOW

NO TRUMPET BEFORE HIM

THE PINK HOUSE

WOMAN AT THE WINDOW

THE MERRY MONTH OF MAY

THE SPARE ROOM

THE Thorn Tree

a novel by

NELIA GARDNER WHITE

New York · 1955

THE VIKING PRESS

FIRST PUBLISHED BY THE VIKING PRESS IN APRIL 1955

PUBLISHED ON THE SAME DAY IN THE DOMINION OF CANADA

BY THE MACMILLAN COMPANY OF CANADA LIMITED

The translation of the song from the Tahitian folk tale
on page 80 is by Ralph Gardner White.

Library of Congress catalog card number: 55-7375

PRINTED IN THE U.S.A. BY THE COLONIAL PRESS INC.

THE THORN TREE

1

IN THE chill of the late November afternoon Marcy and David Doorn stood beside their sister's house. They had come in frantic haste, in their hearts identical sensations of fear, incredulity, horror. They had walked up and down, up and down, in some village, waiting for a car repair, unable to talk, desperately anxious to have the repairs done, to be on their way again. Now they were here, but for a moment they stood, thrust out by some curious silence that surrounded the house, took in the whole landscape. Across the road rose a slope where once sheep had grazed. There were no sheep now, no leaves, no sign of life anywhere. All that the hill pasture held was thorn trees, with their innumerable gray and ghostly branches.

"I'd forgotten how forlorn it was," Marcy said.

Once on the way David had said, "Do you have to wear that suit? It's viciously ugly." She had looked down at the rough purple of her plaid skirt with its gold bars and said, "It suits me." Once she had said, "But the phone. Why doesn't she answer the phone?" And once she had said, "The papers lay there all night." All night she had slept so soundly, and in the morning there the pile of papers had been, and she had opened the oldest first and seen John's picture. "John Esker, noted young composer . . ."

"She knew it was the week end in Virginia. She even talked of coming too," Marcy had said blankly. And that was all. In the town where they had waited, walked and walked, David had gone into the drugstore and, without saying what he intended, tried once more to call the farm. He came out and fell into step with her again, silent.

Three against the world, that defined the Doorns. Marcy and David turned abruptly now and walked toward the door, though the house itself looked as lifeless as the hill pasture. "She's not here," David said with conviction.

"Where would she be?" Marcy asked helplessly, but she saw, with fresh panic, Elspeth climbing the stairs in town, finding silence, finding them gone. She lifted the latch in sharp urgency, and they walked in. The room confirmed their conviction. It was silent, empty. The gray ghostliness of the thorn trees had crept in with them.

They stood there an instant—Marcy, the dark, gypsyish Doorn, in her purple suit, and David, the charming, clever one who looked so like a lazy angel, but was no angel—and they saw all the familiar things: the small sofa by the hearth, the books, the blue plates on the shelf, the cream-and-pale-blue rug before the sofa—all unfamiliar, grayed out. There were no flowers. They had never come into the house before without seeing flowers. Elspeth could take even weeds, a branch of berries, and make something charming and strange come to life in her rooms. There were no flowers now, nothing but this strange silence that denied the presence of anyone but themselves in the house.

"Elspeth! Oh, Elspeth!" Marcy called out, her voice too loud, knowing there could be no answer. The Doorns always came running at the sound of one another's voices.

But silence would have been more comprehensible than the calm, unhurried voice of Elspeth coming from the kitchen. "Yes?"

David put a hand on Marcy's arm. His touch said: Hold it! Don't panic. I'm here.

They walked quickly to the kitchen, to the voice, to a sight they had never expected to see. She might be ill, she might be stricken with grief—that they had thought. But this? Elspeth, the most beautiful, the most talented, the most worldly of the talented, beautiful, worldly Doorns, sat at the old-fashioned round kitchen table with a Bible before her. She looked up but made no move toward them, gave them no greeting, and her hands on the edges of the Bible did not stir. She had on a white blouse and a familiar brown velveteen skirt, but in her face was no trace of the vividness that was the true source of her beauty. A mighty hand might as well have stopped Marcy and David in their tracks, held them powerless.

"What are you doing?" Marcy demanded.

"I'm looking for God," Elspeth said.

David's hand tightened on Marcy's arm, but she said hotly, "*God?* Have you lost your mind?"

"I hope so," Elspeth said. "It's time I did."

"Elspeth!" David said. "What's the matter with you? Why in heaven's name didn't you let us know? Why aren't you answering your phone? What *happened?*"

"Happened?" Elspeth said vaguely. "Why, I came in—and John was dead."

All the Doorns had a thin veneer of madness, their friends would say; but underneath they were eminently sane. One and all, they were artists, but artists who made art pay. This was no veneer.

"But why didn't you tell us? How could you let us see it in a paper? Elspeth, you're scaring me so my teeth are shaking," Marcy cried. "Look, get your things together—or don't even bother. You're coming home with us. You can't stay here. It'll be winter any day now. You can't stay here alone, even if you find God to keep you company."

"But I haven't found Him yet," Elspeth said. She looked down again at the book before her, dismissing them, putting them out of her mind. If the house had put up a wall against them, this stranger sitting there with the face of Elspeth, but not Elspeth, raised it infinitely higher.

"Where's John buried?" David put in baldly.

"In the village," Elspeth said, not looking up.

It was fantastic, this conversation. The three of them had gone skating together the day after their mother was buried. But they had been together, pooled their grief.

Marcy drew away from David's touch, dropped down to a chair across the table from Elspeth. David remained standing, but he put a hand on the back of Marcy's chair, and she was glad for even that protection against this dreadful unfamiliarity. She began to talk, swiftly, protestingly, knowing that this was not the time for words, that she wanted only to put her arms around Elspeth and comfort her. But Elspeth looked so distant, so controlled, so unneedful of comfort.

"Don't be a fool, Elspeth," she said. "You can't will yourself to faith. You know that. The Doorns are heathen and always have been and always will be. It's in our blood. We were born disillusioned. And we've had as much courage for life as most—more than most. If you go all queer like Conan Doyle and Lodge and White—all those people who try to 'get in touch with loved ones'—why, we'll never forgive you, never. You've got too many brains for that!"

From far off came that calm, unfamiliar voice. "But I told you, I'm trying to forget my mind. I'm not trying to get in touch with anyone except myself."

David, from behind Marcy, tried for sanity, said, "Couldn't we have some coffee or something? We're cold and we're hungry."

And Elspeth, who could make a cup of coffee, a slice of bread and butter, seem like a party, looked slowly around the kitchen and said, "I'm not sure there is coffee. It was in that cupboard, but it seems as if it's gone."

Marcy jumped up and ran to the cupboard, running away from Elspeth's voice, reached for the can. It felt light in her hand. "I'll stew it up to make it go further," she said. "Then I'll run in to the village and get some. But we'll have this first. You're not eating, that's what's the matter with you. You think you need God, but what you need is a good meal."

She wished David would talk. David always had words. But David just stood there in a bleakness unlike him and waited for her to make the coffee. Nor did Elspeth speak. It was not till Marcy, with a shaking hand, was pouring coffee into a cup that Elspeth said in that clear, detached voice, " 'For there is hope of a tree, if it be cut down, that it will sprout again and that the tender branch thereof will not cease.' I have been cut down. I have to wait to see if I will grow again."

"Drink that. And I mean *drink it!*" Marcy said fiercely.

David's glance took in Elspeth swiftly, slid away. "A very

fine sentiment," he said, "but a little fertilizer is called for. And wasn't it John who was cut down? Didn't anyone—didn't any of John's folks come?"

"No one came," Elspeth said.

No one? Not anyone who had known and loved John? Hadn't she let *Sebastian* know?

"That was really heathenish," Marcy said. "Even hating funerals, that was cruel. John was important."

Elspeth lifted the cup, put it down without drinking. "I don't want to talk about John," she said.

"Well, you'd better," David said, "if you're going in for immortality in such a big way. And everyone will talk about him."

"John was a genius," Marcy said. "A genius just doesn't fade away to nothingness."

" 'And how dieth the wise man? As the fool,' " Elspeth said.

"Oh, stop!" Marcy cried. "Stop right there. Besides, I don't believe that. The wise man makes a better dying because he lives better. Both are dead—that's all that's true about that. The 'how' is something else again. Did John get the spring dance thing done?"

"No."

"Oh. I suppose the shad-blow blossoms fell too soon."

But nothing showed that that got through to Elspeth. Nothing made contact with that day in April when Elspeth had come up the stairs in town, walked in to find Marcy cleaning silver. She had been so radiant that day. She had laughed so when Marcy said, "I always begin to get ready for a party after the party is over. I had folks in last night, and the silver was a disgrace." "Oh, darling. How like you!" Elspeth had said. She had had on the Davidow suit, soft as a kitten. And she'd said she hoped the shad-blow would last till John finished the spring dance thing he was on. "Shad-blow frightens me. It's so evanescent," she'd said, but she didn't look frightened. "Have you started your novel?" Marcy had asked her. "Novel? But I'm *living*, darling!" Elspeth had said. Only last April.

"Will you go down to the village and get some food? Or shall I?" David said.

"I'll go," Marcy said helplessly. She hadn't said the right words. She hadn't even kissed Elspeth. "You're *sick*," she said, trying even yet to make Elspeth see her, respond in some normal way.

"Yes, I've been sick all my life," Elspeth said. "But I shall get well. It seems so queer, all the things I've always thought so important."

David dropped down to the chair where Marcy had been sitting. He leaned toward Elspeth in sudden urgency. "Then we're queer too," he said. "We've thought the same things important. Look here, girl—"

But Marcy cried out, "It would have been important once—and it still is—that you get down the Italian cups for coffee, or bring in some oak leaves or berries or something, to remember John by!"

"But I'm not remembering John," Elspeth said.

"Go on," David said. "Get some food."

He gave her a look that said he would take over. She could not bear to leave them, and yet she fled, fled from this horrible talk of the heart that left out the heart completely, from this denial of a closeness that had always been as sure as life itself, fled from the thorn trees down the road to the village.

In the store she said, "I can't remember what brand of coffee my sister uses—Mrs. Esker. Do you know?"

The fat storekeeper lifted down a can, put it on a shelf, said, "That's it. How is Mrs. Esker? She hasn't been in since the funeral. Been wondering if she's all right."

"I just came. She's all right, I hope." *All right?* her heart cried.

"Wife wanted to go up but didn't quite know if she'd ought to. Didn't seem to want anyone to come to the funeral or send flowers or anything. Didn't want to butt in, but folks all liked Esker—felt kind of queer, not doing anything, time he died. Folks around here like to act neighborly."

"I think she's just numb. You know how it is. She didn't even send for us. She's numb from the shock, I think. She'll want you to be neighborly when she begins to come to herself. I don't believe she's been eating. Have you got a good steak?"

He slapped a piece of steak down on the counter, squinted at the scales, and said, "Going to miss Esker around here. Nice young fellow, any way you look at it. Used to call for the square dances in the Community Hall last winter—think he'd done it all his life."

"*John?*" Marcy's dark brows shot up in amazement. "That surprises me, Mr.—?"

"Goudge is the name, miss. Caleb Goudge. Anything else you wanted?"

She drove slowly back to the farm. "John, calling for square dances?" she said incredulously.

It was so incredible that it became part of this horrible dream. John hadn't come to the country because he loved the country. He had come for the quiet and had lived all his days with the big black piano in the front room. Through her head went suddenly a melody from "The Ball," which John had written here, in that room at the farm—the beginning of the waltz, when the young girl steps out for her first dance and it seems it is all girlhood stepping into life; a waltz known already, like the Strauss waltzes. . . . But he was no country man. He was urban to the highest degree. With a shiver that made the wheel tremble she realized she was thinking of John as if he weren't dead, as if she hadn't yet taken in the fact of his death. And what was David saying to Elspeth? She began to drive faster. She had been gone a long time. It was too dark to see the thorn trees, and she was grateful for that.

They sat right where she had left them. David looked up at her, but the look was without comfort. No matter what he had said, nothing had changed.

"I would have got onions, but in your present spiritual state I was afraid onions would be too much," she said. She wanted her voice to sound astringent, but it came out flippantly, heartlessly.

It was David, who was not used to waiting on anyone, who rose and took down dishes, set the table. It took forever getting the steak done, putting a salad together, but all was ready at last. They sat in the small dining room that was decorated with good old maps and had a lamp that hung down on a chain over the round table. So many times they had sat here together, a family, laughing, loving one another. It seemed for a moment that now, *now*, the fact that it was just the Doorns, without John, without Sebastian, would crack through this shell around Elspeth, make the tenderness they felt for her, the grief for John, come through, unite them in sorrow. But Elspeth sat there, remote, silent, not one of them.

"You don't want us here," Marcy said suddenly, like a child left out.

"But we're here," David said shortly. "And we're staying for the night. In the morning we're taking you to town and to a doctor."

The faintest trace of humor went across Elspeth's face, enough to make their hearts leap with sudden hope. "A mental doctor, I suppose you mean," Elspeth said.

"That would be my choice," David said. "I'll settle for any doctor, however. Here you are not going to stay."

"I must stay here," Elspeth said.

At the throat of her blouse was a pin of amethysts and diamonds, the round pin John had given her before they were married, which she wore often. Marcy looked from the face she could not bear to watch, looked at the exclamation point of sophistication the pin made against the white. "Oh, darling, don't *be* like this!" she cried.

"Like what?" Elspeth said slowly. "Why are you crying? You ought to be rejoicing that I've come to my senses. It's taken me long enough."

"Is that what you call it?" David asked.

But they were not helping each other, Marcy and David. For the first time their combined efforts were not moving mountains.

"Are you going to keep the piano?" Marcy said. It sounded stupid, but it was all she could find to say.

"The piano?"

"David, you'd buy it, wouldn't you?"

"Of course. But Elspeth wouldn't part with it."

Elspeth leaned back in her chair. Her fine, elegant face was drawn out of the circle of light the hanging lamp made, and was only a ghost face above the wickedly winking pin.

"You may have it, Marcy," she said. "Not David—he has always coveted it."

"I couldn't afford it," Marcy said, seeing David's face with its gay charm blotted out.

"I said you could have it," Elspeth said.

She stood up, but in slow motion, walked away from the table, away from them, through the narrow living room to the room where stood the piano. She did not turn on any light in there, and the house was full of silence.

"And what now?" David said.

Marcy did not answer. She got up swiftly, followed Elspeth. Elspeth stood beside the big black piano with its keys dimly gray in the grayness, stood and looked down in the strangest way at the keys. There was nothing else in the room except a plain table covered with manuscript sheets, and a tall tier of white shelves filled with music. Nothing else. In this room John had written the music for "The Ball."

"Take it away. Take it away," Elspeth said suddenly, sharply. "Take it away now."

"Well, not tonight. I couldn't manage it tonight," Marcy said sensibly, or as sensibly as she could for her hard-beating heart.

Elspeth put a finger down, touched a key gently. It was in the lower bass and made a deep, melancholy sound in the room. Then Elspeth turned, leaning against the piano. "We've worshiped the arts long enough—much, much too long!" she said. "But I've stopped worshiping—stopped forever."

"At least you're able to announce it dramatically," Marcy said. "That relieves me, I must say." Then she turned to Elspeth with a cry straight from the heart. "But didn't you *love* John?" she said.

The brown velveteen skirt was black in the dusky room. Only the pin made a little spark of light. Seconds went by, but the voice came at last. "I loved him."

Oh, David, oh, Sebastian, help me! You must help me! "You act as if you didn't. If you loved him, you can't be like this. You can't. You can't throw away what he left you—I don't mean the piano. I mean—oh, what *do* I mean? His belief, that's it. He left you his belief in life, in the fulfillment of talent. That's your inheritance, darling. That's *John*. He'd hate it if you ran away from life, from writing your books, from—from *us*. Such as we are, David and I and—and Sebastian, we're your family. You can't cast us off, you can't waste us! Why have you cast us off?"

She had said Sebastian's name, said it aloud. But there were only darkness and silence. Marcy Doorn had thought she was strong enough for anything life could do to her, but she was not strong enough for this. Suddenly, like a stage effect in an old-fashioned melodrama, came a scream, an unearthly, half-human scream, quite close to the window.

Marcy froze in the darkness, but Elspeth said without excitement, "It's the screech-owl."

David was there in the doorway. "Oh," he said, "I thought perhaps it was the still, small voice."

Elspeth touched that one key again, and the sad, deep sound reverberated in the room. If she would only speak their language, not let them strike out at nothing. After the sound died away she said, "I think I'll go up. I'm tired."

She just walked away and left them there.

There was no need to speak. David always knew exactly what one was thinking, feeling. Marcy walked past him to the dining room, began to clear away the half-eaten dinner. But after she had piled up the few dishes David said, "Come in and sit down a minute. You'll drop if you don't." And she came willingly.

They sat in the room that had always had such warmth but was now so cold, and could not find words for their horror. But at last David said angrily, "I told you he would destroy her."

"But he didn't. She wasn't destroyed the last time I saw her."

"She is now."

"I suppose shock could do it."

"That isn't shock," David said. "It isn't even grief."

"That's what's so awful. It isn't being brave, it isn't bearing up—it's as if she didn't care."

"Exactly," David said.

"Anyone but Elspeth might go religious. But not Elspeth."

"I told you, she's been destroyed."

"That's nonsense."

"Well, what's become of her stories, the novels she was going to write? Where are they?"

"But she was *living*. She said so. And she loved him, and she was terribly happy. David, I'm *sick*. I can't stand it."

"Why don't we go to bed too? It might seem different in the morning."

Marcy stood up. "I'll do the dishes and then go. But David—it's *John!* Her *husband!* It's *John* that's dead!"

Her voice protested passionately against this house where were no mourning, no sadness, where no comforting was required. Worldly as they all were, they knew what love was. They knew that a love such as Elspeth's and John's couldn't end like this. They knew the great strength of Elspeth, her brilliance and her gaiety, they knew that this was not their sister. David, for all his laziness, his selfishness, loved Elspeth. He walked toward the kitchen, paused in the hall, and she came and stood beside him, saw what he saw, the telephone receiver off its hook, lying there on the little table. David put it back, then said, "We'll do the dishes in the morning. I'm going up."

She went too. She lay in the bed in the room at the head of the stairs and whispered, "How can I sleep? How can I ever sleep again?" The sky beyond the window was pale and cold with moonlight. "He couldn't have called for square dances," she said. And the lusty singing and bowing and stamping that made up square dances came into her head, and John in the midst of it, haughty, remote—*John.*

There was a faint creak somewhere. The thorn trees had got in somehow and were walking up the stairs and down, putting out softly scratching branches to the railing. After the clover and the meadow grass, the thorn trees. Never ones for nature, the Doorns. Then how had she known that, that the soil was dying when the thorn trees took over? The sound made her cold and sick with fright. Anyone in all her world might have gone queer—except Elspeth. And the telephone receiver off—no one could get in. Had she cabled Sebastian? Oh, had she? And how could she give away the piano, just give it away? As if she were trying to wipe John out of her life. Marcy seemed to hear Elspeth say, Sell the piano? Why, John would rise like Lazarus and give me the evil eye if I ever so much as thought of such a thing! . . . "Take it away. Take it away now." We're *made* of music, Marcy thought helplessly. Other people made automobiles and gadgets, but the Doorns made music and books and paintings and fine clothes. Even David, who could charm the birds right off the bough, couldn't talk. He'd been too much an egotist ever to bow to John; he hadn't liked him ever as much as Marcy did. But what would it do to him if Elspeth went away from him? And suppose they took her home—like this? What then?

Didn't she cable Sebastian?

And David Doorn lay and stared at the moonlight on branches and remembered a Christmas after their mother died.

Their father, F.P., had been abroad, and they had had a fear Christmas wouldn't come off. Elspeth had made it come off. They even sang songs around the piano, and Elspeth had the angel from the tree perched on top of her head. She had made it all come right. It was a very clear memory, and nothing else came to take its place. The way they had laughed so, been so gloriously nonsensical, made poems to go with their presents; the way Elspeth sat at the piano and the light made the angel shine in a comical way while they sang "Away in a Manger" . . . Elspeth.

Marcy woke, and it was morning, and the sky was gray and cold from rim to rim. At first she couldn't think why she was here, or even where she was. All night she had lain in the same curl of fear, and her body was stiff. Then all the nightmare of last night came flooding back. Hadn't Elspeth even let Sebastian know? She got up, dressed with cold fingers, went down the stairs and out to the kitchen. David was already there, and Elspeth too. Someone had made coffee. Elspeth?

"Did you sleep well?" Elspeth asked calmly.

Marcy had meant to start this day differently, but she could not. "No, of course not. How could I?" she asked sharply.

She had always loved this big kitchen so. She sat down at the table near the window, where geraniums were blossoming feebly on the sill. She rose and brought water and watered the geraniums.

David couldn't stop mocking either. "Yes," he said, "I'm sure God is all for keeping flowers alive."

"How do you know?" Elspeth said.

"Well, I don't," Marcy said. "And neither do you. But I'd presume the God who made the world and loved His own creation might care."

"Geraniums and people—they're all one thing," Elspeth said slowly.

"Oh, fiddlesticks! And please, not for breakfast! Though I know some people I prefer geraniums to—but vice versa, vice versa. And as soon as breakfast is over we're going to start back to town. And you're coming with us. We don't care whether you want to or not. For our sake you're going to, darling." She tried to make her voice sound firm and authoritative.

"I can't. I've things to do here," Elspeth said.

"You can do them later."

"No. I must stay here." She wasn't argumentative, just calm and final. "In town they nibble at you, they won't let you be whole. I have to be here."

David said suddenly, "Well, stay here, then. But if you get tired of just God for company, you know where to find us. Did you let Sebastian know? Or F.P.? Or didn't you think they might be interested?"

"I cabled Sebastian, I think. I wrote F.P." But she said it so indifferently! She had done the necessary, the conventional things, that was all. "Why don't you go home? I make you unhappy here. I suppose you are meaning to be kind, but I truly want to be alone and I wish you would go." Her voice had authority. She meant it.

"We will. Very shortly," David said.

They couldn't believe it of themselves that they could go away and leave her there. Nevertheless, they did go. At the door David paused, put his hand on Elspeth's arm, said, "You'll come for Christmas?"

"Yes," Elspeth said.

Marcy threw her arms around her suddenly. "Oh, darling! *Darling!*" she cried—meaning: Feel something! Don't be like this! Don't be frozen! We're here, we love you. We loved John. *Feel* something!

But there was no response in Elspeth's slim body, and Marcy let her arms fall, and they said, "Good-by," quietly and went away.

In the car Marcy could not stop crying.

"Sebastian will come," David said at last, but his voice was strange.

"Yes, he'll come," she said. "I didn't say the right things."

"There weren't any right things to say. I said all I knew when you were in the village. There weren't any right things."

"But what's happened to her? Why is she like this?"

"God knows," David said.

They drove through the chill morning then in silence, knowing that the magic circle of the Doorns against the world had been broken—lost in the knowledge, afraid even to speak of it.

They were near home when Marcy said, "Sebastian won't be any help. He's always taken her exactly as she is."

"I know," David admitted.

He would come, John's loving brother. He would leave all his careful research in Paris. He would come, forgetting everything, because Elspeth needed him. They all needed him—he would come to them too, but first to Elspeth.

They were home, the sad, incredible journey finished. They went up the steps with iron rails, opened the door, and went inside the hall Marcy shared in common with Miss Hodge, an interior decorator with the face of a Borgia and the heart of a child. David stayed right behind his sister as they went up the stairs, past all the dim scenes of Paris on the gray-green wall, and stepped into the big living room.

"Well, that's that," David said bleakly.

"Yes, that's that," she echoed.

"Are you all right? If you are, I'll run along."

"I'll never be all right again. But go if you want to."

"I won't if you'd rather I didn't. But I don't want to talk about it any more."

"No, I'd rather you went."

He stood there, reluctant, but she let him go. Their hurt was one, and he would stay if she asked it, but there was nothing more to say.

She went to the window seat and curled up there on the velvet cushions. She saw the old French church, ugly and familiar. She tried to feel at home, safe. She tried to stop shaking. But all she could see was Elspeth's hands on the Bible, all she heard was the sound of a deep note going on and on in a lonely, empty house.

"I ought to call the office," she said, but did not move.

In the apartment below her, in the queer room where periods hopelessly mixed dwelt happily together, where a heavy red leather chair rested on a long, delicate Aubusson, and a Swedish tin tray held sherry glasses, and a fussy Dresden clock stood on the mantel, Bessie Hamlin, who was Miss Hodge's cousin and housekeeper, hooked her cane over the back of the chair with the seat of petit point. Shoving Soutan, Miss Hodge's Siamese cat, out of the chair, she sat down, saying, "I'll bet he killed himself."

Miss Hodge, noting the shoving of the cat with that familiar anger and pain that admitted Soutan loved Bessie's asplike tongue and rough ways better than herself, said, "Don't be a fool, Bessie. Why should he?"

"Something fishy there, you mark my words. They didn't even know till after the funeral. Something very queer there. One thing's sure—Marcy's always been in love with him herself."

"That's preposterous and wicked. Don't you ever repeat that!"

"Whenever he came to town he headed straight for upstairs."

"Marcy fed him," Miss Hodge said tartly. "I think I'll go up and see how she is."

"H'mph!" Bessie said.

Miss Hodge walked away from her cousin, from the sherry, from Soutan, hating Bessie for an instant, hating death, which she could ordinarily cope with but which was not meant for the John Eskers of the world, for the young, the talented. She walked steadily up the stairs.

She knocked, but then walked in, stood for a moment in the darkness, only her wicked dark face showing clearly in a faint stream of light from somewhere outside.

"Are you all right?" she asked.

And Marcy, sitting there on the window seat, stiff with her pain, picked the nearest, the easiest grief. "My brother-in-law died," she said.

"I heard," Miss Hodge said. She came toward Marcy, in her stiff black suit, stiff white blouse with stock. "Child," she said, "you get into bed. Come along now. I'll tuck you in."

Marcy came obediently. The bed was safety. The hot milk going down her throat was as comforting as mother's milk, which Marcy had never known. She gave up to the comfort of Miss Hodge's sensible voice, which was keeping carefully away from her grief.

"You know, your brother is so beautiful. I keep wanting to put him in a Hodge drawing room as decoration. Why don't we produce more gentlemen, I wonder. And how has he escaped matrimony? But maybe he wouldn't seem so much a gentleman if he married. . . ."

And that was astute but not to be answered. Miss Hodge was so ugly and so kind.

"Where did you get this rug, honey? I could use two of them right now."

"Mexico," Marcy said, seeing the edge of the rug, the tannish fur that was so warm to the feet on winter nights.

"Really? Not so fragile as most Mexican things. I like it. It was such a pity about John Esker. *Such a pity!* Go to sleep, child. Go to sleep."

2

LIKE a theme refrain went the words through the city: "*What a pity!*" So young, so talented, so much a symbol of success and romance—*what a pity!* From Milt of the Basin Street boys to the ticket-seller at a Long Island movie house—*what a pity!* From Abel, John Esker's Hollywood producer, to the young man in Brooks Brothers who had sold him the corduroy jacket he had worn for three years before he died—*what a pity!* And "What will she do?" That was for the beautiful Elspeth, so mad about her husband, made to be the wife of a man like Esker. "What a horrible blow for Elspeth! Such a pity! *Such a pity!*" And one at least, Dean Angers, who had worked so hard to get the fellowship for Sebastian Esker's year in Paris, gave first thought to Sebastian, not to genius cut off in its early flowering. "What a pity!" he said also, but he said it for the blow to Sebastian, for whom he had great affection—for solid work cut into, for the pain of his young friend. "*What a pity!*"

Sebastian Esker was not working. He sat with his friend Greg MacPherson under the crooked pines on a cliff at Bandol and watched Beth MacPherson picking up nuts under pines some distance away. He had met Greg on the street in Paris, and Greg had said, "What on earth! You look like death warmed over!"

Sebastian had grinned and said, "I've had the flu."

"Well, for heaven's sake, give up—come down to Bandol with me. I'm leaving in ten minutes. Grab a toothbrush and come along. Beth will love it."

Sebastian had let himself be persuaded, and here he was with his friends, doing nothing but sit under the pines and let the sun soak in and watch the blue of the sea, and talking a little when moved to do so. Now and then he told a story to Lexie, the MacPhersons' little girl. He was fond of the MacPhersons, bound to Greg by virtue of Greg's likeness to himself, his going right on studying when he had a year off. Greg was an economist and was doing a book all full of statistics, and Sebastian, at home a professor of German Literature, worked in the field of linguistics, but they both worked. He sat there now in the long chair and watched Beth's sturdy figure that would be more at home on the Highland moors but that still looked lovely there in its kneeling position against the sky.

Beth straightened, stood up, holding a small blue bowl in her square hands. Her short hair stood up wildly and gave her a look of flight, though her face had great sweetness and serenity.

"I wonder if you know how beautiful your wife is," Sebastian said lazily.

"Think so?" Greg had a jerky and burry voice. "Never thought it showed to anyone but me."

"I never tire of watching her. But don't worry that I will fall in love with her—anything like that."

"She'd never notice if you did," Greg said, pushing tobacco down in his pipe.

"Well, she most certainly would," Sebastian contradicted him mildly. "I'd hate to have David see her, though. He'd get her to pose for him, and the first thing you knew he'd be taking her off to the South Seas or somewhere. I've kept thinking of the pictures he could have made in just this last half-hour—or thought of making."

Greg gave a short, derisive laugh. "I should like to see him try," he said. Then, more soberly: "No, Beth has never been one to succumb to philanderers. But sometimes I think I'm a very prosaic husband for her. She ought to have had someone like, say, your brother John. But she's got me, and I shall keep her."

Sebastian gave him an affectionate smile, said, "Yes, you'll keep her. That comforts me in a world of change, you know. She wouldn't look at me or David—or even John—and one should never make jokes about a faithful heart."

There fell a small silence while they watched Beth. Sebastian thought: I am homesick. The MacPhersons make me homesick. If I can scrape up enough money I shall fly home for Christmas, to see the opening of John's picture—to see them all. I do not think I can stay in Paris for Christmas. It was odd, Greg's saying "your brother John," because John is bespoken—he'd never look at her. Yet I know what he meant about Beth. I suppose it's the flu, but I am homesick.

John might do no more than put a hand on his arm, say,

"Good. Knew you'd come." He might be so absorbed in work that he would not say even that. Nevertheless, John would be glad.

"There's the mail," Greg said.

For the postman was coming along the cliff road on his bicycle, and Beth had gone to meet him, still holding the blue bowl. They could see her giving her warm smile to the postman, putting some pine nuts into his hand, stuffing the letters with her free hand into the wide pocket of her blue skirt. Then the postman shoved a hand into the front of his tunic, pulled out another envelope. Beth stood looking down at it. It looked like a telegram. At last she put it with the rest of the mail, came toward them.

"Anything good?" Greg called out.

She put the bowl down on the rattan table, and both men took handfuls of nuts. She pulled the letters out. "Funny how we watch for the postman like hawks," she said, "when we want so to be away from the world!" She sorted out the letters swiftly, kept two for herself.

Sebastian's landlady had stuffed his mail all into a long envelope, instead of forwarding each separate piece, and it tumbled out into his hands, while the cablegram fell to the ground. He reached down a long arm and picked it up, tore it open first, sat staring at it in a way that made his friends at once anxious.

"Sebastian, what is it? Is it bad news?" Beth demanded.

He looked at them blankly, got up, put the rest of the mail on the table, stuffed the cablegram into his pocket, and strode off along the cliff without a word.

They watched him go, too troubled to read their own mail.

"He's weak as a cat. He ought not to go off like that," Beth said. "Go after him."

"No," Greg said, being one who disliked interference.

They saw him come to the place where the path went down to the shore, and then he disappeared.

Sebastian went down the path, hardly knowing he had left the terrace with the pine trees. The eternal game was going on on the shore. The sky was very blue, and there was a boat with a saffron-colored sail. He walked along the shore, away from the players, came to a rocky spot, sat down on a rock, and stared at the sail. He did not take out the cablegram. Its few words were there in his brain, final and convincing, never to be erased: JOHN DIED YESTERDAY. LOVE, ELSPETH.

He did not think. He waited for the saffron sail to pass a certain point. He had had a day once, the day he knew Elspeth loved John, when there was nothing but darkness in him, a day never to be forgotten or denied; but even that day lessened beside this hour of sickness, which made flu, homesickness, all his past sorrows, nothing. He was not a peculiarly humble man; he knew his own worth and had his own pride; but what humility he had was for his brother's great gifts. All his life he had paid tribute to a fate that had given him a brother such as John Esker. LOVE, ELSPETH. The words were there, graven till eternity, and yet they too were part of the emptiness that stretched out to infinity all around him, for Elspeth's love had all been given. He reached out into the emptiness for John's face, but all that came was the picture of a small boy coming down Mr. Burghardt's steps after a music lesson, a music case in his small hand, his big-eyed, intelligent face much too intent for six. "I can go home by myself," the little boy said. But Sebastian had stayed close by John, crossing the street. He'd stayed close beside him ever since. . . . That picture went away, and there was no other, none of John as he had seen him in the spring. There was only the sail and the great emptiness reaching out on every side. JOHN DIED YESTERDAY. LOVE, ELSPETH.

An hour later Beth MacPherson came straight toward him along the sand. He did not look at her, did not see her. She sat beside him on the rocks but for some time did not speak —could not, so real, even to her, was the remoteness in which he sat. At last she said, "Sebastian, what is it? You ought to come in."

He heard the gentle insistence but still did not look at her. "My brother is dead," he said.

She did not try to comfort him. She made no further remonstrance. She had lost three brothers in the war. She rose and walked away, left him there.

"Didn't you find him?" Greg asked.

"Yes. John Esker's dead."

"Good Lord!"

"He's just sitting there on the rocks. I couldn't talk to him."

"If you couldn't, I certainly couldn't."

"He'll want to go home. He's in no shape to go."

They left the terrace and went into their small, bright house, as if compelled to seek the security of walls.

"Why, he wasn't forty yet!" Beth said in sudden sharp protest.

Greg walked to the window, stared toward the path down the cliff. "Something I found out, quite by accident," he said jerkily. "Sebastian's in love with his brother's wife. Don't mention it. Complication, though."

She did not answer, though she had already half known this, but she came up to him, and he put his arm around her and held her close, being ashamed of their own indestructible happiness.

Sebastian came in after another hour. His long, rugged face was tired and quiet. It had, Beth thought, hollowed out, been graven with new lines in just this little time.

"I have to see if I can get plane passage," Sebastian said, not even mentioning his brother.

"I'll phone," Greg said, making no protest at all. He went at once to the phone and put in a call.

It was while Greg waited there at the phone that Lexie came dancing down the stairs. She was a long-legged, skinny little girl, with a square face like Beth's, not beautiful at all as yet, only filled with a great vitality. She was always excited, and exciting. She ran at once to Sebastian.

It was odd about Sebastian Esker. He made no pretense of trying to understand children, yet children always turned to him, claimed him. He sometimes told them stories, but fairly often the stories were over their heads. Once Marcy, overhearing him, had said, "But she can't possibly understand that!" "Oh?" he'd said. "But she can try. Don't you like to have things a little out of reach?" He took it for granted that this was as true for children as for himself.

Now Lexie took his hand and demanded, "Shall we do it on the terrace?"

But for once Sebastian did not immediately respond. He kept looking at Greg by the phone.

"Do what?" Beth asked.

"He promised. He promised to tell me 'The Blink-eyed Pig' as soon as lessons were over. He promised!" Lexie said.

"You'll have to let Sebastian off today. He doesn't feel well," Beth said.

"He promised," Lexie said again.

Greg turned from the phone. "Friday, unless there's a cancellation before," he said.

Sebastian looked now at Lexie and said, "Yes, I did. Come outside, Alexandrina."

Lexie giggled. She loved having Sebastian call her Alexandrina. She squatted crosslegged on the ground, and Sebastian sat in the chair by the table.

"Begin!" Lexie commanded. Then, more anxiously: "You're not really sick, are you?"

Sebastian neither affirmed nor denied the illness, but began in quiet gravity: "Once in Punaauia there lived an old woman who made her living by fishing . . ."

Inside the house the MacPhersons could hear his voice going on and on, could see Lexie's tense little body leaning forward. Beth began to cry. "I can't stand it," she said.

"Nice fella—stamina," Greg said with his usual understatement. "We'd better drive up to Paris with him, don't you think?"

But Sebastian got the plane earlier from Cannes, and the three of them saw him off.

"I hate to have you going into trouble," Beth said. "I do hate it, Sebastian."

He was not a melancholy man, but he said, "Is there anywhere else to go?"

He shook hands with both of them and said, "You are so kind."

"Come back soon," Greg said, his voice admitting that he might never even see Sebastian again.

"He's coming back to marry me," Lexie said, with her voice bold enough, but her eyes, her whole body, suddenly shy.

"Fine, fine," Beth said. "We consent."

"We're going to have a pig that can talk," Lexie said.

"Professors are very poor," Beth said. "You will have to

learn to save your scraps if you're to feed a pig as well as yourselves."

"I can make scones," Lexie said.

"I foresee a happy life," Greg put in. They were trying to laugh, trying to make it easy. But it was not easy. Greg and Beth MacPherson were too conscious of the emptiness in the heart of their friend, too aware of how much he had loved his brother, too aware of what this would mean to him, both in loss and present pain. They had never seen John Esker; they had never seen the Doorns; but Sebastian had made them all intensely real. Those people were Sebastian's family, the true center of his life, and the MacPhersons knew his greatness of heart, for never once, loving Elspeth, had he shown the faintest doubt as to the rightness of John's marriage to her. Yet there was nothing of the ascetic about him. He was a man, with a man's passion and power.

"Let us know when you come back. We'll drive up to Paris," Greg said.

"I will."

He turned just once, smiled at them, and then he was gone. They watched the plane taxi down the runway, lift, go away from them, into trouble. They went in silence back to their rickety car. In the car Beth said, "I feel so sad. He's the nicest person in our world."

3

IN THE morning, when Marcy Doorn opened her eyes, there was a cold, clear light, but there were whips of dark gray in the sky that looked prophetic of snow. All New York stood out sharply against the cold light. It was the light of sanity, of logic. In this morning you could say: It's a phase. It's grief. She's not the first one who's gone through it. She loved him so terribly, and this is the armor she is putting on against collapse.

Marcy bathed, dressed, ate her breakfast, went to the office, was busy in a rushing way till eleven, pushing away her fear, pushing away even that line thrown out against drowning: *She cabled him. He will come. When will he come?* At eleven Mrs. Boswell came in. Mrs. Boswell was her chief assistant and efficient, but they were not friends. She looked more the head designer than Marcy, and knew it and traded on it and bided her time, keeping an inner fury of jealousy glowing in her otherwise cold heart. The fury was fed by the fact that no Doorn ever thought of himself as less than the head of any project. They were born to be top men.

"Your brother called," Mrs. Boswell said. "You were busy. He'll call later."

On the desk before Marcy was a big drawing sheet with a sketch of a girl in a green dress. The dress was of suede cloth, paler than moss green, and had a band of leopard across the pocket. Marcy looked at it, and the spots on the leopard band began to extend over the whole drawing in a sinister way.

"Thank you," she said, and didn't know whether it had been half a second or half an hour before she spoke.

"Featherly will come at two. All right?"

"Two? Thanks," Marcy said again, and no more. She stared at the spots and waited. Mrs. Boswell went away.

The whole morning's busy routine became meaningless. All she could think of was to wish she were safe in bed again and being given hot milk by Miss Hodge. It was, she knew, a measure of her fear that she had let Miss Hodge look after her, when Miss Hodge had never done such a thing before in all their relationship. The courage of this morning vanished, became dust, nothingness. She could no longer push away the fear. She reached desperately for the lifeline. *Is he coming? Is he on his way now?*

"The leopard on the pocket is all wrong," she told Mr. Featherly.

"But I like it. The young will like it," Mr. Featherly said stubbornly.

"I don't like it. There's been too much leopard. We'll have fur if you like, but pale brown, a thin line of it, something close-napped."

"Nothing will go with that green except leopard."

"It will. You'll see, Mr. Featherly. I can't have my name attached to this."

"Well, it is attached," Mr. Featherly said with a grin. "That was your first idea, and it's right."

"I must have been out of my mind. At any rate, I won't have it." She went over to a table and picked up a pale brown chalk, came back and began to rub over the ink marking the splash of leopard. "See," she said. "Isn't that infinitely better?"

"It's infinitely more subdued," Featherly said stubbornly.

"It's smarter. You could live with it."

"Not the ones we want to live with it. It's dull."

"Nonsense. At any rate, that's it."

She had fought for her first thoughts many a time. Very rarely had she fought for second thoughts. It was, she knew, a defeat that she was doing so now. There was nothing wrong with the leopard except that she had become obsessed by its spots, enlarging, filling her vision.

Somehow the day was done. She came out into the street at five, and Eddie Dunstan was waiting for her. He said, "I'll take you home, sweetheart."

"I'd rather walk."

"Proud, eh? Well, I'll walk along with you. Mind?"

"Eddie—"

"Look, sweetheart, I can't help it if you're news. You could live a quiet life like the rest of us if you didn't enjoy being dramatic. I'm not a ghoul, just a man who takes pictures. In just a month the Tahiti thing is going to be out. I'm going to have a four-page spread on Esker tied in with the picture. They say it's one of the best out of Hollywood—they've outdone themselves. It's news, and it's going to be a moneymaker to boot. The songs, they say, are something—not moon and June and love and dove. Anyway, I'm doing it, and I love you, and you're going to help me. You're going to take me up to Esker's place, and I'm going to take pictures of the house and Elspeth and the piano and whatnot."

He didn't love her. She wasn't his sweetheart. He was just a man going places and using anyone he could along the way. He had always amused her, but all she felt now was a kind of horror.

"I'm not going to do any such thing," she said. "Elspeth's sick, and I'll slit the throat of anyone who bothers her. I'm not fooling, Eddie."

"I'm not fooling either, honey. And I'm used to violence. David will help me out, but I like the Marcy Doorn approach better. David always comes across when it's a matter for the public good, but he looks down that mighty fine nose of his at me, and that does make me obnoxiously pugnacious. Better to avoid it if possible. But David never thwarts Publicity."

"David's having a one-man show in January. Concentrate on that."

"No. You know I couldn't have four pages for that. Esker's a natural."

"John's dead," she said flatly.

"I know. All the same, I could pull it off. Elspeth's photogenic no end, and the place where he worked in the country would be all right."

She paused. It was dark already, and the lights were on.

"Eddie," she said. "If you knew how I was hating you right now you'd be afraid to walk in the street with me. I don't care how much publicity you give to the picture. But if you go down and bother Elspeth or even go near the place in the country I'll— I'm not fooling. You'll regret it forever. I won't have it."

His face sharpened, became foxlike under a street light.

"Come off it," he said. "She wouldn't have married him if he hadn't been a big shot. Would she? Well, even big shots get forgotten soon enough. She ought to be grateful we're keeping him immortal for a month. I admired the guy, you know —admired him no end. He was good. But if you're tops in your field you're tops, and you get in the news. And it's the first time you folks have ever objected to it, in my memory anyway."

"What a lovely picture of the Doorns you are building up. Good night, Eddie."

"Oh, I say, Marcy. Don't *be* like that! Want me to grovel? I can. But you've always taken it straight from the shoulder. You make news. I take pictures. We've always got together before."

But she was walking away from him, and he stood there under the light, staring after her, his sharp face angry and pinched.

In the apartment she tried at once, without taking off her hat, to call David. There was no answer. "He's gone to Alice," she said with a certain wryness. She went through the apartment then, as if she were hunting for something, stood in her guest room and looked at her lovely eiderdown that she had put there in such foolish certainty for Elspeth's comfort. Miss Hamlin from downstairs came thumping up with a box of flowers someone had sent. She was curious, but Marcy only took the flowers, thanked her, let her go thumping away with curiosity unsatisfied. She put her hat and coat away, got a big jar for the chrysanthemums, set the jar on a table near the window seat. Then she just waited—for what? The phone rang several times, for Marcy had many friends, but she put people off, waited. She ate a meager dinner. But what was she waiting for? She wished David would come, but there was only silence, solitude, nothing happening in the minutes except the swift, angry, frightened thoughts that would not die down. At two she went to bed, but even then she could not sleep. She kept hearing Eddie's brash voice, she kept waiting for the phone to ring, for steps on the stairs. Once she dozed, woke, feeling a certainty that Sebastian was there, standing beside the jar of white chrysanthemums. So certain was she that she got up and walked out to the living room. It was quite empty.

In the morning she thought: I must go back. We ought never to have left her, no matter what she said. We mustn't wait for Sebastian. She couldn't have meant really to push us out. She couldn't have meant it.

But she went to the office, outwardly she conformed, did all the usual things. Inwardly she was not present at all. At three David phoned.

"It's snowing," he said. "Why don't you knock off and come home? I'll meet you outside and we'll walk."

"All right. Be right down," she said.

Beyond any moment in New York, Marcy had always loved this moment when the first snow came down on roofs and steeples and all was blurred out in a romantic whiteness. One of her most successful dresses had been conceived as the dress of a young girl walking out with her lover into the first snowfall. But now her only thought was: I wonder if the planes will be grounded.

David turned to her, idle-looking, charming as always, walked beside her.

"I suppose you've been at Alice's," she said. She had wanted his comfort last night, but now her voice was dead.

"Yes. Mind?"

"I seem to. I suppose I shouldn't. David, we ought not to have left her. I don't know how we could have."

"She's ditched us," David said shortly.

"She couldn't. We just thought so—but how could she?"

"Well, she did. The hell of it is, you can't think of anything else. I'm up to my neck in the Bernstein sets, and I have screech-owls screaming in my ears all the time. And what do you say to people? What the devil do you *say?* Everyone asks. Everyone tries to call her up, and there's no answer. Do you say she's gone into a convent, or what? No one can conceive that she wants to crawl into a hole and commune with God. How could anyone?"

"But we don't know what's made her like that. We hadn't any right to leave her, because—because indifference like that isn't *real;* it couldn't be real. We made fun of her."

They walked past three buildings before David said, "We did more than that. Or we tried to."

The snow fell thickly on their heads and shoulders, but they did not mention or notice it. It was they, not Elspeth, who looked bereft as they walked slowly homeward in the snow. They had tried. They had used love as well as mockery.

"Abel's sending someone up. To see if he can salvage anything. The ghoul!" David said in sudden anger.

"I shall go back tomorrow—whether you do or not," Marcy said. "Because I can't stand it, thinking about her there alone."

"Sebastian ought to be here any time—if he could get passage."

"I'm not going to wait for Sebastian."

"Still, I keep wishing he'd get here."

She felt the very sweep of the plane, coming down in the snow. "Oh, David!" she said at last, forlornly.

They had come to the house. It had been over a mile, and they had not been conscious of any time passing. They went up the stairs, into the hall. Miss Hodge opened her door, said, "Mr. Esker's brother came. I thought it would be all right to let him go in."

But Marcy had not waited to hear the end of Miss Hodge's words. She was running up the stairs swiftly, as to sanctuary. She threw open the door and went across the room like a wind, took Sebastian's two hands in hers. "Oh, Sebastian. *Sebastian!*" she said.

She saw the new lines in the rugged, familiar face. "Oh, Sebastian, you look dreadful! Sit down!" she said.

He freed a hand, brushed the snow from her dark curls. Once he had called her "the snow child." His gesture seemed to say it again. But he was saying aloud in a quiet voice, "How are you, David?"

"You're *sick*," Marcy said.

"No. I'm just over the flu but I'm quite all right."

He sat down, however, leaned his head back against the velvet of the chair. "No one answers the phone at the farm. I thought Elspeth would be here," he said. "Where is she?"

"She's there," David said. He looked from Sebastian to Marcy in a kind of helplessness.

"All alone?" Sebastian said. He leaned forward a little in the chair, his dark eyes shocked, questioning them.

"All alone," Marcy said. "She—she doesn't want us. She doesn't love us any more."

"Doesn't love you? Are you out of your mind?"

"She doesn't. She—"

David said, "Marcy's trying to tell you that Elspeth seems very strange to us—beyond the reason of grief. She didn't even let us know when John died."

"Didn't let you *know?*"

"We saw it in the paper. We went down, but Elspeth—well, she was *strange*. We've been counting on your coming. She just doesn't want any help from us."

The emptiness of the moment by the sea enlarged, took in, now, this room, these two people Sebastian Esker had counted on, loved.

"Could I get hold of a car?" he asked.

"You can take mine," David said. "I could have it here in ten minutes."

"We're frightened," Marcy said baldly.

"I see you are. Could I have some coffee, Marcy? And will you see about the car?" Then: "But of course she is frightened too."

"You don't look fit for a drive in the snow," David said. "The first one's always bad."

"I'll manage." Marcy went away for coffee, and Sebastian said, "What happened?"

"I don't know. John's dead, that's all we know. You'll have to see for yourself. She—she's gone *queer*."

"Beyond grief?" Sebastian said. "Wasn't that what you said?"

"Yes, beyond grief. We don't know what to do. She's gone *religious*."

"Would you phone about the car?"

They didn't try to stop him. He drank the coffee quickly, got up wordlessly, and they all went downstairs together. David pointed out the gadgets that made his car the car it was. Marcy leaned against the window and said, "Don't go, Sebastian. Don't go tonight."

"I can't wait," Sebastian said simply, and Marcy stepped

back from the window. They watched him drive away in the snow.

They went slowly up the stairs. Marcy stood there, seeing the chrysanthemums only. They looked sad, a welcome that had failed, cold, like the snow.

"We never said we were sorry about John," she said.

She picked up Sebastian's cup, carried it away to the kitchen. She washed it slowly. For one so sure of herself she looked childish, incompetent, as she stood there by the sink. Suddenly the cup dropped to the sink and broke into three pieces. It was one of her Royal Doulton cups and had a blue band edged with gold and small pink flowers in wreaths.

"What's the matter?" David asked from the doorway.

"Nothing. I broke a cup."

"Isobelle wants us to have dinner with her."

"No. You can—I don't want to."

Reluctantly she put the pieces of the cup into the trash. "Run along!" she said in unexpected fierceness. "You've ditched your responsibilities—so run along!"

"I haven't ditched them any more than you have," David said. "But I do have to have a go with Bernstein in the morning. He was in a rage because I fouled up yesterday. But I'm not exactly enjoying myself."

It was inadequate. He knew it was inadequate and ceased speaking, just stood there in the doorway, waiting for some comfort, some assurance.

She went to him, put a hand on his arm. "Sorry," she said. "It's all so awful. I don't know what I'm saying. It was only —he *loved* John, and all we did was shove our burden onto him, when he's sick."

"He loves her too," David said.

"Yes." She turned away from him, and presently she heard him going away down the stairs. She went in and stood by the window, watching the snow. It had begun to blow now. He would scarcely be out of town yet, but she saw him on a remote country road, saw the windshield wiper going back and forth, back and forth. They hadn't told him anything, only frightened him, put their burden on him. He couldn't imagine Elspeth changed—but it might be, loving her, that he would find the right words. He wouldn't try, as they had, to shock her into life. He would just love her and listen. Only he was ill. They had had no right to do this to him.

"Queer, I've always felt whole," she said to the snow. She meant, without Elspeth, she felt identity slipping away from her—not only identity but her whole world. For an instant Miss Hodge had touched her. For an instant Eddie Dunstan had angered her. Otherwise these last days had been completely unreal—till she had seen Sebastian sitting there, the same, always the same, the rock in a shifting universe. He had been here. He was gone, gone straight to Elspeth, as if they did not exist. No, that wasn't true. He was fond of them. But what would it do to him when he saw Elspeth?

She saw Elspeth suddenly, saw her clearly, spreading out the skirt beneath the bodice of pale blue velvet; heard her say, "But I depend on Marcy for glamor. Isn't it divine?"—making a reputation for Marcy before she had made one for herself. She saw Elspeth at David's first show, heard her say to Ripley the critic, "But this one—I count on you to see this one if no one else does," her face grave behind its radiance, leaving no doubt that she knew what was good, that she depended on Ripley to see the extraordinary as she did—building them up, a part of them.

He would surely be into the country by now. If anyone in

all the world could help her, it would be Sebastian. Wherever he was—in his classes, at the Sorbonne—he was with Elspeth. There was no use in denying that. All the times Marcy had known this anew came crowding against the thickening snow, the falling dusk. Sebastian had come into the office with a little black cat carved out of some black wood. "Do you think she will like it?" he asked so anxiously. The cat in her hands was so smooth—not a cat at all, but the heart of a tree. I like it, she wanted to say. I would treasure it forever. But she said only, "She'll love it." And the winter they were wearing shawls—he came up here with the Chinese shawl of heavy white silk. "Would she wear this?" he asked. "Who wouldn't?" Marcy said. She saw Elspeth walking down the aisle in the white shawl—and everyone looked at her.

"But you did it yourself," she said helplessly. He had. "This is my brother John," he had said. At the Town Hall, that was. There were people all about, but John canceled them out. You saw only John Esker, with his face so fine and sharp, his eyes seeing you only dimly, seeing some other world. "This is my brother John"—saying that this was the best he had to offer. And John shook hands gravely with David, bowed to her—and then he saw Elspeth. Elspeth had on her fur cape, and the wide white lace yoke of her black dress showed like white foam between the edges of the cape. John came out of his other world—no, that was not the way of it. He picked Elspeth up and took her with him to his true dwelling place. All in one look. Sebastian had given them John, but he had lost Elspeth.

"For love is blood enemy to justice," she murmured. And though she had not heard Bessie Hamlin's words, she admitted to their truth. "It was only three days," she said. For three days she too had felt the power of John Esker. On the third day she saw John and Elspeth in the street together—and right then she stopped loving him and began to like him.

"He will eat her up," David had said.

Yet he hadn't. Elspeth had kept right on being interested in all their successes, all their thoughts. She hadn't gone away from them. She'd made John one of them. . . . If life was right, you could bear death. Something horrible had happened to the life in Elspeth—or had she, Marcy, dreamed that night at the farm? No, it was real. Some stranger sat in the kitchen at the farm, bending over a Bible, not Elspeth at all. Was that how they had been able to leave her—feeling she was not Elspeth?

"I am the one who is eaten up," she said slowly. "I am the one."

The doorbell rang. Marcy crossed the room and pressed the buzzer, but without thought.

It was Isobelle. "Hello, darling," she said. "You've been brushing me off all week, and I won't be brushed off any longer."

"I've been a bit low," Marcy said. She could not bring her mind back from the car on the country road.

"I know. But what are friends for?" Isobelle asked.

Isobelle had no beauty, but she had style. One of her front teeth was crooked, and this added oddly to her attractiveness. She had been married but did not live with her husband any more. She thought she knew all the worldly answers and did know a good many.

"If you're a friend, don't condole," Marcy said.

"I won't," Isobelle said, dropping gloves to the couch, sitting down with indolent grace. "I hear Sebastian's come."

"Yes—come and gone." It already seemed years away, his coming.

"He's a lamb, but really a lamb. I wish he made more money. There are plenty of stuffy ones to be professors. He's wasted, simply wasted."

"He wouldn't be Sebastian if he weren't a professor," Marcy said.

"Oh, well, he's Elspeth's anyway. No use even looking across the fence at him. A waste, all the same. Just a bangle on her bracelet. He might be something special."

"He's special enough," Marcy said.

"I suppose Elspeth will live here with you now."

"I don't know. I hope so."

"It was certainly the grand passion while it lasted. She's lucky to have had this much. Five minutes with Frank was all I managed. But then, I wasn't too easy to live with myself. I never wanted the perfect love, like George Sand, but I wanted some faint illusion. Of course, if John had lived to be ninety it might have been a different story. So maybe she's luckier than she knows. Go in and put some make-up on, duck. You look like hell."

"I feel like hell," Marcy said remotely.

"Don't we all? But it's stupid to let it show, darling."

"You don't have to look at me."

Isobelle let her brittle look fade, as she could do at will, became grave. "You know, I've always been jealous of Elspeth," she said. "She's always had everything for nothing. And even this—that should bring her down to the common level—you'll see, will give her something."

"Maybe that is what it will give her," Marcy said slowly, "to be brought down to the common level. It might be a gift."

"Oh, nonsense! She won't be just a widow in black. She'll be the widow of John Esker, the one left from one of those romances they make songs about. She doesn't have to be good or smart or anything. She just turns on that radiance of hers, and people bend their knees."

"Don't," Marcy said sharply. "That's Elspeth you're talking about."

"I know. I know what I'm like, darling. All I have is a sharp tongue to make my way with."

"You don't need to make your way with me," Marcy said.

If Isobelle could have looked ashamed, perhaps she would have looked so now. She got up, picked up her gloves, said, "God bless you, pet! I must run." God was not her familiar. She just used the word. "Don't sit there. You're the one who looks like a widow, darling."

Marcy stared toward the snow. "I can't be funny about it, Isobelle," she said at last, and Isobelle gave her a quick, almost troubled, glance. For Marcy always played it the worldly, sharp-tongued way, never admitting to depths. It was embarrassing to have her voice speaking so honestly and seriously.

Isobelle stood silently in the doorway for a moment and looked at her friend, who did not look back at her.

"Dead's dead, Marcy," she said at last. "It's more comfortable underground than walking around unburied—like me. Like a lot of us. It's stupid to mourn, and you've never been stupid, darling."

Marcy turned from the window. "But I've never felt I was walking around dead," she said. "I've never felt like that. And maybe it would be good for us if we could do a little honest mourning. Maybe we cover everything up too much. If I could cry for John, I would."

"You embarrass me, duck. I haven't cried since the night I was married. Let Elspeth weep for John. It's not your duty. Do you think I ought to drive up to see Elspeth?"

"No."

"I just thought I'd ask. I'd be decent, you know, even if I am jealous of her."

"No," Marcy said again. "Leave her alone."

"And you too, eh? All right, my sweet. But I'll be around when you come out of it. 'By for now."

Isobelle walked along the street toward the corner and a taxi. She did not connect her thoughts with Marcy's love for her sister, with John and Elspeth, but suddenly she said aloud, "Damn Frank!" And after a moment: "Or damn *me!*" For it had been her own doing that her child had been given over to the care of Frank's people. She had felt desperately the need of freedom, and she had attained freedom, but now, walking through the snow away from the Doorns, she wished she had her child. She had the feeling that no one in all the world cared about her.

Marcy sat quite still where Isobelle had left her. "He must be there by now," she said. But she did not let him be there. It was easier to hold him back in the snow.

4

THE SOFT snow that fell in New York fell also on the farm. It made curled whiteness of the brown leaves beneath the maples and caught in every twig of the thorn trees, making them into spheres of incredible intricacy and beauty. The stone wall that bordered the road down the hill soon had a coping of white, and the sills of the old house had small drifts that reached up against the panes.

Twenty miles from the farm Sebastian passed Eddie Dunstan, being pulled out of a ditch by a towing car. Since he did not know Eddie, he passed by with scarcely a glance. Sebastian noticed almost nothing along the road. He knew the road very well, did not need to stop and ask his way. He had the feeling that never once had he paused in this journey since the cablegram was put into his hands under the pine trees at Bandol. Now the urgency had increased as he neared the farm. He was terribly tired, but he never paused.

He came to a stop quietly in the road that led to the barn. He stepped out of the car, went toward the side door that they always used. The snow was coming so thickly that before he reached the door his shoulders were white. At the door he paused an instant. Everything was too quiet. The very house seemed dead. Then he opened the door without knocking, stepped inside.

The house was deeply familiar, as every place in which he had ever known Elspeth was familiar to him—the round-backed Victorian chairs, the maps on the dining-room wall, the silver teapot with the E for Esker that had been his own grandmother's, the chintz-petticoated sofa where, the last time he had been here, Elspeth had curled up in the corner and listened with him to John's playing from the other room, playing that haunting little tune, a tune almost without melody and yet not to be forgotten. It was the one that John had composed for the song the old woman sang as she caught fish in Punaauia—the song that was to be part of the Tahitian movie, the words of which Sebastian had translated himself from the legend of "The Blink-eyed Pig" that he had told the other day to Lexie MacPherson.

Yes, the house was exactly the same. Yet Sebastian stood there, feeling in some foreign land, in a strange house, an intruder, knowing a house is worse than nothingness without its people. There was no John, no Elspeth. Sebastian knew, not even having seen Elspeth, that Marcy and David had been right to be frightened. Nothing could live and breathe in a stillness like this.

Then Elspeth came from the kitchen and stood in the dining-room doorway. She wore the same velveteen skirt she had worn when Marcy and David came, and a high-necked white blouse and no jewelry. She looked just the same, and profound relief went through Sebastian Esker. The relief was short-lived.

"Why, Sebastian," she said with a flatness not unwelcoming, only without surprise, not as an exclamation of delight nor as if she needed him.

Sebastian shivered. He said, "Hello, Elspeth," but he did not put out his hand, nor did she. He slid out of his coat, found a chair to lay the coat across. Still she did not speak, and he said, "I'm glad you're staying here. Come in the other room and sit down." And that was a reversal appalling in itself, for Elspeth was famous for her hospitality.

Elspeth sat in the chair with the carved frame and the pale tan tapestry with its faint blue and rose pattern. Sebastian sat on the sofa facing her.

"It's good to see you, Sebastian," she said quietly. He might have dropped in for tea, not come across the world to her. There was no "Oh, *Sebastian!*" as Marcy had cried from a heart full of grief.

"I hope so," he said as quietly.

"It's comforting that you don't say at once that you want me to go to town."

"To town? Why should you? This is your home. It comforts *me* to have you here. I've never been one to want to clear the house before the funeral's over—getting rid of memories. Was it John's heart?" He said it more sharply than he meant to, out of anger that he should sit here with Elspeth and speak in generalities.

She hesitated, looked down at her hands on the arms of the chair. "Yes," she said then. "His heart just stopped beating."

"Oh. It was never a very good heart—not since the rheumatic fever," he said.

"No, it wasn't ever a very good heart," she said.

The snow walled them in, isolated them, and inside that wall was yet another wall, built against an intimacy that had always been as real as breathing. His "I'm sorry I wasn't here" did not scale the wall.

"No one was here," she said distantly. "I was out for a walk. No one was here."

He heard himself make another generality. "Well, he was always essentially alone," he said, wished the words back, tried for something more immediate, homely. "Where's Mrs. Goodspeed?" he asked. "Doesn't she come any more?"

"No. I don't need her. I'm very competent."

"Yes, I know you are. It's my own comfort I'm thinking of—I want someone to be looking after you. But you were always good at dusting and polishing—and Mrs. Goodspeed would talk so!"

He looked away from the familiar line of her face straight to a film of dust across a cherry table.

"Do you ever think about God, Sebastian?"

His eyes came back from the dust to the tight cuff of her blouse about her delicate wrist. Had there been a faint urgency, a faint sense of reality in her voice?

"Why, no, Elspeth, not any more," he said. "I used to when I was a boy."

"I never did when I was a girl," Elspeth said. "Perhaps that's it—you have to sometimes, and it's only that I'm late. Do you remember when it was the fashion to say, 'God bless you!' at parting? Or, 'Go with God, child'? Just for a little extra warmth—but then being just a plain 'Good-by'?"

"But a plain 'Good-by' is another 'God be with you,' isn't it?" he asked gently.

"I'd never thought—I suppose it is. I came in from a walk

—just a walk through the leaves—and I said, 'God help me, I don't know what to do.' I wasn't calling on God, because there wasn't any God in my world. It was just a cry, because it was too much for me and I had to have help. You aren't laughing at me."

"No. Should I? Do you want me to?"

"They think I've lost my mind. When I say that that is what I must do, they think it all the more. It's very hard to lose your mind, isn't it?"

"I've never tried," he said.

"No, we've always been so sure that cleverness was all, haven't we?"

"No, Elspeth, I've never thought that. But the mind's our balance wheel, after all. Let's not feel called upon to throw our minds over the mill dam."

"We store up our knowledge the way a squirrel stores up acorns—that's all."

"Why not? We wouldn't like being less intelligent than a squirrel, would we?"

"But all the time we're crowding feeling out."

He did not answer, but into his dark, grave eyes there came a flash of the feeling that had driven him here, made him leave the Sorbonne without a qualm, brought him straight across the sea to her.

After the silence Elspeth said, "I can't ever go to town again. I can't."

"Well, stay here. It will be lonely with John gone, but I've never thought loneliness was a bad thing. There's no reason you shouldn't stay here. Only I hope you won't hurt Marcy and David too much. Mind hasn't crowded out feelings in Marcy or David; they love you."

"You don't know what I mean. Those are small, selfish

feelings, where the ego gets hurt. That's not what I mean at all."

"Oh? What *do* you mean, Elspeth?"

"I mean—I mean a place where there isn't any ego. The leaves were skittering everywhere, and you could hear the wind in the chimney—and I said, 'God help me!' And there was God, in everything, right then. You aren't laughing, and I can tell you. He was there in the leaves and the wind, and in—in John, and nothing mattered any more than anything else. And death didn't matter any more than life—it was all one thing. And I didn't matter. I was just a piece of the whole thing. And a leaf falling was the same as John's dying. And all this being important, proving we were more than the leaves—it was all foolish, done away with."

He looked toward the room across the hall, where the piano stood in lonely splendor, and then he said, "Perhaps it's just because I'm a human being, too—but I think John was more important than a leaf, Elspeth."

"To you—not to God."

This was an affront to the heart. He could scarcely bear speaking of John in terms like this. Yet he tried, on the level she had chosen.

"That's our John you're talking about, Elspeth," he said. "Even in the eternal scheme of things—if there is an eternal scheme—wouldn't you think that all the cherubim and seraphim would sing a special paean when the world produces someone like John? Now and then someone comes along who has the power to speak for millions—like John. And even if he were only a milestone in the evolutionary process, he *was* a milestone, he was unique—special. But there's nothing I need to say to you about John."

She did not weep. She did not pour out any tender memories of John. She said tiredly, "Patterns—patterns—we make such patterns. We can't live without patterns. And man and his cleverness—always the main motif. I'm not making patterns any more. Are you hungry?"

He wasn't, but he said, "I am, rather."

He stood up, long, a little awkward, but always establishing himself as a person of authority in his gestures.

She rose also, went to the kitchen, made coffee, got out cold meat, fixed some potatoes for creaming. She was competent. She had not been brought up to cook her own meals, but she did it as if it were nothing. She didn't talk as she worked, and neither did he. He stood by the window and looked at snow making its pattern of the upthrust black limbs of the pear tree, but let her prepare a meal undisturbed.

But when they sat down he said, "If John is no more than a leaf to you there isn't any real point in your staying here. I thought it was because it was the place of your love and deeply familiar and dear. I see it isn't that at all. It shouldn't matter where you are—and if Marcy wants you with her, why not? What does it matter?"

"They try to push me back into my old self. I can't be pushed, Sebastian. I won't be."

"But that ego—if it's as unimportant as you say, why are you protecting it?"

"It isn't that. They make it important. It's the ego they are trying to keep alive."

"Elspeth"—his voice was very gentle and winning—"your old self was a very good one. I'd hate a world without it. And it was the self of John that I want to remember, not a flicker in the evolutionary process. But I didn't come to argue with you. Whatever you do will be right for you. You will have to work it out your own way."

"Yes. It will take the rest of my life."

He hesitated, then asked, "Haven't there been reporters?"

"I think so. I don't go to the door."

"You frightened me, not answering the phone—or the door."

"But I have nothing to say," she said.

She looked very beautiful, sitting there across from him, leaning back a little in the captain's chair, scarcely touching her food, her eyes grave and still; but Sebastian would have preferred her ugly, her face stained with tears, her grooming forgotten. Her spontaneity, her gift of life, had been extraordinary, had been herself.

They finished the simple meal in silence, went back to the other room. Sebastian said, "Let me help you with the dishes," but she said, "Not now."

Then Sebastian looked around the room as if suddenly missing something. "Where's the portrait?" he asked quickly.

Over the plain white mantel had hung for two years now the portrait of John. Marcy and David had had it done as a Christmas surprise for Elspeth. In it John sat at the piano, but the piano and even John's hands were dimmed out, till all you saw was John's sharp, intent face. It had been done by Wickham, who did such striking modern things but had gone completely traditional in this. It was the best thing Wickham had ever done or ever would do.

"I destroyed it. I burned it," Elspeth said with that horrible calm.

"You *what?*"

"I burned it."

He stared at her incredulously, and a chill went up and down his spine. "*Elspeth!*"

"It was mine, wasn't it?"

"I thought it belonged to us all," he said helplessly, staring at the empty space. "It seemed to belong to us all."

A strange look went over her face, something that was not this remote new expression—something that said she was not quite sure of this path she had chosen, something lost and sad beyond words. Sebastian went to her and took her in his arms, and she rested there as if she could not move, though not as one clings with love, just with a complete tiredness.

"Elspeth, Elspeth," he said. "Of course it was yours. You could do what you liked with it. But don't grieve so. Don't, Elspeth. Live the way you want to—but don't grieve so."

He held her close, aware that he was not holding her at all, shocked and hurt to the core, feeling a wild, sharp sorrow for John, a deeper sorrow for her. This was Elspeth, Elspeth Doorn, a very part of his existence. This was her body against his, and yet he might as well have held a wraith. He hadn't meant that she was not to grieve. He wanted her to grieve, to do anything that would show she was feeling, not wandering blindly in some realm of metaphysics alien to her. And with his shock at her destruction of the portrait was mixed some relief that she had shown in some human way that she could still feel. Yet even this—this betrayal of all she had felt for art—was an unfamiliar act. She was not, and never had been, the kind who believed in funeral pyres for widows. She had clung to all her joys and sorrows, enhanced them by remembering them.

Marcy's words, "She doesn't love us any more," hung in the air.

Elspeth drew away from him slowly, said, "How thick the snow is!"

"Yes. I was remembering your first Christmas here in the snow. Will you let us all come for Christmas this year?"

"But you'll be back in Paris."

He let it all go without regret. "No, I'll be here, Elspeth," he said.

There was the sound of a car laboring through the snow. Then the car stopped. Sebastian went to the window and said, "A man's coming."

"Pay no attention."

There was a heavy knocking on the little-used front door. Sebastian moved toward the sound, and Elspeth said, "*No!*" But he went on, pulled back the old-fashioned bolt, and opened the door to the whiteness and to Eddie Dunstan.

"This the Esker place? I hope to heaven it is, or they'll be digging me out of a snowbank come spring!"

"This is the Esker place," Sebastian said. "I'm Sebastian Esker. Is there anything I can do for you?"

In spite of his sorrow, in spite of everything, Sebastian felt a wild desire for laughter. There was something so irresistibly cocky and impudent about the creased, wise face that peered at him out of the snow, that it called for laughter.

"Well, there was something," Eddie said, "but after this Polar expedition I've almost forgotten what it was. I'm not a book agent, and I'd appreciate it if I could just step inside for two minutes and get thawed out."

"Come in," Sebastian said. "I suppose you're a reporter."

"Suppose wrong, then. Mrs. Esker here?"

"She's here, but I will answer any questions."

"I'm Eddie Dunstan. She knows me. I won't say I don't want to intrude, because that wouldn't be so. I do want to intrude—"

"You look frozen," Sebastian interrupted him. "Come in, and I'll light the fire."

Elspeth was still standing by the window. "You know Mr.

Dunstan?" Sebastian asked, but did not wait for an answer. He went at once to the hearth, bent, and put a match to a fire already laid. Flames caught at once on paper and shingles and made a spot of cheer in the room, where dust stood on the tables and floor.

"Yes. How do you do, Eddie?" she said, but distantly.

"Sorry to come here at a time like this," Eddie said. "And I must say Marcy told me not to come. But a man has to make a living, and Esker was top news."

"I thought you weren't a reporter," Sebastian said.

"No more am I. I'm a photographer." He moved near the fire as if he could not help himself, stood there in a shabby, swinging overcoat, shivering a little. "You can have the country," he said.

"Thank you," Elspeth said, almost with irony.

"Big of me, isn't it?" Eddie acknowledged the irony with impudence. "I saw Marcy, and she wouldn't come down with me, but, as I say, I make my living taking pictures, and so I came without permission. It's this way. You know the picture about Tahiti is coming out . . ."

He went on, turning himself from time to time before the fire as if he were on a spit, finally sitting down on the long stool on the hearth, but going on talking all the time, as if he would lose his theme if he ever stopped.

All this time Elspeth stayed near the window. She scarcely seemed to listen.

"You know how people eat up romance," he said. "This would be chock-full of romance—and not phony either. The house in the snow, and the piano, and the portrait Wickham did—think I've got that in my own private morgue somewhere—and maybe you, Mrs. Esker, sitting here by the fire.

You've always been good for a spread, if you don't mind my saying so. Or just standing where you are now—there by the window. Somber and touching—you know. I'm not being flip. Admired Esker—had what it takes, Esker did. Sound ghoulish, I know. But if I'm going to do this at all it has to be now."

"In other words, you're a myth-maker," Sebastian said.

"My trade exactly," Eddie said. "Only this time the myth's already made. Just trying to perpetuate it, that's all."

Elspeth turned and looked at Eddie. Sebastian had an instant's certainty that she was going to ask Eddie about his relationship with God.

"If you'll excuse me, Eddie," she said with distant politeness, and walked out of the room and up the stairs.

Eddie Dunstan gave a sigh, slid out of his coat, and prepared to talk to Sebastian, man to man. "I could fake it, except for the house," he said. "I've got a honey of Elspeth at a New Year's party—that big shindig the Doorns pulled off when David had his first show. Taking it hard, isn't she?"

"Naturally," Sebastian said, knowing that he lied, that she was taking something hard, but not John's death.

"Some folks have the knack of getting their faces in the papers—I mean the papers that count. And it isn't as if the Doorns had money, not what we call money nowadays. They just look like news. The fashion sheets eat up Marcy too—wrap by Doorn, blouse by Doorn, interview with Marcy Doorn just back from Paris. They like it too, you know," he finished a little defensively.

Sebastian gave a faint smile, and Eddie said, "Worried about my cameras. Don't like them out there in the cold. She isn't going to give, is she?"

"No, I don't think she will give. She won't prevent you from taking a picture of the house, though, if you want to—even of the piano."

"No good without her. Have to tie the dead onto the living in a thing of this kind. Wouldn't make a story without her. See, it's got everything—youth, beauty, fame, tragedy. It's got everything. Now I think of it, I couldn't use that picture I've got—looking like she'd just been given Christmas with all the angels thrown in. Marcy's always been more to my taste, though she was snooty as all get-out when I saw her the other day—but for looks Elspeth's the beauty of the lot. Folks like being looked down on—in the papers, that is. In real life it's something else again. David's got that same superior air. Folks eat that up. Where's the piano?"

"In here," Sebastian said quietly, and led the way to the room across the hall. It was very still in John's room, nothing there except the early dusk the snow made, the piano, the manuscript sheets. Sebastian stood there, tall and pale, remembering, seeing it in its emptiness, its nothingness, without John sitting on the bench, looking away from the keys, making such pure sound drift through the house.

"Yeah," Eddie said, as if he saw it all, saw John, saw the emptiness, saw his picture of the room, had already arranged his lights to emphasize the loneliness.

"Where does she keep the portrait?" Eddie asked suddenly.

Sebastian turned slowly, not quite coming out of the grief that overwhelmed him. "The picture isn't here. It's been—disposed of," he said quietly.

"You don't say? Where is it? Who'd he leave it to?"

"It's disposed of," Sebastian said again more firmly and led the way back to the living room.

"Let's see, what's your line?" Eddie asked uncomfortably.

"I suppose you write books or something. Never knew such a family for doing things in the arts."

"No, I don't write books—only a little article once in a while. I'm not news," Sebastian said. "I'm a teacher."

"A teacher, eh? You don't look it. Look important, like the rest of 'em."

"I'm not important to anyone but myself. Perhaps you ought to bring your cameras in."

At this sign of intelligence and mercy in an outsider Eddie was overwhelmed with gratitude. "I say, you must know what it means to play nursemaid to a camera! But I suppose I've got to get out of here and find some place to spend the night. No use lugging them in and right out again."

It was very dark now. The snow too was grayness beyond the panes. "I don't know where you'd go on a night like this," Sebastian said. "You might as well stay here and take what pictures you can in the morning."

"Stay here? And be brushed off by Mrs. E.? No, it wouldn't be any colder in a snowbank, thanks. She's low—naturally she's low. But she's never going to warm up to this project. I might as well forget it and try to get back to town."

"You couldn't possibly," Sebastian said. "I'll help you bring your things in. I'm sure you will be allowed to take what pictures you like. She won't mind—she won't mind at all."

"Says you. It'd be a godsend, though, I don't mind saying, if you could wangle it."

"I won't have to wangle it. It will be, as you say, a godsend. Come along, before it's pitch dark."

Sebastian slid into his coat, and the two men went out into the snow toward the little car.

5

THE TWO men, one so scholarly and gentle, the other so shrewd and straight from Madison Avenue, sat together by the fire. The cameras and other paraphernalia of tripods and lights were piled in the music room. Sebastian had turned on lights, and the room was warmer, more fit for human beings now. Elspeth had not come downstairs again as yet, and the house was quiet.

Eddie lit a cigarette, dropped his match into a cloisonné bowl that stood on the table near the sofa. "Quite another cup of tea from your brother," he said suddenly. "Aren't you?"

"Quite."

"He certainly hit the jackpot young."

"Oh? My brother was a musician from five on, Mr. Dunstan. He worked at it, you know. It didn't drop on him out of heaven—except that he had talent. I've known him to work twenty hours out of twenty-four—and more than once."

"Yeah, you always think the other fellow has the easy job,"

Eddie admitted. "But I've got the files on his education and all that—I don't exactly call it coming up the hard way. Studied abroad and all."

Sebastian did not answer.

"Had some talent myself," Eddie went on defiantly. "Used shoe-blacking on shingles or sacks—not bad, either. I could still do the stuff David Doorn does with my hands tied behind me."

"Are you sure? Now and then David pulls it off."

"Now and then. Startling, mostly, and that's all. Only thing I've seen of his I'd give two cents for is one of New York in fog. He hit it that time, but I presume he'd toss that out as from his early 'traditional' period."

"I bought it," Sebastian said.

"You did? You don't mean it!"

"I've always believed David knew more about the fog in the human heart than we're apt to give him credit for knowing. It was more than just fog over New York."

"Yeah," Eddie said.

"I even see why he and the rest try the geometric nonsense. They're trying to say something that hasn't been said and can't be said in old ways. It seems healthy to me that they try."

"Yeah, know the feeling. Tried to do that old empty mansion—pigeon on the step, dust on the rail, blank windows, all arty. First thing you know you're trying to take a shot of emptiness. Know what you mean."

They sat in silence for two or three moments, Sebastian all the time listening for some sound from upstairs, always conscious that he was waiting, yet at the same time glad for the presence of this brash young man with his insistence on facts, his remoteness from the metaphysical. Or was it remoteness? A young man trying to photograph loneliness, making pictures on sacks and shingles with shoe-blacking. No, he'd oversimplified Eddie, and he apologized in his mind but not aloud.

Then suddenly he began to talk of John, compelled to speak of him. "You see," he said, "it wasn't the way you think with John at all. It wasn't that he wanted terribly to make music or that everything was given to him. We didn't have much money, you know. We gave up everything we had for education, because that happened to be what we believed in. Our father was a musician, but he never made money; he just had a job in an orchestra—competent, not a genius. The conductor was a friend of his, and one day he dropped in. Burghardt was his name. John was five then. I was seven. Burghardt and Father were discussing some number, and Burghardt hummed through a few bars of it. John was playing under the piano, which was his place of safety, and suddenly they heard him sing, in a little voice, those bars—but backward. Burghardt was the one who realized what John had done. He was in the dining room, over coffee. He put the cup down so that his coffee splashed, went in, and pulled John out from under the piano. He was so excited that he became very German. '*Ach, du Kind! Du Wunderkind!*' he kept saying, and he tried again and made John sing what he had sung back to him backward. It was a feat, but seemed nothing at all to John. And he never had a chance to be anything but a composer after that."

"You don't mean he didn't like it?" Eddie demanded in astonishment.

"Sometimes it was a terrible burden to him. He never took it lightly, but it was sometimes a great burden. But we were a family that believed a gift had to be accepted, that talent had to be developed. Five is very young to take on that kind of responsibility."

"Paid off, though," Eddie said.

"Paid off? Yes, I suppose so. Only he's dead, Mr. Dunstan."

"Got it all in—more than most do," Eddie said stubbornly.

"He got music in," Sebastian admitted. "But John knew that he paid for getting it in, for making it all there was."

"He had Elspeth," Eddie said. "All that and heaven too, you might say."

"Shall we go out and see what we can find for supper?" Sebastian said.

A small metal fox hung from a cord to the ceiling light. Sebastian pulled the cord, and the kitchen sprang into brightness.

Sebastian went at once to the refrigerator and began taking out eggs, milk, butter. "This is going to be very simple," he said. "Do you know Marcy well?"

"Oh, I run into her quite often—in a business way. Even at a party now and then."

Sebastian was conscious of the purple edge of handkerchief sticking out of Eddie's breast pocket, tried to imagine Marcy and Eddie at the same party, failed. He got out the eggbeater. Should he call Elspeth now or wait till the omelet was done? Or might not the omelet fall before Elspeth came for it?

"Wait," he said. "I'll see if Elspeth's ready."

He went up the stairs, rapped on Elspeth's door, seeing his own hand exaggeratedly large and insistent against the panel of the door. "Supper, Elspeth," he said.

She came at once. He hadn't thought she would come, but she opened her door and came out into the hall, came with him down the stairs.

"I'm making an omelet. Mind?" he asked. "Eddie looked hungry."

"He's still here?"

"Where could he go to in this storm? It doesn't matter, Elspeth. It doesn't matter at all."

She put a hand to his arm suddenly. "Oh, Sebastian," she said, "it's going away, it's all going away. It's getting not easy any more. I can't come to supper—he lets it all in."

"All he wants is some pictures," Sebastian said, putting a hand over hers. "That's all he wants, Elspeth. It hasn't anything to do with us. He takes pictures for a living, that's all. He's a very decent man, and he won't trouble you—I promise. It doesn't matter what he does, does it?"

"I'm going into little pieces again. People take pieces out of you, Sebastian; they do."

"Not if you don't let them. Not if you don't give the pieces. All you have to be is indifferent. Everything's ready. Come along—it won't be hard."

But the Elspeth he had known could not be indifferent. She gave herself to all, gave of her enthusiasm, her beauty, her talent. She couldn't let a garbage man feel left out. Indifference in Elspeth was a kind of death, and something died in Sebastian as he urged her to indifference.

She came. She even set the table with good dishes and fine silver, the best goblets. The table looked like a party, too fine for an omelet and a salad of greens in a wooden bowl. Then the omelet was done, and Eddie, with his purple handkerchief turned dark in the candlelight, sat across from Elspeth, while Sebastian served as if he had the right—a strange trio indeed.

"Never gone in for ivory towers," Eddie said, when no one else seemed inclined to talk. "Must say this would do, if I never had to leave it—if I never had to get a car out."

"The snowplow always comes," Elspeth said. "It would be better if it never came and the snow could lie like this from fall to spring, with never a footprint on it."

"Bread and butter wouldn't last," Sebastian said practically. "Or would you allow snowshoes?"

"I can make bread," Elspeth said.

"But would you? And you have Mr. Dunstan and me here. Would you want to spend the winter with us? Or would you just shovel us out into a snowbank and lock the door?"

"You had no right to come in," Elspeth said. "Not either of you."

"I had a right," Sebastian said. "John was my brother, and you have always been my friend. I had a right. Eat your omelet and be grateful you didn't have to make it."

"John isn't here any more."

There was something horrifying in the way she said it, pushing them out, pushing out the reason for their being here at all.

"It seems as if he were here," Sebastian said gently. "It seems as if any minute we would hear him play or see him taking down the chess board, or going out for a walk in the snow in the old deerskin jacket. I told you, Elspeth, that I hated throwing memories away. I don't intend to. John is here and will always be here. Salad, Mr. Dunstan?"

"Nibble, nibble, gnaw," Elspeth said with more force, with not quite so much remoteness. "Chew him up into little bits. You think that's what life's all about—cutting us up into little bits so there'll be enough to go around. All things to all men. A picture to you, Eddie—that's what he was. That's what I am. A picture. The great composer who made a glory for your quiet existence—that's what you cut out, Sebastian. And Abel took a bit to pay his taxes with. Nobody lets anybody be whole. Nibble, nibble, year in, year out. How do you expect anyone ever to be himself?"

Eddie put his fork down and stared at her. This was more

the Elspeth he knew, dramatic, alive. He gave a quick, impudent grin, said, "Kind of dull, though, without the butcher and the baker. Kid ourselves if we thought different. If I thought nobody'd ever see my pictures or nobody'd ever hear Esker's music, I'd get mighty uneasy. All this self-sufficiency tripe leaves me cold. Just another name for being damnably selfish, way I see it."

Sebastian folded his arms along the edge of the table. His recent illness had thinned a face already too thin, and he looked gray and very tired. He seemed to have forgotten Eddie. He said slowly, "I've never known you to be cruel, Elspeth. Never before. And it was my understanding, for all I have no connection with God, that God was supposed to be all things to all men. I never took anything from John, except affection. He gave me much, and I think ungrudgingly."

Elspeth stood up. The candlelight seemed to gain strength from her light. "You don't know what I mean. You won't know what I mean," she said. "Do you want to take your pictures now, Eddie?"

Uncomfortably Eddie rose, anxious to be about the job he knew, yet uncomfortable and not so lacking in understanding as Elspeth indicated. "Too right I want to," he said. "But I'd still have three meals a day if I didn't. If you feel I'm taking too big a slice, why, that's it, Mrs. Esker. Forget the whole thing."

"It doesn't matter," Elspeth said dully. "It doesn't matter at all."

So Eddie got out his flashbulbs, set up his camera, went to work. Sebastian didn't help him, but carried the dishes out and washed them slowly. He snuffed out the candles on the dining-room table, went into the living room.

"That was a honey," Eddie was saying. Elspeth was standing

by the window as she had earlier in the afternoon, just standing there, looking out at nothingness, at the night. "Hold it," Eddie said. "I'll do one more." She looked quite capable of holding it forever, quite unaware that two men were behind her in the room. "Okay. Okay. I'll tackle the music room now," Eddie said. "That's all for now."

"You look quite intact," Sebastian said, coming and standing beside her. If his voice had irony, it was irony with pain behind it. "If that is what you want, Elspeth. As for me, there are quite a few bits I'd willingly give away. And didn't he give you glory too?"

"Would you give me a hand, Mr. Esker?" Eddie called. So Sebastian went and helped for a few moments. Eddie worked for a long time, finally put his things together and said, "Now for the outside of the house if it's clearer in the morning."

"Sebastian, will you show Eddie his room? The front room with the white rug."

So Sebastian took Eddie up the stairs. It seemed early to send Eddie to bed. The room had a gay quality—Elspeth at her best. The white braided rug was the only bit of purity. All else was colorful and invitingly bright.

"Glad you got what you wanted," Sebastian said. "The bathroom's down the hall."

"Wouldn't have got to first base without you," Eddie said. "Thanks, fella."

Sebastian said a friendly good night, but as he reached the door Eddie said with embarrassment, "She's in a bad way, isn't she? If I know the Doorns, and I do, she's apt to blow her top any minute."

"It's a bad time for her," Sebastian said slowly.

"Granted. But she's holding it in too hard. Something's got to give. Well, 'night."

"Good night," Sebastian said again.

He went down the stairs slowly, wishing Eddie back with them again. He had loved Elspeth for seven years, and that was a large piece of a man's life. She had loved John, but still their minds and hearts too had always met in some sweet place of intimacy. She had always trusted him. She had always made it seem this was his home whenever he could make it so. Yes, John's glory had descended on them all and been a great part of everything they thought and said and did—not his public glory, but his integrity, his devotion to his talent. Always there, a bright star in their lives. "Something strange, beyond grief," David or Marcy had said. Because he had known her so well, known her with every cell of his body, he knew with a terrible sadness that this was true—this was not grief, this indifference, this putting John with the leaves, this pushing away of friends. This was something strange, beyond grief. He could wish she would blow her top.

Elspeth sat on the stool in front of the fire. Even with the life out of her she was beautiful. She would be beautiful when she was old, Sebastian thought—when she was old, with all passion spent. He sat down. "That wasn't too painful, was it?"

"No."

"Elspeth, Eddie thinks you are about to crack up. He thinks no tears are proof of it. But you aren't going to, are you? You don't even want to weep."

"You're like them all," she said. "You think I have to be in a pattern. Just because I want to find a way of life—"

"It looks more like a way to death," Sebastian said gently.

"It's all one thing," Elspeth said.

"Is it? Elspeth, why did you burn John's picture? I'm not trying to torture you. I have to know."

"I didn't want to look at it any more." But that was just a fact. That wasn't grief.

"Why didn't you?"

"That wasn't John. That was just an idol you set up to burn incense to."

"Nonsense. That was John as we knew him, sitting at the piano."

"But you didn't know him," she said, and with her saying it something seemed to fall away from her, some terrible knowledge, leaving her only a sigh in the room.

"I did," he said, "as much as one can."

"But one can't. One never can. Six years I lived with John. Six years I ate with him and laughed with him and slept with him—six years. And I never knew him at all, never knew him. And then—and then he tried to tell me, and I walked away. I walked away in the leaves, and when I came back he was dead. Dead."

"Tell you what? He didn't tell you that he didn't love you, of that I am sure."

"Sure? Oh, Sebastian, don't be sure of anything! Don't ever be sure of anything! But there is a way, a way to get your pieces all together again, to be whole. There is a way, Sebastian, and I must find it. If you wouldn't come, if you'd keep Eddie out and all the rest. But you have to be alone. You have to, Sebastian."

This was real, this was true despair, and Sebastian's heart felt squeezed. "Do you?" he asked. "But the trouble is, we are made up of people, people we know and love. If we cast them all out we cast out parts of ourselves. Don't we? If everyone goes—we might find nothing left. Nothing at all, Elspeth."

"No. No, there's something left," she said. "It may be something very small, but there's something."

"And what will you do with the something when you find it?"

"You're trying to make me selfish, like Eddie."

"No, you've never been selfish. But you could never make me believe that John didn't love you."

She stood up, came and put a hand on his thick dark hair. "Poor Sebastian. Poor, darling Sebastian," she said in a whisper. He did not move, and after a long time he did not feel her hand on his head, knew she was no longer in the room.

6

QUITE late Sebastian went up to the small slant-roofed room in the ell that contained the kitchen. "This is your room," Elspeth had said to him that first autumn here, making him part of the family. He stood there in the middle of it now, a tall, thin, but strong man in a gray suit a little too light-weight for this part of the world. He was almost too tired to stand, but with that weariness that will not let one rest. Everything stood out too clearly. On the flat-topped desk in the corner where the roof slanted was a *Yale Review* he had left here on his last visit. In the rocker was the red cushion. "But where's the red cushion?" he'd said to Marcy. "Every rocker ought to have a red cushion." And Marcy had brought this cushion, covered in old-fashioned, sprigged calico. His room. They had given it to him. No matter where he was, his heart called this room home.

"Well, Professor," John said, "good for you! But I expected

you today." John had always made him feel expected, wanted. They all had. "Oh, Sebastian, I've made some bar-le-duc! How wonderful that you came so that I can have an excuse to try it! It's much too special for everyday!" And there, oddly, for the first time, he saw John's face as it was this spring. He saw John standing down there by the kitchen window in his brown jacket, his eyes on the pileated woodpecker in the pear tree. "What an auspicious morning!" John said.

It all came crowding. He stood there, letting it crowd, not even turning on the light. The storm had stopped, and there was faint moonlight on the snow and in the room. Eddie would get his pictures tomorrow. It was a measure of Sebastian Esker as a man that he could care, even in the midst of personal grief, whether Eddie Dunstan got his pictures or not.

He reached out now and turned on the light. But the room was no more and no less known in lamplight. He sat down in the rocker, leaned his head back, and shut his eyes against familiarity. He knew now that he had come to a place where all was at stake. He knew that doubt now could destroy the very foundations of his life. He had three beliefs: that his brother John was a dedicated artist and had complete integrity; that John's love for Elspeth was real and a part of that very integrity; that he himself loved Elspeth without covetousness. These were specific beliefs, based on the larger ones that there were such things as integrity, as love, as selflessness.

He did not sit there summing up these beliefs. His mind said: Not know *John?* and: No, you cannot pretend love. "But you didn't know John. . . . I walked away . . . and when I came back he was dead. . . . Poor, darling Sebastian!"

"But I did know John," he said. He sat there and let that knowledge take over. That little boy who could cross streets by himself, yet walking so close to him on the pavement, not taking his hand, but not running away from him either. . . . "I wish you might have a bicycle," their father said. "I wish your mother could go to the mountains for a rest too. But we can just swing John's lessons, son." He sat doing homework while scales went on and on, and then John came into the dining room, said, "Come on out for a walk." How old was he then? Ten, maybe. John made up stories about what went on in strange houses. "They've got a bearskin rug in there and they lie on it at night while their father reads them stories," he said. Or: "Go softly! That's a *sinister* house!" Even yet when Sebastian passed that tall brownstone house, always so dark, he felt dark doings going on inside it. . . . He came running up the stairs after school, and into John's room, where John sat propped up against pillows that year of the rheumatic fever. He couldn't remember ever hearing John complain, though the pain was sometimes so bad. For all those months he, Sebastian, had sat there by the bed after school, playing games, helping with homework; but John hadn't asked him to; he never asked for anything. Only his dark eyes would light up when Sebastian came through the door, saying: You've come. You've come at last. . . . John never asked him to work so hard summers so there would be money enough for lessons; he never asked him to give up college for a year. There wasn't much talk of sacrifice ever in the Esker house. But it was true they banded together to make John free for his gift. It was no sacrifice, and John gave as much as they did—far more, actually. . . . Only once, he, Sebastian, came in, and John sat at the desk with his head down on his arms. Sebastian remembered exactly how young, awkward, and frightened he had been, saying, "What's the matter?" and how John had looked as he lifted his dark head and said, "I am sick to death of music." Thirteen or so, had he been? But it was all one memory, because even the little boy on Mr. Burghardt's steps had been grown.

"I knew you," Sebastian said. Steadily, steadily, all the years, John had gone on, except for that one moment by the desk, fulfilling his talent, writing his music. Single-minded, that was the word for John. When he wrote music, even for the movies, it was good music. When he loved, it was one woman, Elspeth. When he was a friend, he never stopped being a friend. When he counted on you as a part of his life, he counted on you to infinity and beyond. "I knew you," Sebastian kept saying stubbornly, and all the time Elspeth's words went on like counterpoint: "Poor, darling Sebastian"—denying his knowledge, mocking his faith, pushing like some monstrous bulldozer at the very foundations of his life.

A shiver like an echo from his illness in Paris went over him. He got up from the chair with the red cushion, made ready for bed. The bed was cold, and the chill and loneliness were all through him. Once the bed would have been warmed with a hot-water bottle. That was the kind of thing Elspeth never forgot. She had never before wanted just to be a small something by herself, with everyone cut off, gone out of her. He lay there and tried to know with her knowledge what it was she meant, and to let everybody go away from him—John and Elspeth and Marcy and David and the MacPhersons, and all the students who sat in his classes, and his colleagues on the faculty—let them all go, his love, his warm affection, the glow he felt when lecturing before eager eyes. He could not let them go, and knew he could not. But he came near enough to something cold and terrifying so that he felt it in his very bones. It was not peace approached, not any consciousness of identity, but some no-man's land, some nothingness in the midst of nowhere. It was like walking in some ruined city, all its inhabitants dead or fled—no one to hear his voice, no one to say, "That is Sebastian Esker!" Terrible thought—no one to hear, no one to see, no one to care. And identity to establish in nothingness. Terrible, terrible thought.

He was not asleep. He was still conscious of the moonlight touching along the edge of rocker and bureau. Yet the vision of the city was as real as the cities of dreams, and real too was the awful sense of complete anonymity. And then, making it a street anywhere—in Paris, New York, the village down the road—he saw John ahead of him, and John heard his steps, turned and waited, smiling, said, "Oh, there you are, Sebastian! I was expecting you!"

He gave a sigh of tremendous relief and slept. He woke, and the sun was shining on thick snow. The red cushion looked warm and inviting in the sunshine, and the small room was snug and cheerful.

To his amazement he found Elspeth and Eddie Dunstan sitting without restraint in the kitchen. As he came in Eddie said, "Good morning. Well, I'll be out and about my business."

"Help you?" Sebastian asked.

"Thanks, no. Let's keep the snow as pristine as possible!" His thin brows shot up comically at his own remark. He was gone out of the kitchen, whistling a little as he got into his overcoat, picked up his camera.

Sebastian poured himself coffee, sat down, shoving Eddie's cup away.

"And after he's finished I'll go too," he said quietly. "I do see what you mean, Elspeth. I'll leave you alone, and I'll see that the rest do too. Only—Elspeth, if you do find yourself, will you let me know? Even if you're not very big?" His eyes were calm and loving and strong.

"All right, Sebastian." Then, a little sadly, a little warmly: "I ought to have married you, hadn't I?"

Yes, she ought to have married him. He wouldn't have given her much, but he would have loved and cherished her forever and ever.

"No," he said quietly. "You always belonged to John."

"And that is the great sin, isn't it? To possess another, or be possessed by another?"

"I don't know, Elspeth. It's never seemed a sin to me. It may be. But I meant where love is the possessor, the possessed— I know, it's a giving up—and yet when two give up it cancels out, doesn't it? But never mind now. It's true enough that you can't give the self away if there isn't any self."

"You needn't do that," she said, for as he was speaking he had begun to carry dishes to the sink.

"But I want to," he said. "Just this once. After all, Eddie and I are intruders, even if I denied it yesterday."

"They are coming for the piano today," she said, "if the truck gets through. I am sending it to Marcy."

He put a cup down, turned toward her. "The piano?" he said slowly.

"Yes. I wonder if you'd have room in your car for the music in there. I'd like it gone."

There was a silence; then he said, "I'll take what I can," turned to his task again. But there was a sound in his head as of cherry trees falling.

He went into the other room and saw Eddie bent to look at the house through the finder, his overcoat open and dragging at the corners in the snow.

"Are there any cartons anywhere?" he asked.

"In the barn. In the attic."

"I'll wait till Eddie goes, if you don't mind. I somehow don't like to spoil anything for Eddie."

"No, never spoil anything for anyone. Let it all be lovely on top. Let no one see the canker—"

"You said you wanted the snow to cover all. I don't think the world could stand being quite uncovered, Elspeth. It would crack open."

"Then let it. Let it crack open and swallow us all. It is what should happen to us."

"Maybe so, but not in my time, I hope. Isn't there something about 'be ye kind one to another'? You used to know that one."

"I didn't know what kindness was," she said. "I think he's done. I think he'll go now."

He was done. He went. He said to Sebastian in the drive by his car, "Thanks a lot, fella. It wasn't quite what I'd dreamed up, but it's all right. I got some good shots. Want to see 'em before I turn 'em in?" He didn't ask if Elspeth would like to see them.

"I would, rather," Sebastian said. "Not that I'd object. I'm just interested. Could you leave them at Marcy's?"

Eddie grinned and said, "Could do." Then he looked across toward the thorn strees, with every twig and thorn limned in white, and said, "Take it back. It's not my ivory tower, inside or out. And she'd better get out while there's time. I'm not kidding—she's walking on a wire."

"She's got a good balance," Sebastian said.

"I think she's going to fall off this time," Eddie said. "Not that she hasn't got a right to fall as far as she likes—it must have been something, being married to your brother. But I'd drag her out by the hair of the head if I were you."

Sebastian hesitated, then said, "All set? I have to get going myself. Be sure to let me see the pictures."

"I'll do that. Should think Marcy might give up being a career girl and come down and keep her company for a stretch."

"She doesn't want Marcy. She doesn't want us, either. Good-by, Eddie."

It was somehow easy to call him Eddie instead of Mr. Dunstan. Eddie gave him a grin, a grin that said he wanted to say more but knew he was being brushed off and could take it. He started the engine, put up a hand in farewell, went out the snowy drive and started down the newly plowed road in a rush.

Sebastian went in and at once went to the attic, where he found a pile of empty cartons, carried some down to the music room. He said not a word to Elspeth, but with a heavy heart began to put piles of music scores into a box.

Then he was looking down at a sheet in his own handwriting. It was the verses from "The Blink-eyed Pig" that he had sent John, and which John had written the music for. His own comment—"might work in"—was scrawled across one corner.

Cast and catch,
Cast and catch.
It's the little wee fish
In the bunched coral,
In the branched coral.

Bone fish!
Bone fish!
Thou wilt be played and worn out
And I will haul thee in
Upon the raised coral.

John had made Abel come across with a very decent check for that small bit of translation. Sebastian had meant to use it for a present for John before he came back from Paris. But he had come empty-handed.

He put the sheet with others in a box, went steadily on. He didn't know what he was going to do with all these manuscript sheets, but he went on, packed all he could, paused, and carried boxes out to his car, David's car. His body was weak, tired, empty, but he seemed to be working independently of his body. This was John he was carrying; this was John's life, his meaning. Suddenly he paused, went to the living-room doorway, and said, "Perhaps John left this music to someone. Perhaps I haven't any right to take it."

"It's mine. It's all mine," she said.

Still he hesitated. "I didn't ask—but is there anything in the legal line that should be taken care of?"

"No. It's all taken care of. Everything is mine to do with what I will."

"But there won't be anything, if you give it all away."

"You don't need much, Sebastian."

He smiled at her, but briefly, said, "But you wouldn't like to sleep under a tree, Elspeth."

"I could sleep under a tree. I could, Sebastian. But I have this roof over me. There is a lot of money in the bank. There is nothing for you or anyone to worry about."

"My worries are my own affair. I shall worry about what I please. I shall worry about you, because you and John have been—are—very dear to me. But I will try not to let my worry touch you, if that is what you want. Only, you have promised me—"

"I know. You are good, Sebastian. I don't know any other good people. Not one."

"Fiddlesticks!"

"But I don't. It comforts me to have you here. It comforts me more than I expected. But I don't want to be comforted. I don't want to depend on you or anyone. If I let you take over it will be just as it has always been, and I won't change. I must change, Sebastian, or I am done for."

You have changed already, my darling. I cannot bear it to have you changed. Let your face light up just once in the old way, my darling, my beautiful one.

He said slowly, "Once last year, as I came along Third Avenue, a man came down the street, his arms thrown up, his face ravaged, like a prophet's, and he was crying out, 'You're terrible! You're all terrible! You're rotten, all you people! You're terrible, and you're doomed!' He was drunk, I think —he wasn't any Messiah. But he sent a chill up your spine. People just walked along, hardly looking at him. But maybe he had something. Maybe it was despair of the human race that made him drunk; it sounded like real despair. But so long as I know ten good men—and I know more than that—I won't believe in our doom. Change if you must, but don't take away the goodness that's already there. Change in itself isn't anything, is it? Is it?"

"But we are all rotten. We are all terrible—living on top, never real. I am that man too. I am his blood sister. Nothing, nothing is ever true. And Jesus said that the Holy Ghost was the spirit of truth—not a dove alighting, not anything like that, just the spirit of truth. That's what I have to find—the spirit of truth."

"All right, Elspeth. Only—well, this top layer—let's not discount it too much."

"It's all there is to us. That's what it gets to be."

"All right. You needn't tell me when you've found your spirit of truth. I'll know."

He turned away, went back to his task. When he had put as much as he could into the car he said, "That's all I can manage this time. I'll shove along now."

She was standing by the window, where she had posed for Eddie. She said, "You're angry with me."

"No. I'm never angry with you."

A little car came rattling along up the road from town. He could see it for an instant; then it was gone. But Elspeth seemed to stiffen, to go like ice.

"What is it?" Sebastian asked gently. "What is it, Elspeth?"

She turned, her face completely white, and cried out in a human voice, "Oh, Sebastian! I am dead already! I am *dead.* I'll never come to life again!"

"You will. I promise you will," he said, but his voice was unsteady, and he felt he must take her in his arms and love her back to life. "Look, Elspeth—would you mind very much if I got a room in the village and stuck around a while? I won't bother you. But I would be near if you wanted me. If I wouldn't be good for anything else, I would see that you were left alone. I have to take David's car back, but I could come back. Would you mind that—if I didn't bother you? I know you have to find a way of life again. I do understand that. I wouldn't even come to see you if you didn't want me to. But I would like to be near for a while. It's for my own sake, not yours. For the sake of *my* spirit of truth."

She did not answer, just stood and looked at him helplessly.

"I will stay unless you tell me not to," he said after a moment. "I'll say good-by now."

"Good-by, Sebastian."

It seemed to him he could not bear to leave her. But she had not told him he must not come back, and that was surely a concession. He put out a hand, and she put her hand in his, but it was cold, with no friendliness in it.

He found it hard to start the car, paused, tried to remember what David had told him about the mechanism. Then the car started, and he backed out the drive. The boxes were piled so high that his vision was poor, but he got into the road and headed toward the village.

It was a very small village. The post office was in the general store. There were a five-and-ten—a small one—and a bank and a hardware store, two churches, and perhaps thirty houses, a town hall, an inn that didn't look as if anyone ever patronized it, and a liquor store.

Sebastian drew up before the sign of the post office, got out, and went into the store. Mr. Goudge was weighing hamburger and gave him the same squinting look he had given Marcy. He knew Sebastian well from other visits. He wrapped the hamburger, gave change, then said, "Blow about your brother, Mr. Esker. Blow to the town. Can I help you?"

"Thanks, Mr. Goudge. I was just wondering if you knew of some place in town where I could stay for a few weeks—not the inn, if you don't mind."

"Inn's all right. Kind of run-down on the outside, but it's all right inside. Hat Halsey runs it—mightn't think it to look at her, but she's a first-rate cook, and she keeps that place clean as a whistle inside. Takes a lot of tourists to paint that old barn, though. Just tell her Caleb Goudge sent you over, and she'll treat you right. Don't think there'd be any talk, though, if you stayed right up at the farm, if that's what you're thinking about."

"Even so, I believe I'd rather stay in town," Sebastian said.

"Well, you couldn't do better'n Hat. How's Mrs. Esker?"

"All right."

"Seems only yesterday your brother was in—stood right over there by the stove in that old leather jacket of his and taught young Pete Wiggins to whistle. Pete was puffing his cheeks out till he looked like a circus balloon, but nothing came out. We all got a good laugh."

"Did he learn?" Sebastian asked.

"Oh, sure, sure, he got the knack after a bit. I'll say he did! Drives everybody crazy with his whistling."

Sebastian stood there, looking at the stove, seeing John standing there in the old jacket, teaching Pete to whistle. "Well, I'll go over and see Mrs. Halsey," he said. "Thanks."

"Miss—*Miss* Halsey. Never married, Hat didn't."

He walked across the snowy road to the old, unpainted, sprawling inn; walked in. There was a big front lounge, comfortable and old-fashioned, and in it, in the Windsor chair by the side window, sat a woman paring potatoes. She wore her hair in an unfashionable twist on top of her head, and her face was long and had lines down it—lines such as are quite often seen in men but rarely in women. Her hands wielding the knife were long, and the knuckles big.

"Miss Halsey?" Sebastian said.

She looked up with a startled grin. "Yes, I'm Miss Halsey. You surprised me. Don't tell me you want a room!"

"I do indeed. Mr. Goudge sent me over. For several weeks, if I could."

She rose, setting the pan on a stool, said, "Manna from heaven, that's what you are. Don't get many folks come winter. Show you what I've got. Close off most of the place in the wintertime. Couldn't heat it. But I keep three rooms warm, just in case. Let me wash my hands, and I'll be right with you."

She was back almost at once and led him up the broad stairs and toward the front of the inn, opened a door. "This is the best one," she said. "How much did you want to pay?"

"How much would I have to," Sebastian said, "for this one?"

"Well, it's off season—say ten a week. If you wanted to eat here, maybe we could make some kind of a rate. Say twenty-two a week?"

"That's very cheap in these days."

The room was pleasant, warm, and spotlessly clean, and looked out on the main street.

"I'll take it," Sebastian said, "beginning tomorrow. I'm going back to town now, but I'll come back by bus or somehow. It's exactly what I want. Do I pay something in advance?"

"Why, I know you, you're Mr. Esker's brother!" Miss Halsey said abruptly.

"Yes."

"Thought you looked familiar. Seen you often enough in the village, with the young folks. No, you don't need to pay any advance."

She turned and led the way back down the stairs, went into the big room where she had been paring potatoes, sat down, but did not pick up the pan. It looked homely and incongruous, sitting there on a plush-covered chair.

"Sit down a minute," she said. "You look tuckered out."

"I am, rather," he said, "but I have to get on."

He felt drained, tired, and the journey back with the manuscripts seemed something too long to contemplate. There was great kindness as well as shrewdness in the long spinsterish face.

"Five minutes won't matter one way or the other. Sit down," she said again, and he found himself sitting there opposite her. She didn't look maternal, and yet the wings of kindness folded over him and he felt taken care of.

"You don't need to say I'm not much like my brother—I know I'm not," he said with a quick but tired smile.

"Lucky folks never come two of a kind," she said. "Dull world if they did. Wasn't going to say that anyway. I was going to say—much as I'd like a boarder—that if I was you I'd take Mrs. Esker away with you. It's no place for her up there alone."

"I know. But she doesn't want to come."

Now she did reach for the potatoes, began to pare them in long, thin peelings. She began to talk, quickly, not looking at him. "Want to or not, I'd take her. Had a sister—got her yet, as a matter of fact—in the state hospital. Dodie was going to marry Orrin Wilson, and he was killed in the First World War. She took to brooding, and she never stopped. She thought he wasn't really dead, and she waited and waited, and she'd think she saw him in the street, and at last she began to think this one or that *was* Orrin, and it made a lot of trouble. That's the first time I've mentioned Dodie in years, but the other day I was out in the country and I met John's wife walking along the road. Windy cold day, but she didn't have a hat on. Maybe I'm wrong, but she made me think of Dodie. Haven't said that to anyone else, but you look worried."

She had a very sensible voice, but the sense of kindness persisted through its brusqueness.

"I am worried," he admitted. "But she won't come, Miss Halsey. That is why I thought I'd stay near by."

"Ought to do more'n that," she said.

"I've never been in the habit of using my authority on Elspeth," he said.

"Look as if you could, though. Always been a fool for beauty. Maybe because I'm plain myself. Most beautiful girl I've ever laid eyes on. No place for a girl like that, all stark alone up there. You do look like your brother—same shape face. Known him a long time."

"A long time? Well, I suppose six years is a long time. It's gone fast enough."

"Known him longer than that. Stayed here that time he came for the music festival—must be twelve, fourteen years ago. Just a boy, he was—well, in his twenties, maybe. Had that very room you looked at. Always sent me a card at Christmas. Couldn't have been more surprised when he came back and bought here. If I was you I'd go right back up there and fetch her away. She's got a sister in town, hasn't she?"

"Yes, Marcy. It's not so simple, Miss Halsey."

But he was feeling a strange shock. Here? Here in this inn? In this town? John? He remembered the time John had gone to the music festival. Sebastian had worked in a nursery that summer and helped finance John's stay. But surely not here? It wasn't that it was impossible, but it was incredible that John had never mentioned the fact. It wasn't here he had sent money to John. He'd have remembered the name Old Quagatuck.

"Who said it was simple?" Miss Halsey said impatiently. "Here I am taking the bread right out of my own mouth—but that's my advice, all the same."

Sebastian stood up. "All right. I'll try again," he said. "But I still want the room—not tomorrow, perhaps next week. I'll phone you—and, if she won't go, tomorrow. But I wish you were doing the persuading."

"Couldn't do that hardly. I don't even know her, except to say good morning to in the street. Mame Powell went up—she's the minister's wife—but she didn't answer the door. If you should come back—and don't feel bound to—I'll make you as comfortable as I can."

"I'll be back," he said.

So he drove back up to the farm, feeling the uselessness of it, but compelled to try all the same. There was brilliant sunshine, and the snow shone blindingly. It was a day for hope, for clear thinking, but Sebastian Esker drove through fog. All that came clear was a picture of a girl called Dodie going up to strange men in the street, calling them Orrin.

To his surprise and relief he found Elspeth out in the yard, putting breadcrumbs on the snow for the birds. She was bareheaded but wore a short blue jacket lined with red that he had seen before. It seemed such a normal, human thing to be doing, and he smiled at her and said, "I forgot something."

She dropped the rest of the crumbs in her pan to the snow in a small heap, let the pan hang down in an odd way. "What?"

"You. I forgot to take you with me. I'd meant to do that."

She just stared at him without expression.

"You almost argued me out of it," he went on. "Come on in and get some clothes together."

"You promised to leave me alone," she said.

"I'm breaking my promise. I've changed my mind. You can be alone in town as well as here. But I can't see any reason for Marcy and David to be worrying their heads off. Come along, now—I'm not fooling, and I'm not going to be persuaded you ought to stay here. You oughtn't."

"Why not?"

"I said I wasn't going to argue." He took her arm, and she came, but reluctantly, into the house.

"They are coming for the piano," she said.

"What's the name of the trucker? I'll call him. He wouldn't come on a day like this. What's his name?"

"Jed Olsen."

"I'll phone him. What about water? Do you have to do anything about that? Or the furnace? There must be some neighbor who'd see to things. I'll tell you, we'll leave a little heat on in case you want to come back. That wouldn't be too expensive, would it? What's the name of the oil company?"

Then he turned and said half humorously, half angrily, "And don't call me 'poor, darling Sebastian' either. I don't like it. You may be trying to love in the big sense of the word, but till you learn how I wouldn't cast off all the little loves. As you say, it's all one thing."

He went to the phone, began to make arrangements, quickly, competently. He didn't let himself stop, though his hand on the receiver was unsteady and he was terribly conscious of Elspeth standing there in her blue jacket, her eyes as dead as any zombie's. Yet she'd been feeding the birds. And perhaps she was right, for her. Perhaps she would find herself here alone. Perhaps this was completely wrong.

He turned and said, "I couldn't bear it, Elspeth, and that's the truth. I couldn't bear leaving you here. When it came right down to it, I couldn't do it. I want you to do what you want to do—I don't want you pushed around. But I couldn't bear it."

"You needn't shout," she said too quietly.

"I wasn't shouting."

"Everybody shouts. Everybody. You can't be still. I thought

you were going to be quiet—but no, you shout too. How can you ever be still till they stop shouting?—still like David, I mean—not my David—"

"The 'Lord is my shepherd' one."

She gave him a grateful look that almost let him in, said, "Yes, that one."

The truck driver had been forestalled, the oil company given orders, and they stood there in their coats and talked of David as if there were no urgency at all.

"Why have we let it all go by like old wives' tales, Sebastian?—like the wind? When you think that that was the very first moment when someone thought of a loving God—the wonder of it you can hardly bear! Can you? 'The Lord is *my* shepherd'—and the stars over the field, and the sheep asleep, and suddenly 'Why, the Lord is *my* shepherd!' "

David or Marcy would have said with scorn, "Yes, a lovely imaginative moment—if you like fairy tales—and look at the trouble it's caused!"

But Sebastian said only, "But there aren't fields enough to go around, fields all alone under the stars. There's no use pretending there are. We have to make the field, in our heads."

At that moment a car came along the road. It was so still in the house that even the sound [illegible] passing car was noticed. Sebastian turned his head and [illegible] car. It was the same rattletrap of a Ford that had gone up the road earlier. It had an ancient, patched-up look that he remembered. He remembered it too because of Elsepth's look when she had seen it. If he had thought he'd imagined that it was this particular car that upset Elspeth, there was now no longer reason to doubt it, for Elspeth stopped speaking, just stood there, listening, till the sound of its passing was no longer with them. Then she turned blindly, clung to him, cried out, "Oh, take me away!

Take me away! I'm falling, falling, falling . . . Take me away!"

The "falling, falling, falling," was from an old poem they'd loved—the Lawrence poem of the man falling from the hands of God. The God they had discounted, but the symbolism they had taken, and the poem made a lovely sound when David read it, doomlike and impressive.

"But I am taking you. I am," Sebastian said.

She held to him a moment more in silence; then she turned, went quietly up the stairs, packed a few—a very few—clothes, came down.

"I'm ready," she said.

He looked around to see if all the lights, the stove, were turned off. It seemed strange to leave the house with so little preparation, just to leave it alone on the lonely road. There was an instant when it seemed they were, after all, betraying the house, betraying John, betraying Elspeth's spirit of truth. But they shut the door, put the key where the oil man could find it—or anyone else who cared to do so—and went to the car. Elspeth stood quietly while Sebastian made another arrangement of cartons so that the front seat could be free; then they were backing down the drive, heading toward New York.

7

"BUT ABEL'S here," David had said. "He's here, and somebody has to cope till Elspeth comes to her senses. It won't hurt you to come have a drink with him—you know damned well Sebastian won't be back today. He may never come back," he finished grimly.

"All right. I'll come," Marcy had said, and put the receiver down without a sound.

She was there, and the room was full of people. She might have known David couldn't bear having just the three of them hashing over John's music and Elspeth's strangeness. She was used enough to rooms full of people, to rooms full of these very people, but for an instant she couldn't catch on to familiarity, couldn't come to the party. She saw Abel at once, his broad shoulders and his eagle's beak of a face. He was smiling at Isobelle, with a shrewd appreciation of her charms—and her vices as well—in his eyes.

"Hi, precious!" Isobelle said. "Isn't David the angel to have a party? I was about to take the veil!"

Abel's eyes doubted that; then he turned and said, "Hello, Miss Doorn."

She had met him but once, two years ago. It seemed wrong that he should remember her. "Hello," she said.

Isobelle stayed close to Abel and said, "It's your turn to comfort Freddy, pet. His show's closing as of tonight."

If she'd wanted to she could have put Isobelle in her place, could have taken over Abel; but she went over to Freddy, who said in his falsetto voice—such a silly voice—"I was devastated about John. Simply devastated!"

He was devastated all right, Marcy conceded. But it wasn't about John, it was about that curtain, going down, down, down on his hopes, his work. For all his affectations, Freddy worked. "It's wicked, about the show," she said. "There was a minute, there at the end of the second act, when I cried. I did, Freddy. Authentic tears."

Her voice was light, but he gave her a flick of anxious glance, of gratitude coupled with a fear of seeming to care. "Coming from you, I'll take it," he said. "No one could ever call you a fool for flops, my sweet!"

Then someone was saying, "Tell me, how's Elspeth? Where *is* she?" And they talked about John. Of course they talked about John—a memorial cocktail party, Marcy said bitterly to herself. Maybe as good as any wake, yet the steadiness with which the glasses were filled, the sense that all of them were, like Freddy, mourning not John but their own frustrations and disillusionments made Marcy's answers short, her glance evade their glances. "Do you remember . . . ? do you remember . . . ?"—pretending it was real, pretending they had feelings.

Then there was a "Do you remember?" that made the room disappear. "Do you remember the night John and Elspeth did the tango? Will you ever forget it?". . .

"No, it is not possible for an American to do the tango as it should be done," the Spaniard had said.

"Oh?" Elspeth had said so slowly, so wickedly mischievous. And she had put out her hand to John and said, "Shall we?" And David turned to the keys, and people dropped back against the walls, and Elspeth, holding John's hand, stepped out into the middle of the room. Elspeth had on the skirt of Scotch plaid in fine wool, and a white blouse piped with plaid—the last costume in the world for a tango. Oh, the magic of it! For even now it seemed that Elspeth had *been* Spanish, that her fair hair, worn long then, had become black and smooth and high-swept, held by combs; that the dance had been done to castanets. And the Spaniard had leaned against the wall, dark, beautiful, his eyes that had been so scornful surprised, excited. Why had she, Marcy, thought it impossible that John call for country dances, then? Why had she, when he could dance like that?

"You aren't evading me by any chance?" Abel's voice said close behind her.

"Of course not," she said.

He put a strong, purposeful hand on her arm, led her to the little sofa in the corner. "I wouldn't mind so much. It's the way we do things nowadays," he said.

"I don't know why I mind," she said. "I'm exactly like them."

He didn't contradict her, simply said, "We're all more or less alike."

She was used enough to men of power, but Abel's power was like some physical thing there on the sofa beside her. He was as old as her father, but he had the power of the young.

When she did not answer but sat only looking about the room, then down at her hands against the purple plaid suit skirt, he said, "Would you like me to tell them none of them are worthy to black his shoes?"

She looked around and up at his beaked face quickly, said, "I'd like it very much—from someone. But since you are here to make what you can from his remains, I'd rather it came from someone else."

"Shall we put it rather that I don't like waste?" he said quietly.

"Oh, put it in any civilized way you choose!" she said. "Sorry—I don't feel politic today."

"But that is the way I want to put it," he insisted. "I don't like waste, Miss Doorn."

She was silent for some time, then said almost contritely, "No, I don't either."

"Then shouldn't I try to rescue anything I can?"

"Yes. Only it seems the act of a vulture. I am being unpardonably rude, but I can't seem to care, Mr. Abel."

"I don't mind," he said quietly.

Isobelle drifted over, glass in hand, sat facing them on a long stool. "We don't, after all, have a Hollywood producer at every party," she said. "You shouldn't be greedy, darling, even if you have a chance." She gave Abel her charming, provocative smile.

"I was just going," Marcy said suddenly. "You may have anything that's left, pet." She stood up. "Nice to have seen you, Mr. Abel."

"Oh, just a moment," Abel said. "I'll take you home." Then

he smiled at Isobelle and said, "I'll be back," and moved toward David.

"You're not going?" David demanded of Marcy.

"Yes," Marcy said. "Yes, David, I am. And I can get home all right by myself, Mr. Abel."

"I don't doubt you," Abel said coldly. "Nevertheless, I will see you home. I'll be back, Doorn."

She did not protest further but let him get his coat, go out into the street with her.

"We can get a taxi at the corner, I think," he said. "I know you are angry, Miss Doorn, but I have one or two things I want to say to you."

So she let him get a taxi, sat beside him in it, gave the address.

"First, the party was David's idea, not mine."

"I know," she admitted.

"Second, I had great respect for your brother-in-law—still have. If you want to think it is merely because I have made money on him, you will no doubt go right on thinking so. I live with talent, Miss Doorn. I wallow in it, you might say. There is more talent in the world than most people think. You get tired of talent when you live with it day in, day out. John Esker didn't live in Hollywood. He had tremendous personality, but he didn't use it for purveying his talent, to build up himself, as most do. I did not come east for this purpose, but I am here, and I do not want anything Esker may have written these last months wasted. For some reason David is hedging on letting me see John's wife. I have no intention of forcing myself upon her, but I should think it might be to her advantage to see me. Esker was a very special person."

"Yes. I'm sorry. I'm truly sorry, Mr. Abel. Elspeth is ill, that's all. We've been trying to protect her. But I will go, or have Sebastian, John's brother, go and look through what manuscripts there are and see if there is anything. Would that do?"

"It would do very well. Is she seriously ill?"

"Yes."

"I'm sorry. An extraordinary woman. She is still in the country?"

"Yes."

"David didn't tell me she was ill. I had wondered why she did not write. She was in the habit of writing for John, and it seemed odd not to have an answer to my letter. She has a gift for graceful letters. I will appreciate it very much if you will look over his music."

"Here we are," Marcy said. The taxi stopped, but she sat there, looking at David's cream-colored car just ahead of them at the curb. She could see the boxes piled high in the car. She did not even imagine that she might say, "There it is, Mr. Abel. You may look through it yourself." No, it was something else she felt, a dread of taking on disappointment again, a dread of seeing Sebastian's face, of hearing him speak Elspeth's name.

Abel got out of the car, stood a moment beside the taxi, then held out his hand. She put her hand in his, said, "You are forbearing, Mr. Abel. Good night."

"Good night, Miss Doorn."

She had hated the very idea of Abel, but as he drove away she wished him back, felt that he might have been a friend to take her up those stairs, hold back that sinking into despair. She walked alone up the steps, into the house, up the stairs, opened her own door.

Elspeth was curled up in the brown chair, just as she had sat hundreds of times. Sebastian sat on the window seat, his knees hunched up into the circle of his arms, his head back against the window frame, just as David sat so often. Only—only he was not David. His long face looked whittled out of wood, as if the lines down his cheeks could not be smoothed away by any smile.

Marcy went with all swiftness to Elspeth, bent and kissed her. "Oh, Elspeth, you *came!*" she cried. "How wonderful! And I wasn't here. Have you had anything to eat?"

"I've looked over cans," Sebastian said. "That's as far as I've gone."

"Was the driving awful? Oh, Elspeth, you're *here!*"

Elspeth said, "How do you know it's Elspeth?"

Marcy stiffened, but she said, "Darling, you can't fool me. Even if your soul gets as big as all outdoors, I'll know you."

"The stars were big as saucers," Sebastian said. "We got onto a universal plane, Marcy. We're bigger than life right now."

"You can't even see the stars here," Elspeth said.

"But I know they're there," Marcy said. "Whoops—there goes the coffee! You *did* put it on!"

She ran to the kitchen, turned down the fire. She took down cups, went back, and said, "We'll start with coffee, because it's ready, and coffee always helps on universal matters too."

"How about giving Elspeth her supper in bed?" Sebastian asked suddenly.

"Of course. Come on, darling, I'll tuck you in."

"Eat," she said when she brought the tray. "You look mighty fetching in that red trapping you've got on. I might see if Sebastian is hungry."

"He is hungry, but he will never be fed. That's the way Sebastian is."

She whirled and said, "And why? Why will he not? Because

he's given his life to you and there is no return, that's why. If he is a slave, you make him so. You could let him go if you would."

"You can't give freedom—it's in you or it isn't. Sebastian was born a slave."

"And that's a lie," Marcy said. "If you want the naked truth, that's a lie."

"No, it's not a lie. Everything I say from now on is the truth, only the truth. From now on."

"You're not cut out to play *Susan and God*," Marcy said hotly. "You're not the type."

She turned again to the mirror, away from the calm, the maddening calm, of the fair and lovely face. Then she saw the face in the mirror and saw back of the calm something else—was it desperation?

"I'm so glad you came," she said very simply. "Now I'll go feed Sebastian."

As soon as she was in the small kitchen Sebastian came and said, "May I help?"

"No. Sit down. You're dead on your feet."

But he sat down in the kitchen, in the one chair, in her way, right where she could see him, where she couldn't help seeing him.

He didn't talk. He looked too tired to talk. The only thing he said as she worked around him was, "I brought John's music. It's in the car. It was all in before she decided to come."

"You did? Wait."

She went to the phone, called David's apartment, asked for Mr. Abel.

"Mr. Abel, the music is here," she said without preamble. "It's in the car in front of this house—David's car. You'd better have David come and get the car, and you can look the music over there—not here. Could I speak to David again?"

And when David came: "David, she's here. But don't come in tonight. She's gone to bed."

"Thank heavens! Is she all right?"

"No. See you, David."

"Wait—"

But she hung up.

They ate almost in silence. Afterward she piled the dishes up, came into the living room, sat down near Sebastian. He gave her a smile, gentle, loving, a brother's smile.

"Could I sleep on the couch?" he asked. "I don't feel as if I could stir out to look for a room."

"Yes, of course. Is your bag in the car?"

"It must be—no, I brought it up, I think. It's somewhere—with Elspeth's bags, I think."

"I'll get her dishes," she said, stood up, and went to the guest room. The tray was on the floor, and Elspeth was asleep, the red jacket still on. Quietly Marcy lifted the tray, carried it away, went back to Sebastian.

"She's asleep," she told him. "You don't want to talk about it, do you?"

"No," he said. "No. Do you mind?"

"I mind, but it's all right."

"She's not gone crazy, if that's what you want to know. She's in a state of shock."

"Oh? It doesn't seem like shock, Sebastian."

"I know. But it is. Would you mind if I went to bed at once? It's been a long day."

He didn't even argue when she insisted that he take her bed. She got his bag, got her nightgown and robe, left him alone.

Presently she heard a taxi stop in front of the house, and then she heard David's car being driven away.

She wished she had not told David not to come in tonight. She wished he had come up the stairs and comforted her. And what now? Could she just walk out in the morning and leave Elspeth here? Could she pretend it was just any visit? Or would Sebastian stay a bit and look after her? Yes, Sebastian would look after her. Bitter, bitter truth—Sebastian would look after her. He always had. He always would. One little bag—she had brought but one light little bag; she always traveled with clothes for parties, with all the fripperies she wore so well. One little bag. Sebastian was wounded to the core. He looked dreadful.

She half slept there in the chair while all the silly people at the party moved before her eyes, and she heard their voices turning John into a legend. Oh, maybe Abel was right—maybe it was the only way we had nowadays. Maybe we couldn't be simple or real about grief or anything any more. Only—had she ever minded before this? No, she had to admit she had not. But then, she had never been truly frightened before, not in all her life. Shock—she had told herself that before, and now Sebastian confirmed it. But something hammered away, saying it wasn't true, that even Sebastian was wrong this time. This wasn't what shock did to you.

She did sleep, curled up there with her clothes on. She woke to a small sound in the kitchen, was on her feet in a moment. It was Sebastian, with a Scotch plaid robe on, heating up the coffee. He turned and smiled at her. "Sorry. Couldn't seem to sleep," he said.

So they sat there in the kitchen, drinking coffee. She wanted to put a hand out and smooth away the lines down his face. Queer, what he could do to you. He wasn't anyone of great importance, just a professor doing a scholarly job on linguistics. Why did he seem so terribly important? Maybe it was all in that "No" of his; there wasn't anyone she knew, except Sebastian, who could have resisted talking over Elspeth—not anyone. So she sat there quietly and did not prod him, let him drink the coffee in peace.

"Would I be in the way for a day or two?" he asked suddenly. "Then I have to go back to Old Quagatuck. Don't mention it to Elspeth, but I have to go back."

"Go back?"

"Yes. There are a few things to clear up."

"Stay as long as you will. Was the wind wuthering about?"

It was an old word out of the Doorns' childhood that they used of the farm. They had first gone there six years ago when a sad wind was blowing.

"No, it was snowing very quietly."

"I always think of the farm with the wind blowing. We have had fun there, haven't we?"

"Yes, Marcy, we have."

"It seems like a nightmare we will wake up from."

"Marcy—" He waited a moment, then said quietly, "Marcy, you did believe in John, didn't you?"

"*Believe* in him?"

He gave her a strange look, half grateful, half sad.

"Why did you ask that?" she demanded.

"I don't know. Shall we try to get some sleep now? You too. Oh, and if Eddie Dunstan brings some proofs, don't be angry. I asked him to."

"Eddie Dunstan! Oh, no, Sebastian!"

"Eddie's all right. Don't be angry with him. Good night again, Marcy."

So now she went to bed, curling up on the couch. She

seemed to hear the wind wuthering around the farmhouse. But when they had been there together the wind had had a charm. They had been so safe inside by the fire, all together. The wind could not get in. Nothing could get and disturb their closeness. "You did believe in John, didn't you?" What an incredible question!

"I am cold," she whispered to herself, and slept.

8

BESSIE pushed Soutan away with her foot and said, "Well, they had a young man all night anyway."

"Bessie, if I had a mind like yours! That's John Esker's brother."

"Well, he's a man, isn't he? I think I'll take some coffee cake up."

"I think you'll leave them alone."

"Did you? I've got as much right to my curiosity as you, surely. Will you be back for dinner? If you won't there's a chop left for me and I won't have to shop."

"I'll be back," Emma Hodge said shortly. "And I mean it, Bessie, you leave them alone. They're in trouble, and they won't want to chit-chat with the neighbors."

"They won't want to cook either," Bessie said stubbornly. "Get out from underfoot, Soutan! Honestly, this cat is a nuisance, Emma."

Emma's ugly face reddened so that it showed even under

her careful makeup. She leaned down and picked up the cat.

"You'll get hairs all over that suit!" Bessie said impatiently.

"I don't mind. They'll brush off." But the cat was already wriggling away from her hand, and she put it down, picked up her bag, said, "Good-by," shortly, and went. In the hall she met Marcy Doorn. Fairly often they shared a taxi, and they shared one now. Marcy was very quiet, however, and just before they parted Miss Hodge said, "You'll feel better, now your sister is here."

Marcy gave her a quick, doubting look, turned her glance away, said, "Yes, it is a relief."

"It's hell going through this, but it fades, thank God. We do get through," Miss Hodge said.

"But when?" Marcy said. "I don't know, Miss Hodge. I don't know whether we ever really get through."

"Maybe not clear through, but grief can certainly diminish. Otherwise we couldn't bear living."

"And that's sad too, isn't it? Sorry—everything seems sad to me these days. I daresay you're right, though, and that I'll be merry as—what is it they say merry as?—well, just merry enough in another month. I haven't a faithful heart any more than anyone," she finished grimly.

"It's not that, child. It's just nature's way of keeping us from total despair," Miss Hodge said.

They had come to Marcy's corner, and she got out, said, "See you," shortly, and walked off into the wintry street.

Bernstein frowned, put out his cigarette, lighted another immediately. "But this is a drawing-room comedy," he said. He sounded as if it were the hundredth time he had said it. "You're making it sinister enough for Boris Karloff."

David grinned, said, "But all drawing-room comedies are sinister. I like these sets."

"Well, I don't. And no one else will either. What the devil are you trying to do, Doorn? You've always made sets that were gay and civilized. These are like a nightmare. They set the wrong mood, and we can't use 'em. That's all there is to it, Doorn—we can't use 'em."

"Don't, then. That's the way I see this room. That's the way it is, Bernstein. It will give the play more meaning than a room that's all sunshine and books and grand pianos. Aren't you sick to death of people acting in 'appropriate' surroundings? I am."

"This isn't high tragedy. It's a comedy."

"Well, comedy that's comedy can be played against any background. And the better comedy shows up all the more against the somber."

"You're talking about Sarah Bernhardt or somebody like that. We've got Greta Peters and Henry Longo. They're just run of the mill—good enough, but not the stars of all time. They'd be lost with this stuff."

"How do you know?"

"How do I know? I've been in the show business for forty years, that's how I know. If you want to do *The Wild Duck* or something, why, stick to the Village. But if you're on Broadway you have Broadway sets. A stuffed bat under glass on a mantel may seem amusing to you, but it doesn't to me. And antimacassars went out with the ark. And that dark, flowered carpet will turn comedy sour in anyone's mouth, to say nothing of Greta's. Save your dreams for your art shows. This is a play that takes place now, in nineteen-fifty-four—or maybe it'll be fifty-six if you don't get going soon. It doesn't take place in eighteen-eighty in some dank Victorian mausoleum."

"They inherited the place. They didn't buy all new furniture," David said. "That bat was one Great-Uncle Fred stuffed. And that carpet is as good as new, even if it's been down for fifty years. And it was Uncle Fred's mother who made the petit-point for that stool."

"Funny. Very funny." Bernstein lit another cigarette.

"I'm not trying to be funny. That's just the way it was. Anybody can make a charming room—in the modern fashion. But civilization isn't ordered from Grand Rapids. It's made up of traditions, and so is this room. This is what these people came out of, where they grew up. If they've gone all brilliant and brittle, they've done it in spite of this room—or maybe in rebellion against it. Why don't we have Westlake in and see what he says? Bet you ten to one he'll like it."

"Authors!" Bernstein said sourly. "But he's got it all down right here, exactly what he wants. He wants an abstract painting over the mantel. Why the hell couldn't you take one off your walls—nobody ever buys 'em—and put it here? He wants an emerald leather chair right there, and a white rug. He tells you what he wants."

"Ah, but as you say—authors! When he sees this set he'll know he was all wrong, that it has to be this way. And I do sell a painting now and then."

"I don't know who in hell would buy one."

"If no one would, why put one in a house?"

"Because this is a modern play, and that painting strikes a note. That's why. And you're not going to talk me into this one, Doorn. So just turn off your charm and save it for another day."

"All right, Bernstein. Get somebody else, then."

"And pay you too? Damned if I will. Settle down and do what you're supposed to."

"No, you needn't pay me too. Just skip the whole thing. Pretend it never happened."

Bernstein stared at him. It was unprecedented that a Doorn didn't get paid—and paid a little more than anyone else.

"The truth is that you're probably right," David went on. "I'm just in no mood for comedy right now."

"Don't tell me you're in mourning for your brother-in-law! After all the cracks you've taken at him!"

"No. Let John rest in peace if he can. No, I'm just not in the mood, that's all. Get Freeman-Jones."

"Tell you what—get your sister to come in and take a look at this. If she says it'll go, I'll bite. Trust her quicker than I would Westlake. She walked in on the *Fair Weather* sets and put the final touches on, if you remember. Got sense, she has. Ask her in."

"I can't. She's ill."

"Oh—sorry to hear that."

"But she'd like it."

"Sorry to hear that too. But I don't believe it. Imagine her acting this out against this background! But she's the kind of girl ought to have the lead. Greta'll try, but she won't be quite the real thing."

"I said, let's skip it. I'm tired of talking about it. I've done it, and there it is. Take it or leave it."

"Then I'll have to leave it," Bernstein said shortly. "Sorry, but that's the way I see it."

David shrugged and turned away.

Bernstein met Westlake outside the theater and glared at

him angrily. Westlake said, "What have I done now?" in his eager, gay voice.

"That I should live to see this day!" Bernstein said. "A Doorn turning down ready cash! Bats, antimacassars, petit-point stools! Good Lord! Just go in and take a look! Thinks he can pull the strings, thinks he's big shot enough to get away with anything, but I'm not buying any of his private neuroses—no thank you! Just go take a look!"

He stalked away, chewing savagely on a cigarette that was unlighted, and Westlake went in and back to the room where David had his drawings.

"What's up?" he demanded. "Bernstein's in a tizzy!"

"If you don't mind, we won't go all over it again," David said. "He doesn't like the sets, and Freeman-Jones will make some new ones. That's all there is to it, and let's not talk about it."

"But I don't want Freeman-Jones. I want you," Westlake said. He walked over to the table, stared down at the drawings.

"Authors are comparatively unimportant people, Westlake," David said.

Westlake's eyes had been startled as they took in the drawings. Suddenly he laughed and said, "I say! But I'd have to change some lines—I say, these *are* good, you know! These are frightfully good!"

"Yes, frightfully. That's what Bernstein thought."

"You know, this is the first time I've felt excited about the whole thing. Just another play—that's what it's seemed like. I begin to get really excited. You ought to have written the play. It's got another dimension already—makes the people come alive. Don't go away—I'll be back. Got to hunt up Bernstein. Freeman-Jones indeed!"

Sebastian came to the door, and the cat crept in, and Miss Bessie Hamlin said, "I'm Miss Hamlin from downstairs. I thought maybe you could use a coffee cake."

"That's very kind of you," Sebastian said and took the coffee cake, carried it to the kitchen.

"Here, Soutan!" Bessie Hamlin said. Sebastian had not asked her in, but she was in and moving toward the living room, saying, "Soutan! You pest! Come here!"

Soutan had gone at once to Elspeth and jumped up on the velveteen skirt, found it much to his taste, curled up at once, and began to purr.

"Oh, hello, Mrs. Esker! I do hope you aren't allergic to cats or anything. Soutan must remember you; he doesn't make friends easily. Shall I take him?"

Elspeth's hand moved down the creamy fur of Soutan's back. "Leave him be," she said.

Bessie said, remembering that this was a house of grief, "I was so terribly sorry to hear about Mr. Esker—terribly sorry."

Elspeth looked at her, but as if nothing she said penetrated. The look stopped Bessie in her tracks, made her confused and embarrassed. It hadn't been a critical look, nor one of sorrow. It was just indifferent. Bessie tried to begin a little speech about the loss to the country, but halfway through it she could get no further, for Elspeth was merely stroking the cat as if John Esker were someone she had never known.

"Won't you sit down?" Sebastian said politely. Bessie wanted now to get away but she hooked her cane over the nearest chair and sat down.

"Do you not often wish you were a cat?" Elspeth said.

"Well, no, I don't," Bessie said.

"But they have the secret, the whole secret of letting go all the past and living in the now."

"Well, I never wanted to do that," Bessie said uncomfortably. "I like looking back and ahead. That's the heathen's way, isn't it—eat, drink, and be merry, and all that? I suppose that's what this generation's like, but I'm old-fashioned."

"This generation is no different from any other," Elspeth said slowly. "They lug the past around on their shoulders too. Just because they deny it doesn't make it untrue. We're none of us as free as a cat, Miss Hamlin. Why don't you try some day getting rid of all your *things* and see if you'd be anything without them?"

Miss Hamlin gave a nervous laugh and said, "Well, I haven't got any possessions when it comes right down to it. Emma owns all the things. I'm just a poor relation. But, truth to tell, I like things."

"That's what I mean. We carry the past around on our backs—all these *things*. We spend all our time making a past, because we feel naked without one. I don't think that's the way God meant it to be, do you?"

Bessie Hamlin flushed. In her world you just did not discuss God's intent in the drawing room at ten in the morning. It wasn't done.

"Wouldn't know as to that," she said briskly but uncomfortably. "But all the same, I like things. Nothing wrong in feeling secure, to my way of thinking. And I guess you've always been secure, Mrs. Esker."

"Oh, yes, I've had things too. But I shall give them all away," Elspeth said. "I shall take no thought of the morrow."

"Somebody has to pay the bills," Miss Hamlin said sensibly. "Well, I've got to get back." She got to her feet, went over and took the cat, though Soutan put his claws into the brown skirt and had to be dragged away.

At the door Sebastian gave her an odd smile, as if he saw her fright and her confusion, and said, "It's all right. Don't worry!" But when she got downstairs and began her morning's dusting she was conscious that there were innumerable knickknacks to dust.

"What on earth has happened to her!" she kept saying to herself. "What on earth! I knew something was wrong. I *knew* it!"

Sebastian sat down near Elspeth. "I think I will get you a cat," he said. "They are very becoming to you."

She did not answer him, but stood up, said, "I had forgotten how many walls there are in town. I am going for a walk."

"You wouldn't like a cat?" he insisted.

"No. I told you, I want nothing, nothing at all," she said. She went to her room, came back in her fur coat.

"No hat?"

"I never wear a hat any more."

Nothing was said by either of them about his accompanying her. Presently he stood by the window and watched her move up the street. He remembered his dream of the forsaken city. Elspeth seemed to be moving all alone in some such city. And she walked as if quite unconscious of other people, of cars or buildings. He remembered the first time he had walked in the streets of New York with Elspeth Doorn, how suddenly he had been close to everyone in the city, to the very heart of the city itself, how everything had taken on meaning and was new and freshly discovered. He remembered how they had stopped and bought a pot of hyacinths from a monkey-faced man in the street, just because it was spring, and how later they had come face to face with a very pompous oldish man on the avenue, a man born to be president of a bank, to preside at board meetings, to be carted here and there in sleek long cars. But there he was, coming down the avenue, swinging a conservative gold-headed cane. And Elspeth had taken the hyacinth in its pot from Sebastian's hands and gone straight up to the man and said, "For you! It's spring, you know!" The old man had been startled and awkward, but then he had let his face crack into a half-shy smile and he had said, "Thank you, my dear!" and gone on, carrying the pot in the crook of one arm. . . . Now she was gone, had turned some corner. He could see her no more. It was not only that she was out of sight, but that spring itself seemed some childhood fantasy that he would never dream again.

When David came running up the stairs Sebastian was still standing there by the window, waiting.

"Hello, fella. Why so palely loitering? Where's Elspeth?"

"Gone for a walk. Hello, David."

"Alone?"

"Alone."

David gave him his quick, charming grin, said, "That sounded like the last line of the first act—very doomlike and all. Well, at least she's here, where we can keep an eye on her. Thanks for getting the music up here. Abel's taken over the apartment and is pawing through it as if he were a miner after pay dirt. Think she'll be back soon?"

"I wouldn't have any idea, David."

David sat down, stretching his long legs lazily out in front of him. "I'm playing hard to get," he said. Then he sobered and said, "That's not strictly true. I don't seem to care whether I'm got or not. It *is* something of a rat race, isn't it?"

"Still, I'd hate to see you stop running it," Sebastian said.

"Would you, now? Well, I'd hate it myself. And I doubt if I do stop. But I grew suddenly very tired of being pushed around. 'Take it or leave it,' I said. No-compromise Doorn—that would make news, wouldn't it? Being the world's most accomplished compromiser. Is she all right?"

"No, she isn't—I don't know, David. Perhaps she is all right. Perhaps she's exactly in the place she wants to be. But it's a new place, and I'm not used to her in it as yet. I might get to be."

"Don't *you* start compromising now! She is or she isn't all right."

Sebastian did not answer. He walked again to the window. There were only strangers moving in the street. David watched him thoughtfully. It was inconceivable that Sebastian could change too.

"Odd," David said. "I keep forgetting you're John's brother. John always seemed to be quite alone, without any family tree at all. Marcy says we're quite selfish, thinking first of our own troubles. Daresay we are."

"But John was my brother," Sebastian said without turning. He said it sternly, and David gave his back a startled, yet abashed, glance.

"Sorry," he said. "Well, I'll run along. Tell Elspeth I'll be back."

"I will," Sebastian said.

Again David gave him an uneasy look, but Sebastian seemed to have said good-by to him. David was not used to being shoved out, was not used to having a word of his unnoticed. He gave a chagrined smile and let himself out.

And in the streets walked Elspeth, the beautiful Doorn, the radiant one—walked in a dream, walked in a fog of indifference to the actual, up this street, down that, passing all the familiar houses and shops, meeting people, people, people, just missing being hit by bus or car. She had loved New York more than most, felt all its moods, been a part of its excitement. But she might as well have been walking in Kalamazoo or back on the roads by the farm. She pushed all the noise away from her.

"Where the hell you think you're going, lady?" an angry voice came down from a truck seat.

"I don't know where I'm going," Elspeth said.

"You're telling me!" the voice said. The truck went on.

"I'm trying to find a still place," Elspeth said aloud, but no one heard her.

After a while, not remembering getting there, she was in the Museum of Modern Art. She wasn't looking at pictures, but sitting there, as if waiting for someone. A man passed her a couple of times, eying her with interest. Finally he came and sat beside her and said, "Have you seen the Dufy things?"

"No."

"Ought to, you know. Come have a look."

She stood up and came with him and looked at the Dufy things—or she was in the room with them.

"It's so refreshing to find a little humor in art, don't you think?" the man said.

"I don't know what it's all about," Elspeth said.

"Oh, I say, there's nothing incomprehensible about Dufy! Go look at the Pollocks if you think so!"

She stood and looked at the strange man beside her—looked straight at him, though he had the odd feeling that she was looking through him. "I mean I don't know why they do it. All those lines—for what? It seems silly, doesn't it? Why can't they leave things alone? Come with me."

Embarrassed but compelled, he followed her into the courtyard. She pointed to a scrubby little tree that scarcely had room to breathe. "That's a tree," she said. "That's a *tree*. It's not meant for monkeys to copy." She walked quickly away and left him standing, looking at the sickly little specimen competing with skyscrapers.

And in the street, in her own personal fog, Elspeth walked on.

A big man with a big dog on a leash came toward her, the dog a little ahead of the man and tugging hard on the leash. The man saw Elspeth, because Elspeth was one who was always seen.

"You ought to get a cat," she said to him, not pausing. But he paused, said, "I *beg* your pardon?"

"Dogs take over; they pull you about. A cat would let you be yourself."

The man stared at her. "I *beg* your pardon?" he said again mechanically.

"No one seems to think it matters. But it does matter, it matters very much," she said. "Wouldn't it be more fun to be able to walk all alone, without something or someone pulling you? Don't you think God meant men to stand on their own two legs without so much as a cigarette to hold them up? But a cat knows all that."

"May I ask what in the devil you're talking about? Here, stop it, Cappy. Stop it!"

She gave him a smile and walked on.

She came up Marcy's stairs slowly, so slowly that Sebastian thought she would never reach the door.

"You've been gone a long time. Aren't you cold?" he asked.

She sat down, pulling her coat close around her. "That man was right, Sebastian—that man on Third Avenue you saw once. People are so horrible, so terrible," she said.

9

ABEL straightened wearily, stood up. He had a small sheaf of music in his hand, a very small part of the piles of manuscript on the floor about him. He put the sheaf under his hat on a table, then returned and began to pile up the music, put it back in boxes. David did not offer to help him, just sat, smoking, and watched him.

"Are you the executor of the estate?" Abel asked suddenly.

"No. Elspeth, probably. I just don't know."

"Will you find out, please? I can't just take these."

"Oh? Then you're not so unscrupulous as they tell us?"

"Well, I'd hesitate about stealing these right in front of your eyes," Abel said with a tired smile.

"Is there much to steal?"

"No, not much. And perhaps I'll find there's nothing. There are four things here I'm not familiar with. Someone will have to discuss it with the executor—Elspeth or whoever it may be. Is she really too ill to talk?"

"I wouldn't know. She hasn't talked to me as yet. She's in town, you know. I didn't tell you last night, but it seems Sebastian brought her back in that car with the music. But I haven't seen her. The one to see is Sebastian, John's brother. I'll call him, shall I?"

"I'd appreciate it. It would have to be tonight. I'm leaving in the morning."

David rose lazily, reached for the phone.

"Or Miss Doorn—I'd talk with her," Abel said behind him.

But it was Sebastian alone who met Abel at eight-thirty in the French place on Third. He gave a quick look around the restaurant, walked straight to Abel in a corner, saying, "I'm Sebastian Esker. You're Mr. Abel?"

"Yes. How did you know?"

"Marcy said to look for an untamed eagle," Sebastian said.

Abel laughed. "Sit down, sit down. Something to drink?"

"Later, perhaps—not now, thanks."

They ordered, and then Abel fixed his fingers around his glass and said, "Shall we wait till after food for business, or have it with?"

"There isn't much business, Mr. Abel. I've spoken of the music to Mrs. Esker, and she says you may have anything you find."

"Good. But I'm not sure what I have found. I am very familiar with your brother's work—he has always interested me—but there are several things I had not seen. A spring dance number—it looks as if he were still working on it, but it also looks reasonably complete. Two other dance numbers of a very different sort—rollicking peasant dances—and a nocturne called 'Snow'—or Number Thirteen. The dance number, the spring thing, we wanted and talked about last year. It was supposed to be sent in as of last August, but he didn't send it. The others I don't know about. The spring dance was to be background music for a new version of *Snow in April* that we're working on now. The peasant dances wouldn't go in this number, but we could certainly use them later. Nocturne Thirteen—no, but I would be glad to see that it is published. It looks very somber. That is all of value. But something might be done about a uniform edition of your brother's things, as well as record rights for the new numbers. I think, all told, these things are worth considerable money."

Sebastian lifted unsmiling dark eyes and said, "I told you, there is no need for discussion. She said you might have them —as a gift, I mean."

"Good Lord, no! Why, if the records ran into anything like the record sale for the music from his movie, *The Ball*, it would be a very sizable addition to her income. I appreciate it, but of course I couldn't do that."

"I am practical enough about bread and butter to agree with you," Sebastian said. "However, I do not believe she will sell them to you. You may have them, and that is that."

"You astonish and embarrass me. And may I say she has always had a keen business sense heretofore—that this isn't in character?"

"I know. But that's the end of it, Mr. Abel."

The waiter came with their order, and they began to eat in silence. Then Abel put his knife and fork down and said, "When she is well she will change her mind. Suppose we let it go till then. Except for the spring dance, for which we are waiting. Miss Doorn said she was ill; you cannot decide such things when you are ill."

"No, she is not ill—or she is up and walking about."

The gray brows shot up in a question that was not answered. "You're like John," Abel said, "in some way—not in looks."

"No, I am not much like him. Did you know him well?"

"We have met four times in all. Yes, I knew him well. He never did things on order. If an idea interested him he worked on it. It was, I must say, Mrs. Esker who attended to the business, and very good at it she was. Esker might have just given his stuff away—a peculiarly single-minded man. Of all men I have known, the most single-minded." From this big, powerful, eagle-like man the words fell with great weight.

"Perhaps it was his single-mindedness that killed him," Sebastian said.

"Perhaps," Abel said.

"He had rheumatic fever when he was a boy. Its only value was that it kept him out of the war."

"A great value, I would say."

"Yes. Or so I have always thought."

"Oh? You don't think so now?"

"I don't know. I find myself compelled to make new appraisals, now that he is dead."

"I wouldn't make new appraisals of John Esker if I were you," Abel said with what was, for one so ungentle, a great gentleness. "Some musicians make more of a splash, but John Esker was a peak in my universe. He is dead, but the world is not poorer for his having lived. You can't say that of so many. We do a very unsatisfactory job of it, most of us."

Sebastian found himself talking, quickly and movingly, of the little boy John, the *Wunderkind*, the little boy playing under the piano and coming out into his destiny, which had turned out to be that of a brief shooting star—about the years of study, the family's absorption into John's life, the long hours of work.

"He took all we had," he said simply. "Not selfishly. He was never selfish. But we worshiped genius, all of us. For himself he took nothing—for his music, everything. And now it seems to me that he must have needed more for himself, that we made music too much—that it was too much for him to bear, to be the custodian of genius."

"He had Elspeth," Abel said, as Eddie Dunstan had done. All his gifts, and Elspeth too.

"Yes. It is odd; I feel obsessed by the idea that he was very lonely."

"But naturally. Naturally he was lonely. All good artists are lonely. There aren't many good ones. But that was part of it. I wouldn't brood over that—granting that it is sad. Shall we have a liqueur?"

"Yes, I'd like one."

They sat quietly till the liqueurs came. Then Abel said, "If you are thinking he had no life, five or six years of marriage to Elspeth Doorn would be more life than most men get."

The dark eyes that lifted to his, then turned away, startled Abel. There was nothing appeased in their misery.

Sebastian lifted his glass slowly, and it seemed to float away from his hand so that he was surprised to feel the smooth, hot liquid in his throat. If it had been life, why was she giving it all away? Or was it so much life that everything now was dead? "Poor, darling Sebastian!"—giving away even his faith in his own judgment, giving away his love for, his pride in, John, his brother. "Poor, darling Sebastian!" And the portrait burned, the music given away, the piano as good as parted with—and all else too. Walking in the streets in the same velveteen skirt she had worn at the farm, casting off everything, everything. Was that what life did to you? Wasn't life something that fed on itself, did not diminish with death? Could you deny grief if you were alive? "Poor, darling Sebastian!"

"I must go," he said abruptly.

Abel stood up too. He paid the bill, walked out into the street with Sebastian. "You're a professor, aren't you? I think John said so."

It warmed him that John had spoken of him. "Yes."

"We'll work this out between us somehow. It is impossible that Mrs. Esker shouldn't profit in some way—and foolish, considering the state of the nation."

"Someone must pay the bills," Sebastian agreed, echoing Bessie Hamlin.

"Could I have your address? Mrs. Esker doesn't seem to answer letters. I'll put the thing in writing so you'll have something to go on."

Sebastian paused in the street, took out an old envelope, and wrote his name and address on it. Then Abel held out his hand, gave a firm handshake. "Good night," he said, "and don't brood. It isn't called for."

He walked off quickly, a big man, undiminished by a big city. As he moved he shook his great head, said, "Two of 'em—doesn't seem possible!"

David came and found Elspeth sitting up in bed, in the red jacket. He pretended not to see the Bible against the blanket.

"Charming! Charming!" he said. "You ought to wear red more!" Then the old freedom of speech could not be restrained, and he said, "You don't look a bit like John the Evangelist!" He sat down in the little chair covered with yellow chintz.

"Do you remember Mother much?" she asked surprisingly. She hadn't even greeted him.

"Remember her? I was twelve when she died. I was normally bright."

"I can't remember how she looked."

"You ought to. You're very like her. You know that. You've seen her picture often enough."

"I know. But Mother herself—I can't see her moving or hear her speaking. It's strange—it's all gone."

Marcy came in and sat in the other chintz-covered chair.

"Elspeth can't remember Mother," David said. "Odd—you don't look senile or anything, darling. It wasn't so long ago."

"I remember her," Marcy said. "She was sad—beautiful and sad. I suppose she didn't see much of F.P. But it seems now that it went past that. I wonder why."

"I remember that pale blue velvet thing she used to wear, with a coral band around the cuffs," David said. "I remember the time she said, 'But children should not be so free. You are children.' We did run wild, I daresay. I used to puzzle about that one—freedom being the natural element of children."

"Or is it?" Marcy said. "The freedom of savages."

"It makes the process of civilization quicker," David said.

"But can you hurry the heart?" Elspeth said. "You put on the shell sooner—but there's the heart, still untamed, undisciplined. Mother was right, if she ever said that."

"Oh, she said it. It was after that time when we had Miss Snow for a governess and we had worked up some hoax on her. Mother thought it was cruel. F.P. thought it very clever."

"Yes," Elspeth said slowly, her hands still clinging to the black edges of the Book. "I remember Miss Snow. I remember her better than Mother. She sniffled. And she went away right after that. I remember her standing by the curb with her old bag, waiting for a taxi. I remember her very well, and the little hairs that always draggled out of the knot at her neck. That's what I mean. The heart doesn't grow at the speed of the head."

"I am not quarreling with our bringing up. I am grateful for it," David said.

"But your heart has never grown up," Elspeth said. "You're just as you were when we teased Miss Snow."

"Oh, not quite," David said dryly.

"Yes, you always get exactly what you want, just as you did then. But that's not the way the heart grows."

"How do you know what he wants?" Marcy said with some abruptness. "How do you *know?* We were brought up not to show the beatings the heart took. I think you're making some sweeping statements, Elspeth."

"How childlike and far away you look to me," Elspeth said in a low voice. "When I was small I could do something with my eyes—see things little and far off at will. You look like that—very, very little, and a million miles away. Like looking through the wrong end of the telescope."

"But we're life-size, and we're here," Marcy said sensibly and stubbornly. "You can't push us that far away, darling. We're here."

"I'm not pushing you. That's where you are."

"You know," Marcy said with sudden determination, "I think that's the way John saw the world—except when he was with you. He always saw you, full size. But the rest of the world, no. Maybe that's what being an artist is, seeing everything clear from a long way off. Only—only there's something that doesn't seem in character. Mr. Goudge said he called for square dances last winter. I can't get that out of my head. Did he really?"

Elspeth could not have snubbed Marcy more deliberately. She picked up the Bible and bent her head to its pages.

"Speaking of discipline," David said wryly, "even we were taught to answer questions when we were young. You might as well get used to hearing John's name mentioned sooner as later, for you will certainly hear it."

Marcy frowned at David, got up, and moved toward the door. Just as she came to the doorway Elspeth said, "Where's Sebastian?"

David too had risen. "He's tending to your business for you," he said sharply, "as usual. The business of living does go on, you know. He's meeting Abel to discuss the music that's left."

"Oh, yes," she said. "I wish he'd come back."

"Why?" David demanded. "Because he doesn't badger you? Because he likes to let you have your own way? You aren't the one to talk to me about getting your own way, are you? I suppose you think you pay for what you get? I suppose you think a smile to Sebastian is enough for all he does for you?"

"You don't have to pay Sebastian. Everything is free," Elspeth said.

There was no answer to that, even from David. It was true. He walked out of the room after Marcy.

"I think I'll go home and paint," David said, walking restlessly about the living room.

"Tonight?"

"Yes, now."

She picked up an ashtray on the table, a silver ashtray from Peru with a llama in the bottom. She looked at it as if she had never seen it before. If I just gave it away, someone else would have it, she thought. What difference who has it? I'm glad I have it, because it is beautiful and is not just anything. It is part of me, and the curtains are part of me, and the yellow chintz in the bedroom and my china with one cup broken —they are not things. They are the me that likes the beautiful. It isn't that I am taking heed of the morrow or laying up treasures for my children—oh, *what* children? There will never be any children. But I will not go back on the things I love, even if they are inanimate.

"All right. Go and paint," she said aloud.

He hesitated. "Do you think she would see Dr. Morov?"

"No, I do not think she would see Morov. Or if she did she would change him into something not Morov."

"Perhaps we should have left her at the farm."

"Perhaps we should. Run along, David. It is late."

Still he did not go. "Was that true—about the square dances?"

"That's what Mr. Goudge said."

He stared at her, then got his coat and went without another word. She just stood there, holding the ashtray, looking down at its loved lines, feeling the love that had gone into making it, the artistic purpose. Surely artists did add to the world? You could not cast them off as if they were nothing, as if all art were wrong and useless. You could not. To make this ashtray was as much worship as any prayer. Or to make a dress—or a painting or music. Or to write a book. Was it all only a futile attempt to make man meaningful when he was nothing of the sort? No—no, it wasn't. It gave man meaning. If all men just sat and did nothing, or just looked at nature, would the world be better? An act of worship? Worship of what?

She put the ashtray down, thrust hands into the wide pockets of her skirt, walked to the window. She felt the great weight of woman waiting for man pressing down on her shoulders, on her heart. But it was true, everything was free with Sebastian. He never had to persuade himself to be kind; he never did the expedient thing—he was kind. Yet it wasn't that he was spineless; it wasn't that he was a slave, as Elspeth had said. How could his giving be free if he were a slave?

She saw him below in the snow, the snow already turned a city gray. He came up the steps, and she looked down at him, seeing him foreshortened. She felt a sudden swift anger at Elspeth; then the anger turned against a world that could make a love like Sebastian's count for nothing. Then the anger turned to sorrow as his steps came up the stairs. She remembered the moment when she had in the mirror seen Elspeth's eyes—eyes not indifferent but lost in some sorrow past her, Marcy's, imagination.

"Hello," Sebastian said.

"Hello."

He slid out of his coat but left the coat on a chair.

"She's not asleep yet. You could go and say good night," Marcy said.

But he sat down, saying, "I will in a minute."

Did he too hesitate? Had dread entered even his pure heart?

"How did you get on with Abel?"

"Very well. I liked him. I didn't expect to."

Then he leaned his head back and closed his eyes. But almost at once he opened them again, got up, and went back to Elspeth's room. He did not stay long, and Marcy could not hear what he said. He came back and took the same chair.

"I didn't expect to like him either," Marcy said. "But I did. I think he loved John—if a man like that ever loves anyone."

"Yes, I think he did."

She had seated herself on the arm of a chair. She leaned

toward the table, picked up the Peruvian ashtray, then came and put it into Sebastian's hands. "It's for you," she said.

He looked up in surprise. "For me? It's not Christmas yet."

"I know. I just wanted to give it to you."

"Thank you," he said. "It is too good for ashes. I like it very much."

She remembered when she had first seen him, at the Gowans', where there had been an evening of chamber music. "And the Eskers—Sebastian anyway," Judith Gowan had said. He had been so absorbed in the music. She had watched his face through the whole evening, because something about his absorption moved and disturbed her. The rest of them were more or less alike in feeling music something that ought to be listened to—oh, liking it, knowledgeable about it, but listening to it as one of the things that are done in certain society. But Sebastian had not been conscious of the other people at all. He just listened. And then when the music was done he turned and saw Elspeth.

I might be invisible, she thought, for all he ever really sees me. Yet other people saw her. Other people liked her gypsy face, her gaiety, her Doorn charm. For Sebastian she was Elspeth's sister, that was all. He was her friend, but he never really saw her.

"Sebastian," she said, "it doesn't seem like shock to me. I think I would know if it were shock."

He didn't contradict her but said, "Let's just wait—if you don't mind, if you can bear waiting."

"I don't think I can bear it."

"I know. But is there anything else to do?"

"I don't know. I keep feeling I could shock her back again if I just knew how—if I just knew the right words."

He stood up, still holding the ashtray. He didn't put it

down absently, discount it. He held it and said, "Good night, Marcy. I think I'll turn in now."

"Good night."

She went in to Elspeth. "Would you like something before you go to sleep? Something to drink or eat?"

Elspeth had tossed the jacket to the foot of the bed and lay there, still and beautiful. "No, thanks," she said.

"I'll open the window, shall I?"

"You needn't wait on me, Marcy," Elspeth said. "Don't act as if I were an invalid."

Marcy laughed and said, "All right. Open the window yourself. Good night."

10

SEBASTIAN went up the steps of the old brick house he had known since childhood, rang the bell. As a boy he had been afraid of Mr. Burghardt, and even now, when they met as men, some exaggerated idea of the importance of Mr. Burghardt lingered in Sebastian. He remembered so exactly Mr. Burghardt's emotion over John, because emotion seldom showed in Mr. Burghardt. There was nothing of the stock German musician in the man. He was very tall, cadaverous, unmerry. His eyes were coldly blue, and he had never so much as covered their sharpness and blueness with glasses. He opened the door now himself, the same tall, disciplined man Sebastian remembered of old. He did not look surprised but put out a swift, bony hand, said, "Sebastian. Come in. It is Sebastian, Mama."

That "Mama" was his only concession to sentiment.

Mrs. Burghardt came swiftly, in her wheel chair, tears of welcome already on her round face. She could furnish sentiment in plenty. "I told Papa you would come!" she said as Sebastian bent and kissed her.

The crowded living room was so familiar it was like coming home to enter it—the books, the music, the photographs, the cello in the corner, and that other familiar off-key thing, the arrangement of everything a little lower than would be right in most houses. This was to facilitate housekeeping for Mrs. Burghardt, who had been in the wheel chair for years but did not let it interfere too much with anything. She went around the house like a streak in her chair, washed dishes, dusted, visited with her friends. Once a week a woman came and cleaned. Otherwise, she managed.

"Did you find Paris changed?" Burghardt asked.

"A little. I wasn't there long."

"And so engrossed in the umlaut or the glottal stop, I presume, that you scarcely saw the Louvre," Burghardt said.

Sebastian smiled, sat down in an old leather chair, said, "I was saving it for a rainy day."

"You'll go back?" Burghardt demanded.

"I suppose so. If my money lasts till I get there."

Mrs. Burghardt turned her chair with incredible swiftness, went away to the kitchen, came back with a plate of fruit bars in her lap. "You eat some of these, Sebastian," she said. "Just you eat one or two. I made these for the holidays, but you might be back in Paris by then."

Sebastian gave her a warm smile, took the plate and set it on a stool, helped himself to a fruit bar. There was always food given here, hearty, rich food. The first time he had been here he had eaten pfeffernüsse.

"Papa doesn't want to talk about John," Mrs. Burghardt rushed on.

"Then let us not," Sebastian said quietly. "I came to talk of him—but let us not. There isn't any need, Mrs. Burghardt."

"He was too young to die!" Mrs. Burghardt said protestingly.

"He is nevertheless dead," Mr. Burghardt said in a cold, angry voice.

"He was too young!" his wife said again, like a chorus. "He was only a boy!"

Then she thrust the plate toward Sebastian again with an anxious "Take another. Take one!" And Sebastian took a fruit bar, held it in his hand while the powdered sugar with which it was coated made a small sprinkling of snow on his knee.

"But that isn't true, is it?" he said. "He was born old."

Mr. Burghardt's frighteningly clear blue gaze took Sebastian in slowly. The look contained a whole bird's-eye view of John Esker's life, said that grief for John was not an easy thing and had to contain this musician's knowledge of the life ended. It forbade speech, any speech without this knowledge. Then he rose, and his tall figure moved, skirting the wheel chair, toward the piano. He gathered up bulky manuscript pages from the rack, came back, and stood there with the sheets in his hands.

But he said nothing, just stood there, the bony knuckles showing at the edges of the pages, looking down sternly at the black notes.

"What is it? May I see it?" Sebastian said at last.

Still Mr. Burghardt did not release the sheets. "It is the First Symphony by John Esker," he said. "The first two movements."

"Now, Papa, there is no need to blaspheme," Mrs. Burghardt

said, and indeed the silence, then the cold unforgiving tone, were like blasphemy against a God who had not allowed this work finished.

Burghardt thrust the manuscript into Sebastian's hands, and Sebastian looked down at it with eyes that at first saw not. Then his vision began to take in the slow opening movement, saw how the force began to grow. He put the manuscript down on his knees and said, "But he spent the summer on Nocturne Thirteen—he called it 'Snow.' A somber piece called 'Snow.' "

"Excuse the tears. I cannot help it," Mrs. Burghardt said. "If he'd only got it done. 'I'll bring you more in the autumn,' he told Papa. He put his hand on my hair—he always liked it that I still have braids. He said, 'Till autumn, Marguerita'—and yet it was so sad, like a good-by forever. Papa says that is nonsense—he'd got such a big thing out of him, and he had a right to be sad—but it went through me like a knife, as if it was good-by forever. You remember if you want, Papa—I said so that day."

And all the time Burghardt's tall, angry figure stood there, silent, but charged with his anger. Sebastian kept looking down at the swift black notes that were so much John that he could see John's slender hand making them.

"Was Elspeth with him—when he brought this?" he demanded suddenly.

"No. He came alone. The poor child! It will kill her."

"It will not kill her," Burghardt said then.

"Don't mind Papa. He is jealous of that one," Mrs. Burghardt said. "He has not even been to see her. It makes him angry that he heard the news from a stranger."

"Hollywood!" Burghardt said with brief savagery.

"For Hollywood or whatever, it has been good music," Sebastian said.

"Better than deserved. But not this. I may be old, but I am not senile, Sebastian. I still know good music." He took the music from Sebastian's hands, as if Sebastian had no right to it, carried it back to the piano.

Sebastian dusted the sugar from his knee, said, "I must go." He stood up. "I will come again," he said helplessly.

Burghardt came to the door with him, came out on the steps. His anger was still in him, but it was an icy anger, kept in, a remarkable anger for a man of his years, when, in the normal course of events, nothing matters quite so much as it once did.

"Was it as she says? Was he sad?" Sebastian asked abruptly.

"Women," Burghardt said coldly. "They always like to feel they have had prevision of events." Then he thrust out his hand again, said, "Get back to Paris."

"But was it that way?" Sebastian insisted.

"Precisely," Burghardt said, turned, and went into the house without another word.

Sebastian walked along the street. There had been something about that word "Precisely" that made the dull weight of misery on his heart heavier. He could discount Mrs. Burghardt's words, but not this one word. And why had none of them known about the symphony? How could they not have known? How not spoken of it? But would it not have been true that creation of that sort would have left John drained and sad? Did it have to be true that there was an extra sadness? Nor was it true, as Burghardt had implied, that the music for Hollywood was only a way of earning money to serve the beauty that was Elspeth. Elspeth would have been the first to be excited at the thought of a symphony begun. Once she had written: "John is having one of his terrific bouts of concentration. I never see him—or he never sees me," and that must have been it. "Precisely . . . precisely"—why did the word confirm so finally that there had been a sadness past the normal?

It was true what Burghardt had said, Sebastian Esker was a man who might eschew the Louvre for research on the glottal stop, even as now he eschewed the glottal stop for another kind of search. If he had not known John, he had never known anything. Yet all the time, day and night, he was conscious that there was some gap in his knowledge, that ever since Elspeth had said, "But you didn't know him," he had felt something sure gone out of his life, something heretofore never questioned, never doubted. He knew he was a man, not a child given up to illusions. He knew that his faith in Elspeth and his faith in his brother had to be one thing—that ever since those words he had been searching, searching for another John, with Abel, with David and Marcy, with everyone he met. Nothing had changed his love for John, but he had to know what had done this to Elspeth.

He had not realized where his feet were taking him but suddenly found himself before the old bookshop door. John had come here often in the old days. He collected any old book of folk songs he could find, and now and then bought a book on medieval history. A bell rang when the door opened, and from the shadows came Mr. Smith—a plain name for the wise little gnome of a man who lived here with his books.

"How do you do," Sebastian said. "I'm Sebastian Esker—you won't remember me, but I came with my brother once or twice."

"Wait," Mr. Smith said and disappeared, came back presently with a ragged old book of songs, put it on a dusty pile of books. "Will you take that to your brother, please?"

Sebastian picked up the book, stood staring down at its pages a long moment. Then he looked up and said, "My brother is dead."

"Dead? Did you say *dead?*"

"Yes, dead," Sebastian said.

The word went on interminably in the untidy old shop. Mr. Smith turned away with a fumbling movement, then said almost crisply, "Well, it is the way of all flesh."

"I will take this book," Sebastian said.

But Mr. Smith reached out and took the book from Sebastian. "There is no need. He cannot read it now," he said.

"But I would like it."

"One sixty-five," Mr. Smith said.

Sebastian counted out the money, but Mr. Smith did not put out a hand for it, and Sebastian laid it on top of some books on a table. "He counted on this shop," he said then.

"I'm seventy-three; he might have counted on it once too often," Mr. Smith said dryly.

There seemed nothing to do but take his book and go. Then Mr. Smith said, "He came to argue on philosophic principles that matter very little to me at this stage. But his style of argument was civilized, and that one finds a surprise in these days."

"Oh? And what principles was he interested in?"

"Does it matter now? If you are dust, free will ceases to be important. I no longer read books explanatory of the growth of conscience. I have a rudimentary conscience and take care of it in a rudimentary way. And what has conscience to do with music, may I ask?"

"It might have a good deal to do with it—according to your talent."

"Pardon me. But I do not feel equal to further argument on the matter," Mr. Smith said. He was not rude. Rather, he seemed lost in some deep pit of pessimism. "I daresay I shall miss him," he said suddenly, "but at the moment I think: Well, another one gone—and that is that."

Sebastian picked up the book. "Thank you for saving this," he said and made his way out with no restraining word from Mr. Smith.

He didn't know why, but he felt Mr. Smith was as distressed as Mr. Burghardt. But Mr. Smith was not a sentimental man, and he would never go so far as to admit it.

He started back to Marcy's. He could take no more of this sort of thing today. His purpose was not shaken, but he could take no more today.

Yet he didn't go back. He suddenly signaled a taxi and made his way to Marcy's office. He found her just starting out to lunch. When she saw him there was an odd confusion in her face, almost a reluctance to speak to him. It was gone in an instant, and yet he knew he had not imagined it. All his nerves were sensitized today. "Come have lunch with me," he said.

"Wonderful!" she said.

They found a place of no consequence near the office, sat down, and ordered something.

"I thought you were going back to Old Quagatuck," she said suddenly.

"So I am—in a day or two. Am I in the way? That's a very fetching and silly hat."

"I like hats silly. Where's Elspeth?"

"I don't know. I went to see the Burghardts."

"Why I hate to leave her alone I wouldn't know. You can see she's relieved at the very thought of getting us all out of the house. But the minute I'm away I wish I were back."

"I know. She would say, 'Why do you try to dig John up?' That is what she would say. That is what she has said."

Marcy gave him a quick glance. "And why do you?" she asked, but gently.

"I have to. I seem to hear him calling to me from the grave. That sounds very melodramatic, doesn't it, Marcy?"

"From you it does."

"Yes. But I am listening all the time."

"And does he speak?" she asked.

"He speaks. He says, 'I died without finishing my work. I wasn't ready to die yet. I died with a terrible loneliness in my heart.' That's what he says over and over. You know I don't go in for fantasy, Marcy. I never have, have I? I'm a man with feet on the ground. And yet I hear this cry all the time, waking and sleeping. Elspeth doesn't hear him at all," he finished flatly.

"Oh, you know that now," she said slowly. "No, she doesn't hear him. That is what makes gooseflesh rise all the time. If it weren't for John, though—if it weren't that it's *John* who is gone—oh, I don't know what it is I want to say. Only that sometimes she makes sense to me. I hate it that she does, because it would mean my whole life was nothing. You can't bear to feel that, can you? But I come to the office and I start to work, and suddenly it's all nonsense, and the adornment of the body is so artificial that I can't even care about it one way or the other. But I cannot feel like that and earn my living. And I have always cared about making designs—I have *cared*. It's been exciting. If you weren't excited you couldn't do it. And it's part of civilization; I've never felt ashamed of being civilized. I hate her making no effort to be civilized—and yet—and yet—"

"Even primitive peoples mourn their dead," he said quietly.

She put her arms along the edge of the table, said, "You always came to help him when he needed it. It is that you can't bear, Sebastian, that you can't help him now."

"No, that isn't it, Marcy—though that is hard enough to bear. Did you know he had started a symphony?"

"No. Elspeth never told me."

"Nor he. He never mentioned it, though he wrote fairly often. Burghardt has the first two movements. Why didn't he tell me? Why didn't Elspeth tell you? Do you think it is true that we took pieces of John for our own glorification, that we nibbled away at him, as Elspeth says? That he knew this, or believed it? It didn't seem that way, but perhaps that is the way it looked—perhaps it even looked that way to John."

"Oh, nonsense! Of course we gloried in him—how could we not? But if—if, as Elspeth likes to imagine, all that glory were stripped away, we'd have still loved John. Only I find it hard to imagine John without it. He was born for glory."

"Yes, we expected it of him, didn't we? Perhaps he didn't want it."

"I don't believe that. He worked too hard toward it."

"It's strange—I would have said I knew his every thought. It may be I did not know him at all."

There was the usual bustle of noise, of dishes clattering, voices rising and falling, that is part of any restaurant. But Sebastian's words fell into a pool of quiet.

"I have to get back," Marcy said.

He beckoned the waitress, paid the bill, rose, and came with her. "I wasn't very good company, I'm afraid," he apologized. Then he smiled at her, his old, deeply friendly smile, and said,

"And don't stop making dresses, Marcy. I always think of you drawing away so dashingly, making clothes more exciting. I like to."

"That's a comfort," she said and was gone.

When he came into the upper hall he saw the pile of mail on the little table, and on top of it a big envelope with "Eddie Dunstan" scrawled across one corner. He picked up the envelope and went into the living room. Elspeth was not alone. Isobelle sat there, curled up in the corner of the sofa.

"Hel-*lo!*" she said with her quick, delighted, but somehow malicious smile. "We were just talking about you. How lovely to see you! I was just telling Elspeth here how wonderful it was to have you at hand to pick up the pieces."

Elspeth's hand stroked the brown of her skirt. She had worn this skirt ever since she came. Her blouses always looked white and fresh, and this one was white as snow. It had a high collar with a little foolish ruffle of lace at the bottom of the collar.

"There aren't any pieces," she said. "I am all one thing."

"We do departmentalize our lives too much, don't we?" Sebastian said easily. "What a word! Like 'contact' and— I have vowed never to use such words. But I am against building little rooms in our minds for different friends, different activities, shutting one door before you open another. Let's have all the doors open all the time."

Isobelle gave a mock shudder. "Oh, let's not!" she said. "That would never do. It wouldn't indeed!"

"If you were whole it would do," Elspeth said. "It is because we are not whole that it terrifies us so. To be all things to all people—we laugh at that; it seems indecent; but that is *it,* that is what we must be. If you are one being, you cannot be a hundred beings. This is it, this is I—all of me. Take me or leave me. I am not gay for this one, sad for that—I am both at the same time, the same for you, the same for Sebastian, for anyone who comes near."

Isobelle stared at her in some alarm. "Now that's nonsense, darling, pure nonsense. I hated Frank—yes, that's the word for it. I hated him. Suppose I let that hate show every time I looked at sweet Sebastian here—or at you. Come, come, let's keep some doors closed, pet—for decency's sake."

Elspeth looked at her, and it was that look from the wrong end of the telescope. "But I can see the hate," she said. "It shows. I hear it in your voice when you mock at children, when you mock marriages that stick together. And when you keep going like a whirlwind all day, all night—"

"Oh, that will do!" Isobelle cried. "If this is what you mean by no doors closed, deliver me from such a house of life, my sweet!" She made a brave attempt to give her usual mocking little laugh, succeeded quite well.

"So pray we all," Elspeth said. "Deliver us from evil. Make us whole. Be the center of our being, O God. Let Thy light shine through all the doors."

Isobelle sobered, gave Sebastian a look close to fright, but she said lightly enough, "Has she gone out of her mind?"

Sebastian merely let a smile crinkle the corners of his eyes, said nothing.

"Yes, I've gone out of my mind," Elspeth said. "I don't live there any more. The mind keeps busy shutting doors, building up monuments to our cleverness. The mind, the mind, the mind! How sweet it is, that crooked front tooth of yours, Isobelle. So childlike—God will forgive you much; God will pity you for not straightening that tooth."

"It's not a matter between me and God," Isobelle said dryly.

"I was too vain to wear braces on my teeth when I was young. That's all, darling."

She picked up her gloves and rose. "I came to tell you how desperately sorry I was about John," she said, "but I'll save my condolences till a more suitable moment. And I trust you can't read my mind right now."

The brittle words made no stir in the room. Isobelle didn't say good-by, but walked to the door, and Sebastian came with her, went down the stairs and out on the front steps with her. He said nothing. What was there to say?

"I thought Marcy was taking this too hard," she said suddenly. "I see she wasn't. David didn't want me to come."

Then she grinned and said, "Well, into the whirlwind! Nice to see you, Sebastian, in spite of the company you keep. Fantastic!"

"Nice to see you," Sebastian said mechanically. "Come again."

She moved down the steps, then looked up at him. "I was sorry about John," she said simply, and walked away.

A half-hour later she was sitting in a cocktail lounge and saying, "But I've just come from there. I mean it literally. She's gone crazy. . . . No, I wouldn't have believed it either. If ever anybody knew all the answers and the right strings to pull, it was Elspeth. . . . She just sits in a trance and makes pronouncements about the soul and God and such. . . . It's rather horrible. . . ."

And soon after that Freddy, with whom she was having cocktails, was having dinner with his mother and said, "I hear Elspeth Doorn's gone off her rocker. Heard it first hand—she's here. Funny Marcy didn't tell anyone—or perhaps it isn't funny if that's the truth. Hard to imagine."

"I don't believe it," his mother said.

"Isobelle said so. She'd just been there and seen her."

"Oh, Isobelle! She likes to be melodramatic."

"She seemed to mean it."

"I'll go see her myself."

And Freddy's mother went to the theater that night with her ex-husband, with whom she kept on very friendly terms, and said to him, "Freddy tells me that Elspeth Esker's lost her mind. I don't believe there's a word of truth in it. An extr'ordinarily well-coordinated girl."

And the ex-husband mentioned it to a man in his office next day. The friend said, "Incredible! I wonder if Sam knows?"—Sam being a publisher who had always loved Elspeth too.

It doesn't take long—not long at all, even in a big, impersonal city.

Sebastian didn't mention Isobelle to Elspeth. He took out the pictures and spread them on the window seat. He sobered, seeing how good they were. "Don't you want to see Eddie's pictures?" he asked.

"No," Elspeth said.

He looked down at the picture of the woman standing by the window. The stillness of the pose suggested grief, suggested the forlornness, the desperation of a heart alone—or would, if you didn't know that the stillness was something else altogether.

"What are we supposed to do with these? Will Eddie pick them up?" he asked.

"What?" She had gone to the desk and sat there, pen in hand—writing what? Writing to whom? "Oh, I suppose he will get them."

He looked a long time at the picture of the forsaken piano.

Was he reading more into it than Eddie had put there, than was actually there? This was the bereft soul, this thing of wood and ivory and steel. He put the pictures back into the envelope with a swift, angry movement, got up and went over to the record player, found some Chopin records he liked, and put them on, without asking Elspeth whether it would disturb her or not. He sat on the window seat and listened.

He felt extremely tired. He had talked all day, it seemed. And to what avail? All that had come through was the John he knew, the John he saw so clearly, with the sharp, pure lines, the straight, thin nose, the sensitive but pale mouth, the hollowed plane at the side so that the front plane was a narrow and sharp-cut triangle—the face that bespoke self-containment, did not let the world in. Not know John?

"I was sorry about John." Isobelle had meant it. For all her slickness, her brittle charm, she had meant that. They were all sorry. They had all loved John, or respected him. He had turned to no one who had not felt this way about John. No one—except Elspeth. Even Marcy grieved more than Elspeth.

"Have you heard from F.P.?" he asked suddenly.

"No. He will take some time over his eulogy," Elspeth said. "Write a letter to save and show—the perfect tribute." It was as human a thing as she had said, and for some reason his heart felt lighter.

"I have to go away for a time," he said. "Will you be all right?"

She put her pen down, said, "Go away?"

"Yes. I have some business. Of course, if I can be any help here—but I can't, can I?"

He did not turn. He did not see the curious blankness of her face. "No, you'd better go about your business," she said slowly. "I must help myself."

11

DAVID DOORN often made his own breakfast, but this morning he woke early and went out. After breakfast he went to a florist's he often patronized and said to the girl who was just opening the shop, "I wonder if you'd call Ridgefield, Connecticut, and see what they have right now? I want something sent to Mrs. Henry Garrett, but not just any old plant they think I might never see." The girl was a new one; Miss Mack would have understood perfectly.

"And the address?" the girl asked.

"Old Hickory Farm," he said shortly.

She went at once to the phone. She had brown hair, worn in a flopping pony tail, and her hand on the phone was a sensible, boyish hand that looked as if it had worked hard. She spoke in a brief fashion. Then she said, "Oh, no, that wouldn't do at all. . . . Anemones? That would be right." And she turned to David and said, as if Alice were just any person and his devotion to her but the merest politeness, "The name for the card, please?"

"No name," he said shortly. For an instant her gray eyes widened, but she said, "No card," briefly into the phone, put the receiver down.

"Thank you. Anemones were exactly right. I'm surprised they had them," he said. Then he looked around and said, "While I'm here I think I'd like something sent to my sister—something gay. *Not* poinsettias. How about that—pitcher and all?"

"I'm sorry. That's part of the shop decoration," she said.

"Well, you could get some other pitcher for the shop, couldn't you? I'm willing to pay for it."

She looked hesitant. "That's a rather special pitcher," she said.

"That's why I want it. I'm sure it will be all right. Miss Mack's a good friend of mine."

She took the pitcher and put it on the desk. It was bluish white, with faint blue lilies sprawled on it. It was filled with sprays of freesia. Then she gave a rueful smile and said, "Of course Miss Mack would sell it. But I found it myself and I wanted it here. I didn't even pay much for it, but it's a love of a pitcher. I should have taken it home."

He gave her his most charming smile, said, "I'll tell you—send it, and then I'll bring it back. The freesia belongs in it, but she won't even notice if I bring it back. I promise."

"*Would* you?" she said with gratitude and relief in her voice. She had a brusque sort of voice, but now she sounded child-like.

"I would. Mrs. John Esker . . ." And he gave Marcy's address.

The girl's hand paused on the order pad. "Oh," she said, as if he had suddenly become real to her. Then: "You needn't bring it back."

He felt oddly irritated, and he said, "Don't tell me you're one of the moonstruck mourners of John Esker too!"

She gave him a quick look of pure disdain, said, "And your name, please?"

"Sorry," he said. "I didn't mean John wasn't worth mourning. The name's Doorn, David Doorn." And he gave his address. She gave not a flicker of recognition as she wrote, and that was irritating too. There was a smudge of ink along one of her fingers. She pulled a slip off, handed it to him, and he shoved it mechanically into a pocket of his topcoat.

"Thank you," he said briefly, then smiled at her and said, "Look, don't be angry. I've been coming here since I was knee high, and I say anything I like to Miss Mack. I didn't mean to be rude."

She smiled back, but not too warmly. "This is only my third day here," she said. "Miss Mack said, 'Show a personal interest, but stay impersonal, if you know what I mean.' And I thought I knew. But it's difficult. I ought to have handed over the pitcher without a murmur."

He grinned, said, "No, that was exactly the right approach. Make the thing seem special, and, the more special it is to you, the more the customer wants it. That was very good, and Miss Mack would have approved."

"But I shouldn't have shown that I mourned John Esker, should I? Because that goes into my personal life, and I'm not selling myself—to explain it I'd have to tell you the story of my life, which of course I haven't any desire to do. But I did do the Mrs. Garrett thing all right, I think—never showing

I'd ever heard of her or your grand passion, but managing anemones. I think that was good." Her eyes mocked him a little.

"You must have had a good time going through the files with Miss Mack," he said tartly.

"Educational," she admitted. Then: "Was there anything else, Mr. Doorn?"

He almost said, "I wouldn't mind hearing the story of your life," for he had a knack for sudden intimacies and could charm life stories out of people at will—often did, just for amusement—but this time he merely said, "No, I think not," turned, and went out the door.

He was not as amused as he might hitherto have been at the thought of Miss Mack telling the girl with the ink on her finger about David Doorn and Alice Garrett. And he thought the girl had better get going on her impersonal regime soon, or Miss Mack would send her packing.

He went back to his rooms, got his smock on, and began to paint. He had work to do on the sets, for Bernstein had conceded reluctantly that they might do; but he went to work on a big canvas. Once the phone rang, and he scowled, though he had never been averse to interruptions.

At eleven the doorbell rang, and he said, "Damn!" and went on working. But the bell kept ringing, and at last he went to the door, paintbrush still in hand.

It was Alice, her beautiful dark eyes expectant, wistful, as if she had had to come but recognized at once that she had come the wrong day.

"I just sent you some flowers," he said with what was, for him, stupidity.

"Can't I come in?"

He opened the door, said, "Come in, come in, of course. It startled me so, as if I'd produced you by just mentioning your name at the florist's. What are you doing in town?"

"Oh, the children—everything got too much for me. So I said I'd come in and do some Christmas shopping." Then she gave him an honest look and said, "But I really came to see you. And you're not glad."

"Not true. Wait, let me get my brushes cleaned up. Let's do something very special."

"No, go on painting. I'll watch you. That's all I came to do, David."

He put his free hand around her wrist in a way he had, and led her along to the studio. "Sit down and look at me," he said, "but for ten minutes only. I can't waste the day painting, you know."

She sat in the carved chair he used for models. It had at the moment a backdrop of rose-colored velvet, and her black coat made a good line against the rose. But she slid out of the coat, and she had on the orange wool. Ordinarily David would have cried out in pain at the orange against the rose, but though he touched her hand in a loving way, he turned at once and went to the picture, began to paint.

She put up a hand and pushed dark hair back in a confused gesture, then leaned her head back and saw the back of David's fair head, the shoulder lifted, the stained blue smock swinging free. She saw this, saw it with love and a deep familiarity, before she saw the picture. For a long time now he had taken the edge from her boredom, her unhappiness; he had made life possible. Her husband was successful but dull, dull, dull. What had begun as a brief flirtation had become a habit and was now more real to her than her actual marriage. Once David had asked her to come away with him, leave her home, her dull husband, her children so like their father; but she had had some noble ideas about keeping her home intact, and so it was this way. And even the husband accepted him as almost a part of the family. But they had never had an unexpected hour together like this before without a quick delight on David's part, the eagerness of one to whom a wonderful gift has been given. She was sensitive to true delight, and she, for the first time in all their relationship, wished she had not come. Yet it was true enough that if he had welcomed her she would have been content just to sit and watch him. For an instant she shut her magnificent dark eyes, the only lovely features of an otherwise plain enough face, feeling with sick incredulity the premonition of the death of something she had thought would last forever. She felt old, at least middle-aged, a suburban mother and housewife. She opened her eyes and saw the picture.

She did not analyze her sensations, but the death was repeated in her heart nonetheless, and she looked straight into the pit of loneliness. The picture was not done, but it showed its intent very clearly. It was a big picture, thirty by forty or so. There was a twisting tunnel of green light through a jungle. The tunnel itself was something of a tour de force of painting, but she did not think of that. In it, on the floor of the jungle, but still in the cleared green light path, was the very small but clear figure of a man, just an ordinary modern man in a tweed suit. It might have been David, it might have been anyone. But all the rest was in some other world of huge, sinister leaves and twisting vines. And out of the ugly growth enormous prehistoric creatures peered—a brontosaurus, great lizard-like things—and overhead, flying through, not above, the green, the dead, sick green, was a bird, a wide-winged, prehistoric bird.

David was a painter of gaiety. His modern paintings were full of light and laughter. Whether they had meaning or no, they seemed to have the effect of making people happy. But this—this would make no one happy. No one would laugh at this. David's brush was making the horny saw of a dinosaur's back, making it carefully, not with sweep or abandon, but with a terrific concentration.

Alice Garrett looked down at her hands on the orange wool —good hands, carefully tended, strong hands, not useless at all. They looked far off to her, not her own hands at all. "Dear God," she whispered, "it's over. It's all over. What will I do now?" And she saw herself old, sitting at a bridge table, being polite and bored, her children married to people like their father. Yet David had taken her wrist between his fingers in the old way, the touch that meant he chained her so, in spite of all. Old. I am old, she thought. She was two years older than David, and two years had never seemed anything at all. Now it seemed a generation. Straight here, like a bird, she had come, sure of a welcome, as sure as of anything in her life. He never forgot the children's birthdays. He had sent her flowers just this morning. What kind of flowers? Why was she so sure, so sure that it was over? Yet she was sure. She ought to rise and walk away in a proud way, not looking back. But she sat there in utter stillness and watched the loved hand at work.

And why had she come today? What so special had happened to make the necessity greater than on other days? Nothing. Nothing at all. Henry had taken out a small flat leather notebook that he always carried in his pocket and written down in it that he must take the 4:21 home tomorrow because they were having cocktails with the Mastersons. And she had seen the notebook become enormous, reducing to a schedule all friendships, all happiness. At 6:14 turn on your cocktail smile. At 7:28 turn it off again. At twelve on the dot lock the front door and say, "Well, time to turn in."

"I think I might go up to town and get a little Christmas shopping done," she had said.

"Good idea," he'd answered.

She hadn't seen David since the night he came to her after John Esker died. He had been terribly depressed. Henry had been home and had offered him a drink and sat and talked with him as if David had come just to see him. And yet she had known David found comfort in being in the same room with her. Once he had turned and smiled at her. At midnight he had said, "I'll have one more drink with Alice, I think," establishing the fact that he couldn't be put on a schedule, yet dismissing Henry to his. He hadn't talked so much, but he had needed her then as much as this morning she had needed him. But his very hand, moving so carefully yet surely, said that he did not need her now, that he was not even aware she was there behind him in the carved chair.

She was lost in the hideous green jungle of the picture and knew the plight of the little man who had no chance at all, none at all.

It was two hours later—and two hours is a long time to spend in that place where Alice Garrett had been—when David turned, put down his brush. "Good Lord!" he said, admitting he had forgotten her. "Have I been a long time?"

"No," she said. "But I do think I'll run along now and do some shopping."

"I'll come with you." These were words out of an old, gay novel that had lost its gaiety.

"No, don't. It's to be very humdrum—no Christmas spirit in it."

"Oh, we'll make the spirit!" he said coaxingly. "Yes, I must come, whether you want me or not." He reached out a hand, drew her toward him, rested his face against her hair. She held her hat tightly in one hand, aware that she was crushing it, and aware too of the smell of paint and turpentine. "You don't give me much time," he said. "We must make it count, darling."

As if she had this moment come, as if she had not already given him all the time she had to give, or would ever have.

She drew away from him, said more gravely than she was wont to speak to him, "No, don't come, David. I came to see you. I've seen you. I'd rather remember you here."

"I don't like the way you said that—like a long farewell," he said. "You can certainly eat lunch with me at least."

"Not today, if you don't mind. I'll be in again. Be good, David."

It was a usual good-by. If he had let her say it and be gone —but he turned toward the picture and said, "It's good, isn't it? It's damned good."

"If you say so. It makes me feel I've been to hell and back."

"Yes, it's supposed to— And *back*, did you say, darling?"

But she couldn't talk about the picture. Nor could she go like this. She put a hand out and touched his arm. "Thanks for the flowers," she said.

"Don't go. Please don't go."

But she went. She gave him a smile that was left over from that other time, just went away and left him there in his blue smock, his eyes tired from his long stint of painting.

He did not go back to work but cleaned his brushes, scrubbed his hands, took off the blue smock. He was as aware as she that things had not gone right, that he shouldn't have gone on painting, that he had failed her in eagerness. He always knew such things. Yet he had not dreamed that anything could end between them. She was his safety and his comfort, and she had never failed to please him in some way. He liked being thought of, thinking of himself, as her faithful lover, without having the responsibilities of marriage. She had never been demanding, and as much of himself as he gave, he gave her freely, without strings. But he was disturbed that she had seemed hurt. Hurt she had been, and no doubt because he had spent these few extra minutes away from their private concerns. Then he looked up and straight at a clock that said ten minutes to two.

"Oh," he said flatly. "Oh."

When Miss Mack, plump and quick, came in in the middle of the morning, her new girl said to her, "It isn't true about Mrs. Esker. She's still with her sister. Mr. Doorn sent her some flowers there."

"Oh, David was in, was he? Well, I heard it on good authority. Maybe they keep her in the attic." Her jolly laugh boomed out for an instant; then she sobered and said, "Probably just gossip. David's a mighty pretty boy, isn't he? Pays up slowly, but he pays. Who else was in?"

The girl got her pad, reported. At one name Miss Mack laughed and said, "What, so soon? That's an appeasement bunch of roses. About once in three weeks they have a knock-down row, and it's always roses afterward! It's only been two weeks this time. If they break up it'll be money out of our till. . . . The Gilson boy—why do they go so for orchids for their first girls? Lots of things prettier than orchids. But you'd think they were giving them the moon. It isn't as if he had the money, either. Next time—might be months before he saves up for the next binge—but next time try to steer him into sweetheart roses or something. Sorry I missed David. We always have a good heart-to-heart. But no doubt he appreciated somebody young for a change—though if he heard your name was Fanny he'd give you only a cold glance. That *is* a dull name."

"Do you think so? I like it all right," Fanny said defiantly.

"Well, might call you Lisa or something for the trade. You've got a good haughty look—ought to have a haughty name."

"But Fanny's my name," the girl said stubbornly.

Miss Mack laughed, patted the girl's hand, and said, "You're all right, Fanny. We'll get along fine."

Then she squinted from far off, because she refused to wear glasses, and said, "What's this—'and pitcher'?"

"That's it—and pitcher. He bought the blue pitcher the freesia was in. I charged him for a special messenger."

"Right. Let him pay for his fancies—not up to Ridgefield, I hope!"

"No, to his sister's."

"H'm. Golden flowers for a golden girl. Now that was a pretty little flight, eh? But David certainly knows the right touch. Lost her mind or not, she *is* the golden girl! But don't think you can overcharge David. He knows to a penny the price of a bow—or a special messenger. Smart cookies, the Doorns, one and all."

"I don't think he's too smart if he spends his life sending flowers to a married woman," Fanny said.

Miss Mack laughed heartily. "And that's where you're wrong, honey. A hopeless passion's not half so expensive as providing for a wife and five kids."

"It's still not smart. Ten years from now it will just be silly."

"Guess you can safely leave that to David, child. David would know how to slide out when the time comes. Bone selfish, that boy is, but I like to look at him. Hello, Miss Selkirk. Is your sister out yet?"

When Marcy came in late that afternoon Elspeth was not there. Sebastian said, "She's gone for a walk."

"Why not you too?"

"She didn't want me," he said with a rueful grin. "Want to read this? I think it would be all right—she gave it to me. F.P."

She took the thin airmail paper into her hand. "He didn't let himself go as far as a cablegram," she said dryly.

She sat on the arm of the sofa, not taking off her hat, read in her father's dramatic script, half printing, his condolences.

"My dearest daughter" it began, and Marcy paused there, something lost and sad coming to her dark eyes. Yes, Elspeth had always been his dearest daughter. He was very good at pretending there were no differences in his feelings for them, but here it was, in black and white.

My dearest daughter:

I carried your letter about with me all day, finding no moment free for reading, but looking forward to it none the less. Tonight after the performance I came straight home for a change and read it. And all day long I might have been sharing your grief! You said so little. But what are words now? When a star goes from the sky the world is very black. And John was a star. Since we have never gone in for the mystical, I cannot say you will meet in Paradise. You've had your paradise, my dear child. It must suffice. Would it comfort you to join me here in Rio for a time? It would comfort me. My impulse was to cable you the funds for flying down at once, but I have to admit that at the moment my bank wouldn't allow it. I feel sure you have funds, however, living as you did so quietly in the country, and John being one of those born to make money—or Marcy would lend you money, I'm sure. Do come, I will count on it. This is terrible, going on about money when all I want is to comfort you. But I know you are full of courage and will meet this too with fortitude. Words are such stiff things! Bless you, my darling. And come.

Marcy put the letter down and said, "I've known him to do better."

Sebastian looked surprised and said, "Perhaps it would be a good thing for her to go."

"Don't be stupid. You're not stupid, don't pretend it. At her own expense? The comfort would come high. Of course he thinks it would add immeasurably to his prestige to go about with someone like Elspeth. The only hitch is that he would be embarrassed to tears to take this Elspeth about. She didn't take it seriously, did she?"

"No, I must admit she didn't. It might have been the grocery list. She just handed it to me and said, 'F.P., taking time out,' and she got her coat and went out."

Marcy frowned. "I don't like it, having her wandering about alone. Who sent the flowers?"

"I don't know. She's safe enough. And if she isn't there's nothing we can do, Marcy."

"You mean God looks after children and fools? There she is now."

But it was Eddie, come for his pictures. His sharp fox-face belonged anywhere but in Marcy's civilized drawing room.

"Hello, angel child," he said to Marcy impudently. "Still mad?"

"I don't suppose it matters," Marcy said. "But I'll never ask you to do a job again so long as I live."

"Not till you need me, anyway. The shots weren't bad, though, now were they, sweetheart?"

"They were good," Sebastian said. "Very good indeed."

He got the envelope and handed it to Eddie. "Thanks for letting us see them."

"What did she think of 'em?"

Sebastian gave him a smile and said, "She didn't look at them."

Eddie looked close to embarrassed. "Didn't, eh? Look, Esker, how *is* she?"

"All right."

"Well, that's something, anyway. I must say it was a relief when I knew she was here. She'd have been for the booby hatch if she'd stayed up there in the sticks another week! No fooling, Marcy. She was on the edge."

"Have a drink?" Sebastian said for Marcy.

"Thanks, fella, got to be on my way. Marcy here might put poison in it, anyway—way she's feeling right now. You'll love me again, sweetheart. 'By now!" He went running down the stairs, a little man always on the run.

"I like Eddie," Sebastian said.

"You find it easy to like just anybody," Marcy said. "Is there anyone you don't like?"

"Why, angel child!" he said in Eddie's voice.

"I wish she'd come back."

"As a matter of fact, there are a lot of people I don't like. I'm just not articulate when it comes to expressing dislike, that's all. But I like Eddie."

"Who?"

"Mrs. Boswell."

"*Boswell?* For heaven's sake! Why?"

"Jealousy and hate come out of her like a cloud. I rarely go to your office any more because I don't like seeing her beside you."

"Boswell—of all people! But you needn't hate her. I can cope with Boswell."

"You asked me. I'm telling you. Does there have to be rhyme or reason?"

"Who else?"

"One of my colleagues last year—a record-keeper. Always worrying about cuts—never a thought to human beings. I used to watch till he got by of a morning, so I wouldn't have to walk to my eight-o'clock with him. Does that whittle me down enough?"

"It makes you different," she said. "But I don't mind. Just don't hate us."

"No. And hate isn't the word. Or is it? We'll let it go at that if you like."

"I hate a lot of people. Or I hate just people for being what they are."

"But you love a lot of people too. That's what I've always liked about you—you could love so wholeheartedly."

Marcy crushed the letter from F.P., shoved the letter into her pocket. "I think I'll walk down the street," she said forlornly. "I might meet her."

"You'll do no such thing. Leave her alone, Marcy. Do leave her alone."

"But no one—no one—ought to be so awfully alone as Elspeth," she said.

12

MRS. BOSWELL lingered a moment at the desk. She was not in the habit of intimacy with Marcy, and it was difficult for her to put on the guise of friendship to cover cruelty. But she managed it quite well.

"Why don't you take some time off, Miss Doorn?" she asked with an alien gentle kindness.

"Time off?" Marcy said impatiently. "What for?"

"It must be so hard to put your mind to work," Mrs. Boswell murmured. "I mean with all you've gone through lately."

Marcy put her hand up through her dark curls, leaving them disheveled. "Oh. Has Mr. Featherly been complaining?"

"Oh, no. Of course not!"

Marcy bent her head to her work again as if the conversation were done. It was not done. Mrs. Boswell went on softly, though her eyes were green slits as she looked down at Marcy's bent head.

"It would be inhuman not to be upset," she said. "It was terrible about Mr. Esker, but, after all, death is final. You can't quarrel with death, can you? But this business of your sister—that I do not think I could endure. I know we're more sensible nowadays about mental troubles, but there's a hangover from the dark ages in most of us, all the same. And she was so brilliant! I just thought, if I were you, I'd want to get away for a while."

She had Marcy's attention now. Marcy was looking up, straight at her. "And where did you get that piece of gossip?" she demanded coldly.

"Oh, *is* it gossip?" Mrs. Boswell said with a show of relief and a little shiver of pure pleasure at having got through to Marcy's vulnerable spot at the same time. "How awful of everyone to spread it around then! I suppose so many people are envious of her—but that's cruel if it isn't true!"

"Clouds of hate," Marcy murmured. "I see what you mean." Then, straight to Mrs. Boswell: "Thanks for your consideration. Would you mind calling a messenger boy? Get Johnny if he's free." And she bent to her work with finality. Mrs. Boswell reddened and left the room.

But she had shocked Marcy none the less—she would have been pleased to know how deeply. David? Isobelle? Miss Hodge or Bessie Hamlin? Bessie Hamlin probably. No, Isobelle.

"It's true. I ought to go away," she admitted, but she stayed stubbornly at her desk till lunchtime.

With her proudest look she walked out into the street and toward the restaurant where she had eaten with Sebastian. The behemoths of the snow-disposal force had done their job well, and gone was the whiteness that had made New York a fairy-tale city. All was gray and wet.

Clouds of hate. . . . She had told Sebastian she hated a lot of people, but it hadn't been true. She hadn't even hated Mrs. Boswell, simply discounted her, recognized her jealousy but felt above it. But now she shivered in the wet wind, and at the same time knew a wave of gratitude toward Sebastian for recognizing evil that touched her.

"Suppose I took her to Rio," she said suddenly. "Suppose I just bought the tickets and took her. It would cost a lot of money, but I could get it somehow." Then she shivered again, imagining Elspeth greeting F.P. with "I am looking for God."

She bumped straight into Sam Weston as he came out of the restaurant. "Hello, Marcy," he said.

"Hello, Sam."

She would have gone on in, but he detained her. "Sorry I've just finished. I wanted to talk with you," he said. His blue eyes behind sparkling glasses were anxious and kind. Someone else came through the swinging door, and they had to step to one side to let him pass. "I heard some distressing news yesterday," he fumbled on.

Her body felt inexpressibly weary, as if she had just put on heavy armor and her flesh did not have the strength to wear it. She meant to laugh, but she said, "Who told you?"

He was a fat man, nothing romantic about him at all, but he had always loved Elspeth, even if hopelessly. "Just from a man who happened to drop in at the office. No one you know. It's true?"

She looked away from him. "Did you send the freesia in the blue pitcher?" she asked.

"Freesia? No, I didn't. What do you mean, Marcy?"

"Oh, I don't know. Why don't you go see her, Sam? She's at my place."

His glance was both shrewd and sad. "You must be terribly

worried, to send me," he said. "Or perhaps you think, because of Joe— Joe's quite all right, by the way."

"No," she said. "I thought maybe— You've always believed she could write. I thought maybe you might get her to writing. Though I doubt it."

He hesitated. "Should I phone?"

"No. She's always there."

She went on, wishing she couldn't remember Sam's brother Joe, wondering if somewhere, unknown to herself, had been the memory of Joe. "And for God's sake, handle Joe Weston with kid gloves," David had said. "He's just out of some psychiatric place." And Joe Weston had stood in that room with no glass in hand, though everyone else was drinking—just stood there by the mantel, in full view of everyone, as if he were testing himself to do just that; smiled if anyone spoke to him; said almost nothing. And she had thought: Sam shouldn't have brought him. He can't take it. How would it be if you had to take it forever, the anxious greeting, the averted glance, the ear attuned to expect aberration? She had been hurt for Joe Weston and still remembered the brave, defiant face. Yet Sam said he was all right. But what was all right?

If just some man she didn't know had told Sam, then all the ones she did know said it too. She could hear the word going around as if she had contributed to it. "Did you hear . . . ?" "Can you imagine . . . ?" and so on and on. They knew so many people. They didn't frequent the night-club spots—only rarely. But first nights knew them, and symphony concerts and art shows and the like. Joe—Joe Weston.

At three, without any explanation at all, she went out of the office and took a taxi to Isobelle's apartment. Isobelle didn't spend much time there and she would no doubt be out somewhere now. But she opened the door herself.

"Why, darling! Where did you drop from? How divine!"

Marcy did not smile. She came in, said, "No, thanks," to cigarette, to drink.

"What's on your mind, pet?" Isobelle demanded.

Marcy had not taken a chair. "I just wanted to know if you have been saying around town that Elspeth's lost her mind. I just wanted to know," she said.

Isobelle let her match go out, lit another slowly. Then she said, "But she has, hasn't she?"

Marcy stared at her, then turned toward the door.

"Oh, don't be like that!" Isobelle said impatiently. "These things happen to all of us. No use pretending they don't."

Marcy said, "Let's not even pretend to be friends any more, Isobelle. Good-by."

"As you like," Isobelle said. "But I thought we were friends, not just playing at it. It's terrible, but I don't see what's gained in denying it."

But Marcy had gone, closing the door quietly behind her.

It was still early, but she went home. Something in her cried out to be there with Elspeth, protecting her against—against what? The Isobelles of the world? What? Something else within mocked her because she knew Sebastian would be there too, said, "Are you making your concern for Elspeth the outward symbol of a much deeper compulsion?" She hated being confused about her own thoughts. Long ago she had said, "Well, that's that," about Sebastian Esker. She had said it and meant it.

They had handed this trouble to Sebastian, asked him to shoulder it. And in some ways it had been a great relief to think of him there at the apartment, looking after Elspeth. In some ways it was, she admitted, a terrible pain.

But she went straight home. Sebastian wasn't there; she

felt it as soon as she opened the door. But Sam Weston was there, sitting with one hand up in the air and three fingers of it held down by the other hand.

"Hi!" he said absently. "But hush, I'm counting. Queen Anne's lace, butter and eggs, plantain—that's forty-six. Solomon's seal—did I say that? Eglantine—bet you didn't think I knew that one! Mitrewort, wintergreen—ha! Fifty. I could go on for hours." He grinned at Marcy. "I'm trying to prove to Elspeth that she has no monopoly on the lore of the fields. Why, I was raised in the country!"

"Were you really, Sam?" Marcy said. "I never knew that."

"To tell the truth, I didn't spend my time on wild flowers at that period," he confessed. "It was during my brief period of living in Westchester County that I became so knowledgeable—trying to justify living out there, but I didn't make it, and settled in near the job. I'll tell you something that may surprise you, though. I generally walk to work if the walking's good. On the way there I pass fifteen windows with flowers in. I admit that most are cut flowers from some florist; still, they're there, and prove something—you think what. But two are geraniums and seem to prove something more."

Elspeth looked quite friendly. "You forgot tansy," she said.

"Didn't forget it. Don't know it," Sam conceded. "But don't forget, my girl, that if you ever write a book on nature I'll be able to check. You can't dig it up out of encyclopedias, either—I'd know that. Well, I must run along." He got up and held out his hand to Elspeth.

Elspeth hesitated, but then gave him her hand. "Good-by, Sam," she said.

"Come again," Marcy said.

Sam walked right past her, looking at her but not seeing her. He was gone—his comical figure, his round, pleasant face, and kind eyes, dignified by pain. Yet his voice had sounded so normal, so friendly and commonplace, as if it were just any conversation between him and Elspeth.

"I like Sam," Marcy said casually. "I used to laugh at him, I know, but I like him."

"I wonder where the geraniums are," Elspeth said.

Marcy said tartly, "Considering the fact that you didn't even water the ones at the farm, you're a good one to be worried about where they are!"

"It was stupid having flowers inside," Elspeth said, "when there was all the world growing right up to the door. And let's never make lists. Let's never do that. You don't know flowers because you can make a list."

"But you might," Marcy said. "You don't know that Sam doesn't know as much about flowers as you do."

"If you make lists you're only saying, 'I know more than flowers do. See how clever I am, learning all that!' Flowers don't try to show anything—they just are."

"Who sent you the freesia?"

"The freesia?" Elspeth asked vaguely. "Oh, David, I think."

"And I didn't see you doing much communing with nature when I used to go to the farm," Marcy went on half angrily. "If you took walks or went skiing it was with people. If you ever looked at wild flowers it was with an idea for decorating the house. You looked at nature through the window, but you didn't commune with it, whatever you may have come to believe of yourself."

"No, I didn't," Elspeth said. "That was before I knew what nature was. Before I knew I was part of it. How can you know here, where they whisk the snow off so soon, whether you are in winter or summer? How can you know the rhythm of the sun and moon when you never see the moon, and the sun only dimly through smoke above skyscrapers? You can't feel the earth turning around, and you get out of rhythm, and your faces show it—everybody's face shows it—nervous and sharp and asking, asking all the time why you're going so fast, but not knowing you can slow up, that the earth won't forgive you if you don't."

"Well, we always have the hand-organ man and roller skates to tell us when spring comes," Marcy said dryly. "And there's something about walking up Fifth Avenue in October that always makes me know it's October—even a few dry leaves skittering. And men like Sam who see geraniums in windows. There are vestiges left, darling. I haven't forgotten the moon."

"But you don't live with it," Elspeth said.

"And we have E. B. White to remind us," Marcy said with a grin. "I don't know what you're trying to do—make me dissatisfied with my life, or what. But I make a living in the city. And I have to make a living. I couldn't design clothes on the farm, you know. I like designing clothes. And you needn't try to philosophize about it, either. I have to eat and have a roof over my head, and I wasn't trained to dig potatoes—or raise chickens. And even if I had a mint and didn't need to work, I'd stay in cities. They have a rhythm too, and it's my rhythm—and used to be yours. It used to be yours even in the country. You didn't have your meals with the sun but had a civilized dinner at seven or eight, *with* candles."

"But I was wrong. I'm changed. I'm truly changed, Marcy."

Marcy got up and pulled off her hat, stood swinging it. "And there I agree. I quite agree," she said. She wished her voice were steadier. "Where's Sebastian?"

"I don't know."

Marcy went away, hung her coat up. She felt battered and sore all over. She stood staring at her face in the mirror, and she said, "What now? What do I do now? I don't know what to do." And where was Sebastian? Out in the gray streets, listening to a voice calling?

Still, when she went back to the other room she said sensibly enough, "David's getting awfully big-hearted, sending freesia. And what a darling pitcher! Miss Mack's getting smarter."

She could see David so clearly, standing in the shop, sending flowers to Alice. Well, he might as well, while he was there—leaving it to Miss Mack—well, no, he was fussy about details—but still, just an afterthought left over from sending flowers to someone else.

"Would you mind if we had our usual Christmas at-home?" she asked suddenly. "It would be quiet enough—just old friends, friends of yours and John's too. I think we ought to if you wouldn't mind too much."

"It doesn't matter," Elspeth said.

Even that was no good. It would be better if it did matter, if Elspeth said she couldn't bear it, if she even said she wanted to go back to the farm for Christmas. Just "It doesn't matter" wasn't enough. Other Christmas parties went flashing through Marcy's mind, parties so gay that everyone counted on them, parties with Elspeth in the very middle of them, making everyone laugh, making everyone feel happy and part of the party—oh, that was a great gift to throw away! Perhaps they weren't much, all these friends; perhaps no one was so much when it came right down to it, and yet—and yet they were their friends, the people they knew, that they had had fun with. Weren't friends part of the rhythm? A lifetime of being attuned to tansy wasn't enough; it wasn't. And a month ago

Elspeth would have been the first to say so. Marcy could hear her saying it. "Tansy? Certainly I live in the country—but *tansy?* I'm still a human being, Freddy! I'm no weed."

"Or maybe you'd like it if we all went up to the farm for Christmas," she said quietly. "We could, you know. If that would be better."

"It doesn't matter," Elspeth said again indifferently.

Downstairs Bessie said, "They're gathering already. She's had a man there all afternoon—that fat one we've seen there before."

"Why shouldn't their friends come?" Emma Hodge said. "They've always had lots of friends dropping in."

"I wonder what they think of her? She's certainly very queer—not herself at all."

"Under the circumstances you wouldn't be yourself, either," Emma said sharply.

"Well, I wouldn't sit and talk about cats if my husband had just died. She gave me the creeps."

"You mightn't want to talk about your husband. What have you done with the plates?" There had been two Dresden plates on the mantel for ever so long.

"It's such a clutter there. I put them away," Bessie said. "We've got so much truck in here there's hardly room to turn around."

"But we don't turn around on the mantel," Emma said. "I like them there. Where are they?"

"Now don't be silly. I put them on the top shelf, and they're safe enough. It looks a lot better without so much there."

Emma went to the kitchen, climbed on a chair, and got the plates.

And that morning Sebastian Esker had gone away from the faintly pleading light in Elspeth's eyes, gone about the city with a dogged persistence, listening, listening. He knew the light was only a reflection of an old light. He knew his reluctance to leave her lay not in her desire that he stay. "Wist ye not that I must be about my Father's business?" Almost he said the words to her, but he did not, for she did not really care whether he went or stayed or what his business was.

There were so many people who knew John. Or were there? So many who liked to speak as if they knew him. But who did know him? Burghardt. But not yet could he go again to the crowded living room, be moved so unbearably. And not in Burghardt's room dwelt the unknown John.

All day long he wandered through the city, as unseeing of the city as ever Elspeth could be, but listening with an ear for some strangeness of tone, for words behind words. And all had first to say, "What a pity!" And he had to say, yes, it was a pity. And twice he had to say, of Elspeth, "Oh, no—that's nonsense. I just left her." When he said that he felt he must get back to her at once, that she must not be left alone with her ghosts. Still, he kept steadily on all the day long.

He saw Mrs. Kovacs, who used to clean for them. Why? Because she had always had a fierce, protective affection for John. She was old now, worn to the bone with cleaning other people's houses, but still fierce, still indomitable. She had a picture of John in her clean, stuffy little parlor. She'd never been much on talk—a doer, was Mrs. Kovacs. He went away, remembering only the floor.

"Now, not one boy in a million would have done that," she said. "Come in with his muddy overshoes on my nice clean floor. I was doing the upstairs, and when I come down there he was on his knees, cleaning it all up. You don't find boys—nor grown-ups either—that thoughtful very often, I can tell you. He was a real thoughtful boy. Only he never would eat enough. It worried me the way he pecked at his food. You always had an appetite, but he, never. He never forgot me at Christmas—never once. You'd think, getting up in the world like he did, that after a while an old woman who scrubbed floors wouldn't mean nothing to him. But he never missed."

Sebastian had never missed either, because Mrs. Kovacs had been so kind when his father died. They couldn't have managed without her. But he knew there had been some special quality to the kindness of John. He did not feel resentful, only a little sad as he went away from Mrs. Kovacs, seeing John on his knees in the kitchen.

The glory, yes, that had been everywhere—John, proud, aloof, the genius, too young to die. He turned away from that John. And at Mrs. Kovacs's there had been John the boy, still the boy in the old woman's heart. But even she proudly displayed the fine photograph Sebastian had once given her.

He found Jimmy Terrant in a bar. He'd known him since boyhood—a cellist who'd taken lessons from Sebastian's father long ago. Once their father had been late for a lesson, and Sebastian and John had played some game with Jimmy on the kitchen table, some foolish game of cards—and had been friends with him ever since.

He went back to a table with Jimmy, and Jimmy said, "I can't get over it. I can't make myself believe it. Meant to get up again all summer—one thing and another, I didn't make it. Last time I saw him was in March. Certainly didn't seem sick or anything then. Took me to this shindig in the Community Hall in the village. Surprised me; he never seemed to mix with the natives, not so far as I knew, but here he was, calling for the square dances, knowing everyone's name—maybe getting the feel of it for some music he was doing—I don't know. Never saw him so on top of the world. A right guy if there ever was one. . . ."

But even that was not strange. "For the rhythm," John would say, his eyes crinkling at the corners. No, he wouldn't explain anything, but you'd hear the rhythm in something after a bit, authentic, recognizable.

There was an instant, just an instant, at Andrea and Axel's. "And now he'll never see her drink out of the cup," Andrea said, and she turned from the crib, from the new baby under the pink blanket, and went to the kitchen and took down the silver cup and kept looking down at it with the tears running down her face. "Why, it was just the other day—just the other day he brought it," she kept saying. Then she put the cup down, wiped her sleeve across her eyes, and said, "You know how it is with us, Sebastian. We play life for the laughs—you know—especially being pregnant. Only John never laughed. And some folks bring blankets and doodads but don't remember if it's a boy or a girl—and John came and brought this cup, with the name and the day and everything, and I can't help crying every time I look at it. He wasn't even my friend, especially—really just Axel's." It was there, just at that instant, that he felt the moment important, that this was the John who called.

And then the day was almost over. He didn't know why he gave up listening and went to David, except that he couldn't listen any more.

"Thank God!" David said. "You've saved me from collapse. Come in and have a drink."

"Just a cigarette, and then I'll get on," Sebastian said. "Don't tell me you're working this hour of the day?"

"I've been working since six this morning," David said. "Just an exercise in concentration. I feel giddy. I'll have a drink. Sure you won't?"

"No, thanks. Are you doing something new? Could I see it?"

David poured himself a drink slowly, eying the amount in the glass with a great eye for exactness; then he put the glass down and said, "All right. I don't mind you. But Isobelle's on her way over with some private tragedy. Don't let her in under penalty of death."

The picture was nearing completion—at least the jungle greens, which had been laid on only lightly when Alice had seen them, were deep and sinister, and the tunnel of light stood out dramatically against the huge leaves and twisted branches.

"I suppose they'll say it's a retrogression," David said in a more nervous way than he was in the habit of using. "I went through my surrealist stage."

"They?" Sebastian said, but without emphasis. The day, which was an accumulation of all the days since the cablegram had been put in his hand, was heavy on him. Too exactly he was the little man in the green tunnel. He turned and went back into the living room, and David followed him, but with a look of faint hurt in his blue eyes.

"You don't like it," he said flatly.

"Like it? It is. It just *is*," Sebastian said. Then: "It would be difficult, I should think, to show the predicament of the human race in line and color, in squares and circles and triangles—extraordinarily difficult. When critics see it, I think they lie; what they see is the predicament of the artist. It's not the same thing, is it? Oh, I can see the weariness of using old symbols—I can see that. I feel it in words sometimes. Yet I haven't given up words. Oh, let it go. You must be very tired. I think I won't stay. I don't want to see Isobelle, if you don't mind."

"But she's here," David said. "Sorry, but she's here."

She was there, all furs and scent and smiles, but her eyes did not dance so mockingly as sometimes, and, if she could ever be called nervous, she was nervous now.

"You were cruel not to come!" she said. "I thought you were being unfaithful to me. But I had to see you. I simply had to. I'm feeling dreadful, and please give me a drink, and fast. I'm terribly low."

Sebastian stood up. "I really must run along," he said politely. "Sorry, but I must."

But Isobelle put a small hand on his arm and said, "Sit down. Sit down. You're my defense. I'm so glad it's you here instead of one of David's lesser loves. I'm your Great Love, am I not, sweet? Thanks. . . . Lord, how I needed that!"

"What's on your mind?" David asked.

"Freddy—he's the only one I told. And Freddy's known you all for years. And it's true enough, isn't it, Sebastian? I didn't do it in maliciousness, as Marcy seems to think. I think it's silly and really mean of her—really stupid, to take it that way. We've got past the day where we keep skeletons in the closet and hang our velvet frocks over them and never, never, never let anyone *know*. Haven't we?"

"Make some sense, Isobelle," David said.

"I've known Marcy ever since kindergarten days. It hasn't anything to do with loyalty. You'd think I'd stabbed her in the back. But you know, you both know that it's true, and I don't see that there's anything wrong in admitting the truth. It's a terrible pity—I could howl with rage at fate. All the same, you don't cut off your friends for saying it's true. Elspeth *has* gone queer in the head. She just has. I can see why and pity her; all the same, she has gone queer. And Sebastian, you were there when I saw her, and you can't say she didn't show plenty of evidence of it. Am I being hysterical? It really got me down, having Marcy come in with that choose-between-me-and-not-keeping-your-mouth-shut air. I've always been terribly loyal to Marcy. But—oh, David, darling, I am *so* upset. What *is* it, David?"

David reached over and took the glass from Isobelle's hand, set it down on the table. "Run along, Isobelle," he said coldly. "Run along and have your cocktails with Freddy. I'm really very busy."

"*David!*" she said, and for an instant her reproach was real.

"I mean it," he said. "Shall we go now, Sebastian? Just wait till I wash up, will you?" He walked out of the room and just left Isobelle standing there.

"The Doorns," she said bitterly after an instant.

"He's upset too," Sebastian said with pity.

"But it isn't that it isn't true," she said quite calmly and coldly. "It's just that the Doorns won't have it true to *them*. She's as crazy as a loon. *Isn't* she?"

"No, Isobelle, she isn't. But sometimes I think I am."

"Do you mean to say that you think all those utterances of hers the other day were normal? I shook like a leaf for hours. All the same, I am upset—about Marcy. You don't like losing a friend all in an instant like that. There aren't so many good ones, you know. Oh, to hell with it!"

She turned toward the door. "I don't know why I'd expect *you* to back me up," she said as she went. "You, of all people! Well, be a closed corporation if you like, but don't expect people not to talk, because people will talk."

She banged the door, and Sebastian had said not a word in comfort or reproach. He did not wait for David, knowing David did not want to go anywhere with him, nor did he want to see more of David right now. He let himself out quietly and went away from David, from the picture, from the ugly scene in the gay room, but not from his thoughts, which were always with him. He hurried a little, feeling he had been away from Elsepeth for a very long time.

13

AND IN the city, all over the city, they lay awake that night with thoughts going round and round in circles, or dreamed troubled dreams related yet unrelated to the day's events.

"But you can't serve two Gods at once," Marcy's stubborn mind said over and over. "She looked hurt, but you can't. That's a fundamental—even with a God. It's like being a cannibal, eating your own kind like that. She looked hurt. I know she doesn't really like Elspeth, but she always professed to like me. I needn't have said 'pretend.' Clouds of hate, clouds of hate—I never believed before that anyone hated me; perhaps no one does until you know it—does that make sense in a Bergsonian way? Sebastian says to wait. But that's what we can't do. We have never waited for anything; we've gone straight on, no matter what. But he's been waiting all these years. He has the habit. And what is he waiting for? No, maybe he isn't waiting. Maybe he knows there's nothing to wait for, maybe he's just being. He goes on teaching and studying; he always has. He has a kind of life outside her, and yet—and yet— David, you looked so odd, so lonely—or does everyone look lonely to me these days?—with the pitcher hanging from your hand. That was odd, taking the pitcher back. That was very odd. I can't wait. I don't know how. Well, you've waited all these years for Sebastian, as he has waited for Elspeth—if you call that waiting, if you call it anything but accepting something you can't do anything about. I'll have to have the Christmas party—why will I? Just to show everybody I am not afraid? Is that why I've got to have it? But I am afraid. *Is* everything all right with you, Joe Weston? And what if there is never any miracle and she never comes alive in the old way? What do we do then? I wish she didn't half make sense. But people with no inhibitions do make sense sometimes. It isn't sense for *her*, that's the trouble. You can't cast overboard everything that made you and survive. You just can't. He never sees me, as I never saw the hate—does it mean *I* don't exist? If I went in now and sat on the edge of his bed and put my hand on his hair, he might take me in his arms and comfort me, as if I were a child, but I still wouldn't be seen. Does he really believe she is all right? That waiting is enough? No, he doesn't. But then, maybe you *can* serve two Gods. Sebastian does; he has this God of Love for Elspeth and the God of his love for John. Which voice calls the loudest, the one from the grave or her voice? Oh, *Sebastian*."

And Sebastian lay in a tunnel of light, yellow light instead of green, and could not rise or go to answer the call of anyone. And yet the calls kept coming, from here, from there, insistent, pleading; but he could not move. Beside him, only a foot away, lay a silver ashtray with a llama carved in its base

The ashtray was calling out in a small silver voice, but he could not move his hand toward it. Hush, hush. But it went on crying. He turned and opened his eyes to the square of pale night light that was the window.

All the people he had seen through the long day flowed through his mind, but they flowed past, not pausing long enough for him to say, "That's it. Wait—that's *it.* That's the John who's done this awful thing to Elspeth. There he is." Never anyone like that at all. All that had come was that young John on his knees, cleaning a muddy floor; that John calling for square dances; that John who brought the silver cup. And then he had a clear picture of Elspeth at the farm, cutting up the canvas, stuffing it in the fireplace, standing and watching it burn. *Oh, my darling, don't be so hurt! You won't get over the hurt this way, not by being someone else. You're you. Take the hurt, hold it. You have to. You can't pretend it isn't there. Or let me hold it for you. Let me . . .*

Emma Hodge tossed and turned. Once she leaned over the edge of the bed and peered down at the blue cushion, put there for Soutan. But Soutan was not on the cushion. He never was. "But where would she go?" she asked helplessly, angrily. "You can't get a divorce from your cousin. I'd give her alimony—but where would she go?" Then she gave a self-mocking grin. "And who'd get my dinner, such as it is?" she asked herself. It wasn't good though, she insisted, to keep hearing Bessie's cane tapping, tapping, even in the night. It wasn't good to get in such a fury over the plates, nor to take the chance, with her tendency toward dizziness, of climbing up on that chair. But they were her plates—it was her house, wasn't it? "But where would she go?" she said to the empty cushion, to the empty room, to her empty heart.

And Fanny Drake lay in the room in her parents' house, the room that she paid rent for, and without resentment, for her folks had a tough time of it by and large—and why not; she wasn't married, and yet she had to be independent, and they wanted her at home, even if they did want her to pay for room and board too. And she was in the midst of the old snowstorm. "No," she told herself, "stop. Don't live it again. It's no use. It's just no use." But she was coming out of the movie and the snowstorm of the movie, and the girl who had been to her first dance, gone to it through the snow—and John Esker's music was still in Fanny's head, the music of the dance. Oh, such music! Or it had seemed wonderful, but maybe any music would have seemed wonderful. And she was in the outside world in another snowstorm, and it seemed as if the two were one thing and she was in the middle of happiness, just as the girl had been, and she said, "Oh, Cory, it's snowing!" and she'd been so terribly happy, and right then —oh, why right then, when she was so lifted up out of all the plainness, the run-of-the-mill difficulties of living, why right then did he say, "Fanny, I think I ought to tell you, I'm going to be married—quite soon"? He didn't pretend he hadn't cared about her, that they hadn't had fun together, that there was no reason to tell her—he was decent, Cory, he didn't want to hurt her—but all the same, there, in the middle of the snowstorm, in the middle of the music, he had told her. And why shouldn't she cry when she heard the music? Why shouldn't she cry for John Esker, who would never lift anyone up again as she had been lifted up that night? She would take roses from the great cooler, she would know all the loves of the neighborhood, she would learn to be impersonal at the right time, but never again—and the pitcher *was* important, because she had almost really cared about it, and it had seemed as if she would never truly care about anything again, so long as she lived. But what would it have been like to be married to a man who could make music like that? What kind of a dying was *she* feeling now? How terrible for her—and yet it wasn't the same as Cory's saying "quite soon" in that firm yet sorry voice. It wasn't like that. For it hadn't been a person that died; it had been hope. And some people just played with love and with hope too, like that David Doorn, who thought the world was just to wait on him. He had a beautiful face—but no face any more meant anything. Cory had been dark and plain, but his was the one face—and in the snow—*oh, stop, stop, don't do it all over again, don't do it!*

"It's two. Couldn't you have managed the coffee a little earlier, Alice?" Henry said. "I have a job, you know." And he locked the door and came up the stairs.

"Yes, it was a long evening," Alice said from above him on the stairs. "It was a long, long evening." And slowly down the hall, past Nick's and Carol's rooms, they moved, like two people walking in a trance of habit, and made ready for bed. Alice rubbed cold cream on her face and heard the sound of Henry's spitting as he cleaned his teeth in the bathroom.

"And if you're going to play bridge at all, why can't you play a good game?" Henry said.

Isobelle put up a thin arm across her face and gave a small whimper, like a child whimpering for its mother in the dark.

Mrs. Boswell, Agatha Boswell, lay wide awake and stretched her long legs as far down under the sheets as they would go. She felt beautiful, successful, satisfied, as if the mirror had told her her enemy was dead and she was now the only one with beauty and power in all the world.

David Doorn lay awake and watched the sky turn a lighter gray. "Let's be famous," Elspeth had said, "like the Brontës or the Sitwells oı one of those lots." As if it were only to be wished, to be suggested, and the thing were as good as done. Only they'd done it—or she had done it. Of course they'd had some talent. They came by that naturally—nothing to be proud of. "First we'll get you 'discovered,' David. You can draw like an angel; we'll make a thing out of the discovery. . . . Oh, let's be *famous!*" "You really need a spot of cash," David had said. "Nonsense! You don't need a thing—or anything we haven't got," Elspeth had said. Oh, it took some doing. They worked at it—but like a game. They made a terrific game out of it. They got there too. The fabulous Doorns, they were called. With nothing but some talent and a zest for life, looks—well, they all had looks. That helped. "And now I can't show it to her," David said to the gray sky. "I can't even show it to her." He knew exactly, in his sensitive way, why he had done the picture—because he had been rejected, made nothing, by Elspeth. He had never been able to tell her what happened to him when he saw the news item. He might never tell her now, because you could not talk to her. You'd think I was Lord Byron, with a yen for Augusta! he thought angrily. It wasn't like that at all. He hadn't liked her marrying John, but he'd got used to that. It hadn't stopped anything. He had done the picture to show her he had not been nibbled at—something so good she had to see it. And now he couldn't even ask her to come and look. "I ought to have slapped Isobelle's face," he said.

The light grew brighter, and he could see the pitcher he

had brought from Marcy's place and which now stood on the dresser across the room from his bed. . . . Elspeth used to come in and say, "But that's magnificent—that's the best yet!" Or: "Make it shock a little, darling. Her hair's so red—have the chair purple, a real and violent purple. It will make the nerves jerk."

He got out of bed and in his pajamas went into the studio and pulled on the light. He stared at the picture. It was demanded of him that he know whether it was good without being told so by Elspeth or anyone. "I've pushed the world out. So what?" he said angrily, staring till he was cold. He went back to his room, showered, shaved, dressed, went in and began to paint, without breakfast. He felt light-headed, and yet his hand was extraordinarily steady, his eye sure.

Elspeth Esker woke and looked around her. Asleep, she had had the look of a dead saint. The look stayed when she awoke. Yet she rose and dressed carefully, brushed her fair hair, fastening it up in the way she always did it, intricately, yet looking careless—but all as a nun might go through the motions of putting on her habit exactly, seeing that the band across her forehead was snowy white, that the folds of black fell just so, that the chain and cross hung straight. The woman in the mirror had nothing to say to the woman outside it.

Then she went out to where Sebastian was having coffee and toast all alone and said, "Would you take me skating?"

He almost dropped his cup, but he said at once, "I'd like to. When? Right now?"

"Soon. When I've had coffee."

"An egg—I'll boil an egg for you," he said.

And they actually went up to Central Park, he carrying Marcy's skates for Elspeth, and when they got there he rented skates, and she put her hands in his, and they skated out through the gray morning. It was a school day, and there were no children about, only a few skaters. Elspeth wore an old brown skating jacket of Marcy's, and her head was bare. She moved like music, like the wind, and Sebastian thought: I ought to be happy; I haven't been so unhappy in God knows when. Yet they moved together in rhythm, and her hands were not reluctant in his.

"How John loved to skate!" he said. "He couldn't ever go in for football, that sort of thing, but he skated as he breathed, as he wrote music. I've always been so grateful that you had the pond at the farm. Do you remember the pond?"

"Hush," she said—just a whisper on the cold air, no pause in movement.

But he went stubbornly on. "I think of the pond often—how deep the snow lay in the pines up at the north end, and the moon like day, and our little fire. . . . No matter what, there have been some moments of pure happiness."

"Children at play. Drive slowly," Elspeth said.

"No, I wasn't a child. None of us were children," he said. "We knew quite well we could be run over; we had fun none the less. I remember how John made the treble clef sign and one note of a symphony—one note—and it seemed as if we heard the music of the spheres. That's poetic, for me, isn't it? But that was how we felt; that was what it seemed like. And the walk back to the farm, with Marcy singing up ahead and the notes coming back to us, so pure on the white air; and you and John walked hand and hand, and I trailed behind and felt happiness floating back to me from you all. . . ." He was skating more slowly now, and his words had a tempo to match their speed, slow and stately.

"And this isn't happiness?" Elspeth asked.

"No. It isn't," he said. "Sorry, but it isn't. If I was not a child then, I am less a child now."

She paused, made a small circling movement, faced him, hand still in his.

A middle-aged woman was making hard going nearby, a thick scarf dangling, her feet coming down so heavily, as if weight generated skill and speed. Yet her anxiety, her persistence were touching.

"No one hears me," Elspeth said in sudden forlornness. "No one listens."

"I hear you," Sebastian said.

"You're all so busy going ahead—going back. It's all one thing. No one hears me—no one."

He held her gloved hands tightly, said again firmly, "*I* hear you. Does pizza sound too earthy to you?"

She laughed, and the sound startled him. "I'd love some," she said. They began to skate toward the building.

But when they had their pizza, Sebastian couldn't eat. Elspeth did, however, and as if she enjoyed it. "I was hungry," she said.

"Good. I'm glad there's something here and now that you're not indifferent to."

They moved out into the homeward way.

"But you told me to be indifferent," she said at last.

"Did I? Yes, I know. I take it back. I've been meaning to take it back ever since I said it. I don't want to be a God who could say, 'There falls a leaf,' with the same concern in which He says, 'There falls John Esker.' I'm a human being, Elspeth. So long as something matters to me, I cannot but feel it matters to all men everywhere. We all go to dust, true—but I shall continue being interested in men more than in leaves.

Don't look like that, Elspeth. And I shall talk about John. You must remember that: I intend to talk about John."

She looked at her gloved hands, did not answer. In silence they reached home, in silence went up the stairs together.

Elspeth went to her room, and Sebastian sat at the desk in the living room and wrote a letter to Lexie—a gay enough letter, considering his sober thoughts—signed it: "Your devoted fiancé, Sebastian Esker."

He forgot lunch, and when Elspeth brought some on a tray he was surprised and moved.

"I'm going away tomorrow," he said. "Is there anything you'd like done before I go?"

"Away?" she said. Then: "There's nothing to do."

"I'll be back," he said.

"Yes, you always come back," she said.

He had not believed of himself that he could ever be other than gentle with her, but the vague acceptance of his presence in her voice drove him suddenly harsh. He stood up abruptly. "And you know why," he said, "and don't pretend you don't. I come back because I love you and have from the first time I ever saw you. You know that very well. I *care* what happens to you. And I cared about John. I still care about you both. And God forgive me for ever telling you indifference was the way through trouble. It's the sin against the Holy Ghost, that's what indifference is. Maybe you can excuse it in leaves, but never in men. I don't forgive it in you, Elspeth. Why, even Isobelle cared more than you! Even Isobelle!"

She let her hands rest on the back of a chair, but otherwise she was very still, and though she looked straight at him she did not come closer, in either body or spirit.

He tried to take the violence from his voice, but vestiges

of it remained. "Elspeth! John *loved* you. He was not just a leaf to you once. He *loved* you. For some reason—God knows what—you don't believe it any more. But you have to believe it. And don't talk about no one hearing you; you don't hear me either. Elspeth, *he loved you so*."

She did not move from behind the chair. "Darling Sebastian," she said gently.

Anger turned him around, made him address the envelope on the desk in black, savage strokes. When he looked up again she had drifted silently out of the room.

14

DAVID DOORN walked into Miss Mack's, the uncovered pitcher swinging. He put the pitcher on the little wall desk, said, "Hello, Miss Mack. Where's your henchman? I brought her pitcher back."

"But you've been billed for it. I suppose you want a rebate?"

"Naturally. And I thought I might take the wench out for lunch. She doesn't look properly fed."

"I like the child. I don't let her go out with philanderers," Miss Mack said. She couldn't help smiling at David because she couldn't help liking him, but she meant what she said too.

"Oh, I only philander at the cocktail hour. I was thinking of an automat."

"H'mph! I doubt if you even wait for your orange juice in the morning," Miss Mack said. "Oh, there you are, Fanny. Mr. Doorn wants to take you out to lunch. I'm no guardian, but I ought to warn you that he means no good."

"And wash the ink off your finger," David said.

She gave a glance toward the pitcher, did not hesitate at all before she said, "It would save the price of a sandwich, I suppose."

Then she put out a hand and looked with surprise at the ink along one finger. She reached around the corner of the back door, took down a coat. "I just washed my hands. It's indelible," she said. She wore her hair in the pony tail and looked schoolgirlish. "Back in an hour," she said to Miss Mack.

"I warned you," Miss Mack said.

"No need, no need. It's obvious enough," Fanny said, and David swung the door open and let her out. It was like him to do things like this, on impulse, and he nearly always succeeded in fulfilling his impulses.

Miss Mack, bulky, rouge on either cheekbone, watched them go up the street. She frowned. Even in the little time Fanny had been here, she had shown she had a mind of her own, that she couldn't be fooled much by anyone. She had gone with him, a stranger, just as if she had no will at all.

Only a few doors from Miss Mack's Fanny said, "This will do."

They were before a small chain restaurant. David said, "Oh, no, it won't do at all. I'm more fastidious than that."

"It will have to do," Fanny said. "It's not bad at all—really a come-up from a drug store counter. You don't have to sit on a stool or anything like that. I only *sell* orchids, you know—anemones and such."

He gave an unwilling grin, and they went into the restaurant, found a booth, sat down. All too quickly a pert waitress was there, waiting for their order. Fanny ordered a sandwich and coffee, and David, after some frowning appraisal of the menu, ordered the same.

"They're too efficient," he said. "There won't be time for the story of your life if they do everything at such a speed."

"In my circles," she said, "we don't go in for that sort of thing much. Proper working class people we are, sir, and no time for being neurotic."

"I work too," he said. "Do I look like a rich playboy?"

"To be truthful, yes," she said.

"Good. That's my aim. But I work too—work damn hard."

"But still take time out for minor pleasures," she said.

"Oh, yes. Of course. Wouldn't want to get stale."

And there the sandwiches were, plunked down before them with no nonsense, the coffee shoved across before their faces, slopped a little in the saucers.

"Oh, sorry!" the waitress said. But Fanny, as if she had done it many times, took a napkin from the metal container, soaked the coffee up. Then she grinned and said, "Reminds me of my greatest humbling. You know, you don't have to spill coffee. If you don't think of it, you can even wave a cup around in the air. It's being careful that spills it. But I tried a demonstration of that once, at a party. I was helping set the table and carrying in fruit cup—don't raise your brows; fruit cup's all right. So I gave this demonstration of how not to spill. 'Like this,' I said. 'Just don't think of it!' and I waved the cup around, and, to my surprise, the fruit flew all over the room and made the most unholy mess! Don't know what that proves, but it always makes me laugh, remembering my own astonishment that my theory didn't work!"

David laughed. "Trouble with theories," he conceded. "Is that the major event in your life?"

"One of 'em. Makes you walk wary, an experience like that."

"And then you got this personal-impersonal job, and we're up to now," David said.

Fanny drank coffee that still looked scalding hot, then said with no flippancy, "Did she like the freesia?"

"Well, if we're to be strictly honest, no. I doubt if she even noticed it."

"Oh. I'm sorry. I thought it looked lovely."

"It did. Which brings us to the nub of the matter. Why were you mourning John Esker?"

She bent her head, and the pony tail gave a funny bob as she did so. Then she looked straight at him and said, "Do you know, I don't find this sort of inquisition funny. You wouldn't want me prying into your affair with Mrs. Garrett, would you? Not that I ever even knew your brother-in-law—nor your sister either. They're just people in a book to me."

"A good book?" David asked.

"Sad, anyway," she said.

"Rather," David said. "Odd—it started out such a gay tale. By the way, the Garrett angle is out. That's free."

"Oh. Well, it did seem a waste."

"And that's a very flip judgment, isn't it? How do you know whether it was a waste or not? How do you know my very heart's blood didn't go into it?"

"If it had you couldn't discuss it with a stranger."

"Oh, you could. Isn't it true that you tell your secrets to seatmates on a train? Or to shipmates? Not plane-mates—that's too fast."

"Not I. Not I, Mr. Doorn. Are you done? If so, I must get back."

"I don't think your hour's up. I'd like some more coffee, wouldn't you?"

He ordered coffee without waiting for her answer. Then

he folded his arms along the table and gave her his sweetest smile. "My sister Marcy would like you," he said. "I must see that you meet. She doesn't like many of my—shall we say 'pick-ups'?"

"You might as well say it," she said crisply. "But you needn't introduce me to your family, Mr. Doorn. In fact, you couldn't, could you?"

He smiled again. "Just what is your name, anyway?"

"Fanny Drake."

"Dreadful name, Fanny."

"Miss Mack said you'd not speak to me if you knew it. But that's my name, Mr. Doorn."

"I wasn't asking you to change it. Dreadful, all the same. Suits you in a way—goes with that silly hair-do. Yes, you and Marcy must meet. What would you say to cocktails some Friday?"

"No, thank you," Fanny said.

"How blunt you are! You prefer characters in books, then?"

"Some characters. Look, Mr. Doorn, I don't know what you think you're trying to do. I don't know why I'm having lunch with you—except that I didn't feel like an argument. But this is it, Mr. Doorn, the beginning and the end of an amusing acquaintance. I do work—and I don't mean work in your sense of the word, but a nine-to-five job day after day, for forty-two dollars a week. It's fun to see someone who has his picture in the papers, but I haven't any ambition to travel in your crowd. And I don't want to meet your sister. In this coat? You see, I have my pride." She was grinning in a mocking way.

"It isn't much, is it?" David conceded. "Good enough for the shop, but it isn't much. But Marcy—well, you ought to see the awful purple suit she runs around in most of the time. Elspeth, now—she's the one whose clothes look like something. But I wasn't asking you to go for a wardrobe inspection."

To his surprise, she stopped her nonsense, her mockery, and said simply, "The truth is, I heard your sister had had a mental crack-up, and it made me sorry for you. That's why I came. I thought if you sent flowers it couldn't be true, but I heard it again this morning. If it's true, I *am* sorry. That's personal, I know, but I mean it."

He stopped smiling too, stared at her.

Then he reached for the check, stood up, shrugged into his coat. She pushed her hands into gloves, went with him out of the restaurant, pausing with her back to him while he paid the bill at the cashier's window. He didn't say a word till they got to the shop. It was only a little way but seemed long. Before the shop he paused, plainly not coming in.

She said, "Thank you," formally though nervously.

"You're welcome," he said.

"I'm sorry," she said.

"Yes," he said. "God knows why. For the trade, it's a lie. Between you and me, Fanny, it's true. As you say, it's a sad story. Good-by now."

"Good-by," Fanny said.

He turned abruptly, walked away from her up the street.

"Good gracious! He hasn't made you cry already!" Miss Mack said impatiently. "But I told you—"

"Oh, I know what he's like," Fanny said, hanging her coat up. "Only everything is so horribly *sad*. I wish someone would laugh—you know, good old belly-laughs. Doesn't anyone any more?"

"Well, all I can say is he's better even than I thought if he can make you weep over his misspent life as fast as this," Miss Mack mumbled. "Especially when nobody ever enjoyed misspending more than he does!"

"It isn't him—he—it's just everything," Fanny said. "I'll take over now if you want to get your lunch."

Miss Mack, big bosom preceding her down the street, puffed a little along her path and said angrily to herself, "Why, the so-and-so! The young squirt! I'll give him a piece of my mind, I will at that!"

On Marcy's table in the morning was a note: "Had to get an early bus. Hope I didn't disturb you. I'll write or phone. Sebastian." Not "with love"; not even "sincerely"—just that bald statement and his name. She went into her own room that he had been using. It was neat, with the used sheets folded in squares at the end of the bed, no sign that he had been there at all. Then she saw that the ashtray was gone.

She heard the whispering sound behind her, and Elspeth was standing there, dressed for the day. "What's the matter?" Elspeth said.

"Not a thing. Sebastian's gone off on business somewhere. How tidy it is!"

"Yes. Everything in order—everything in neat little packets, like the parts of speech. He doesn't want anything to overlap, like using a noun for a verb, as we do sometimes. And everything overlaps. Why not let it and not *be* so tidy?"

"I couldn't agree more, but I don't agree that Sebastian's like that. He lets everything overlap too much. You're making him a pedantic, dry-as-dust professor, and he isn't that. You know he isn't. You make such generalizations, darling. I wonder if he made coffee. Seems as if I smell it."

He had made coffee, and Marcy ate breakfast quickly. Then

she said as carelessly as she could, "And what will you do all day, without Sebastian?"

"I don't know. Don't give me a thought."

"All right, I won't," Marcy said. She got up, put her things on, picked up the portfolio that was her constant companion, went out and down the stairs, calling a careless " 'By now."

And how could she not have known it when he put the note on the table? How could he have gone out of the house without her very bones crying out in protest? He was gone, gone to Old Quagatuck. Why? What business did he have there? It wouldn't do any good to go and stand by John's grave. For you can't talk through six feet of earth and a coffin lid. You just can't talk any more.

On her desk was a note saying: "Dunstan at ten. Bazaar pictures."

"Who sent for Eddie?" she asked Mrs. Boswell.

"Why, I did. You always have him."

"I like him," Sebastian had said.

"Did you want someone else? I took it for granted you'd want Eddie."

"It doesn't matter," she said and turned away from Mrs. Boswell's sleek, ingratiating, complacent smile. She wanted to hate Eddie, but it suddenly ceased to matter at all. "Tillie here?"

"I think so. Yes, she's here. She's dressing now."

Tillie was Marcy's favorite of all the girls who had worn her clothes. She was so devastatingly young and provocative, a pin-up girl, if there ever was one. Marcy went into the showroom, and Tillie stood there in the red and white dress —such a foam of white, such a red red.

"Good. In fact, enchanting," Marcy said. "Oh, hello, Eddie."

"Hello, honey child," Eddie said. "All is forgiven, eh? And that's today's glamor girl? I'll vote for you, Tillie. Is that rig what college girls wear to their first prom? Damned if you don't look it, but you know you never made the eighth grade."

Tillie giggled and said, "Barnard, 'fifty-six."

"Oh, come off it. I knew you when," Eddie said.

Then there was the business of lights and angles, and the tiring process of pictures. And after the red and white there were the suit and the blouse with the big bow under the chin —and Tillie standing with books by a window.

It was after Eddie had gone, hours later, that Tillie, in her ordinary clothes, which were a reasonable facsimile of what the best-dressed college girl wears, stood by Marcy's desk and said, "Will I need to come again, Miss Doorn?"

"I think that's all, Tillie. It went very well, I thought. You looked lovely."

Then Tillie said, "I *might* have been Barnard, 'fifty-six, only instead it's night school and night school and night school. I'll be old when I get a degree." Her voice had a bitter note. But then she flashed her usual brilliant smile and said, "But I'll get it, Miss Doorn. I sure as hell will!"

Marcy gave her a swift, searching, yet surprised glance. "I'm sure you will," she said. "But why do you want to?"

Tillie hesitated. "I don't know," she said. "Only I've said I would, and I will. Most of the girls think it's wonderful to have your picture in all the magazines. But it's not so much, is it? It's just a way to earn money, that's all it is. And after a while I won't be pretty. No one's pretty forever. I want to teach school. Everybody laughs when I say that. But it isn't a joke, Miss Doorn. I do want to."

"And you *will*," Marcy said gently.

Tillie gave her gamin-like grin and went away with her day's pay stuffed into her shoulder bag.

"Well," Marcy said. She was surprised and touched. She'd used Tillie four or five times now, and she'd never even known she went to night school. Queer, her saying that today. "Oh, you're still here, Eddie?"

"Just going," Eddie said. "Sweet kid, isn't she? Just what you need when you're tired of this mad whirl of living."

"Not what you need," Marcy said tartly. "Or what you'll get, either. And she's going to be a schoolteacher."

"For crying out loud!" Eddie said. "What for?"

"She says it isn't so much, having your picture in the paper," Marcy said tartly.

"Is that so? Depends on what paper and who took the picture," Eddie said. "Not so much, eh?"

"I thought that would be good for your morale," Marcy said.

Eddie's traps were piled up beside him. He looked at her shrewdly and said, "You know, I thought you meant it when you said, 'No more pictures from Dunstan.' I thought you really meant it."

"I did," Marcy said. "I meant it—but it suddenly didn't matter. Skip it, Eddie."

"No use cutting off your nose and the rest of it, eh? Look, kid, how's your sister? Is she okay? Can't help thinking about her."

"She's fine," Marcy said shortly.

"Says you. She ought to marry the brother. Now there's a right guy—smart, too, in his way. Early days for that, I suppose, but he's a right guy."

Marcy wished he would go. She wished she could put her

head down on the desk and weep. But she said, "He likes you too, Eddie."

"He does? You know, that makes me feel good—hard-shell Eddie, with a heart like butter. Well, I'll say this for him, he doesn't look down his nose at you like your charming brother —and maybe you girls too. You can get to him. Treats you human. Well, so long, Marcy. Be seeing you around somewhere."

At the door he turned and winked at her and said, "What do you want for Christmas, sweetheart?"

"A little Christmas spirit would be nice," she said shortly, not looking up.

He gave a cackle of laughter, said, "See what I can do—scarce, though," and was really gone.

The phone rang, and it was David. "Where is everybody?" he asked. "No one answers the phone at the house."

"I don't know. Sebastian's gone away for a few days. I don't know where Elspeth is."

"Gone away? What for?"

"I don't know. Business of his own. I'll go home now."

"Somebody ought to be there," David said. "Want me to run around?"

"No. I want to go anyway."

"Nice to have a job like that," David said. Then: "I wish she'd stay put."

"Why should she?" Marcy said and hung up.

But her sharpness was not for David. It was for the worry that was there all the time, every minute of every day and night. She wasn't tidy. It overlapped everything else, the worry. It spoiled everything. Mrs. Boswell would look pleased, would say again that she ought to go away for a while. But she just picked up her portfolio and went out of the office, without saying anything to anyone.

She came into an empty apartment. Yet Elspeth had taken nothing with her. She would be back. Only it made you feel sick to think of her wandering about by herself, vague about all real things, wandering in some world of mysticism. Marcy went slowly down the stairs and asked Bessie if she had seen Elspeth go out, if Elspeth had left any message.

"Yes, I saw her go out," Bessie said. "Maybe an hour—maybe two hours—ago. But I was busy; I didn't speak to her."

"Oh, thank you," Marcy said and went back up the stairs, away from Bessie's curiosity. But Elspeth had gone out before. She went out almost every day—somewhere. Where? With Sebastian gone, it seemed different, as if nothing stood between Elspeth and some disaster. Yet she hadn't gone with Sebastian every day.

"He might have said 'love,' " she said.

Then Elspeth was coming up the stairs. She came in, in Marcy's old jacket, carrying Marcy's skates. No one had told Marcy of the other skating expedition. She stared at the skates. "Good for you, darling!" she said almost at once.

Elspeth put the skates down on the floor, sat down, with the jacket still on. There was color in her face, and she looked very beautiful. "I flew home too," she said.

It bothered Marcy that she understood her sister instantly. Oh, you might get the connection between skating and flying quickly enough, but there was more to it than that. They had used to pool their dreams of flying, and Elspeth's favorite flight was along the river, over the boats, through fog. Marcy often flew down Fifth Avenue, and David swooped between skyscrapers. They used to astonish strangers or friends with quite factual-seeming accounts of these flights. But they were always completely aware of what was fantasy and what was not—and so, after the first uneasy surprise, was any listener. But there was something about the way Elspeth spoke now that made you doubt whether she knew she was talking of a dream world or not, or whether she really knew that she had lived years since the days when they had had this Flying Association.

"Oh, I do love skating!" Marcy said. "Let me come too on Sunday. We had such fun on the pond. Remember?"

"I don't have to remember. It's all right there," Elspeth said with a small movement of her hand that seemed to make the pond materialize right there in the room.

"You couldn't remember what Mother looked like," Marcy said shrewdly.

"No. Odd, as if she had never been. Maybe she never was. Maybe there was nothing between us."

"But there was," Marcy said. "There was something. But we never listened to her. We liked it better to listen to F.P. Though I am sure now that Mother was much wiser than F.P. ever was or ever will be. As a matter of fact, you're very like her, more now than ever before, if you know what I mean—if you *would* know. She did all the gay outside things, but I remember her as being lost."

"Oh. But I'm not lost, Marcy. Because I don't walk in your path doesn't mean I'm lost. You seem the lost one to me."

"Well—at least I know it," Marcy said. "We were too wild, too untamed, for Mother—too smart, we thought. But I remember when she was sick, right at the end, how one day I went in and sat beside her bed and she turned and smiled at me—you know, not with any mask on, not making the best of a bad relationship, but lovingly, the way a mother smiles.

She didn't say a word. But I remember that smile and how ashamed I felt. But I didn't say so. It was as if she had told me that it was all right, I wasn't to mind not having been a loving daughter, having been an un-understanding, rebellious, wild daughter. In the long run I'd know—and somehow I do know, Elspeth."

"That's you. She never smiled at me," Elspeth said. "But it doesn't matter. We want all the relationships arranged in order; we want everything finished and just right. And it just isn't, and never will be, that way."

"I never had the telescopic view," Marcy said shortly.

"No. It's a pity," Elspeth said.

"But I'm just not a bird—nor am I a monkey swinging through the trees, if that's where we remember the sensation from. I walk on two legs, and I walk on earth. You see, I remember back farther in time than you do. I remember when we were just earth, if you want to go all out for that kind of reasoning. Anyway, even if I like to skate, the ground's my place."

"I know. A pity," Elspeth said again.

"I don't mean to argue," Marcy said more humbly. "I don't know what gets into me. I'm edgy these days. I miss John. Sometimes it seems as if I miss him more than you do. Though I know that's not true—it just seems that way. But when I saw the skates it went through me like a knife—how trite, but that's how it was—how John loved so to skate, how he looked on the ice. And sometimes at the office I look up and expect to see him coming in to say you are here and will I meet you for dinner. He looked as if he could forget your very existence, but he never did. You were always grateful the way he remembered. I do miss him terribly."

"Well, he's there somewhere, if you just want to look," Elspeth said flatly.

"Oh, I don't want his spirit. I want John. And I'm not in the habit of hunting for spirits."

"Weren't you hunting for Mother's?"

"But I don't think there's any communication, even if I found her," Marcy said stubbornly. "Anyway, I wasn't. The finding was only something in my own head, that's all. It was my spirit, really, I was hunting for."

"But when I hunt for mine you think I've lost my mind," Elspeth said.

Marcy got up. She ran her hands through her hair, making the curly mop stand up ridiculously, in a way she had when disturbed. "I know. I know. Only—oh, darling, it seems such a damnably lonely place where your spirit lives!"

"Not lonely enough," Elspeth said, and her voice was cold and far-off.

Marcy went to the kitchen and began to get something ready for dinner. She could hardly see what she did for the tears that would not stay back.

Suddenly she went back to the living room, a saucepan in her hand. "But didn't you *love* John?" she demanded.

She had said these very words before, at the farm—baldly, demandingly, she had said them, and been answered. Why did she have to say them again? Because she couldn't bear it that Elspeth did not mean the same thing by "love" as she did. She could not take this talk that sounded like something and yet never, never went to the heart of grief.

"Love him?" Elspeth said. The words came slowly after a long pause. "Love him?" And that was all. Marcy waited, but that was all. She wanted to force an answer from Elspeth, but she could do nothing but stand there helplessly, waiting till she knew at last there would be no more, and then she turned and went back to the kitchen. She knew now exactly what Sebastian meant about the voice calling. *Someone* had to tell them what had happened, and Elspeth was never going to.

15

ON THE next day Sebastian Esker drove Miss Hattie Halsey's car up to the farm. Most of that early snow had melted away, leaving only patches in corners, beside rocks. The countryside looked forlorn, waiting for the next snow to cover up the brownness, the grayness.

"I didn't exactly keep the room for you," Miss Halsey had said wryly. He liked the tartness of her tongue, her uncompromising homeliness. He liked it that she wasn't young. "Well, I don't get out much—you might as well use my car when you need one," she'd said. And "Eat hearty, young man!" He had slept as he had not in weeks.

He found the key where it always hung, in plain sight, went into the empty house. He felt grateful that they had left the furnace going. It would have been too awful to come into an ice-cold house. The warmth made it seem as if someone might live here again sometime. Nothing else proclaimed it, however. The geraniums were brown and withered on the kitchen sill. The cupboard doors were closed on the gay yellow dishes. The music room was terribly empty, with the piles of music gone, only the piano there in the gray light of winter.

He walked through the rooms, but all was tidy, if dusty. In the little room under the eaves the *Yale Review* still lay on the table. He picked it up, even read a paragraph from a review, put it down again. The bed where Eddie had slept was clean and made up. When had she done that? he wondered—quickly, wiping out their presence, and then she had gone out to feed the birds. . . . In her room all her possessions seemed still to be there, as if she had no need any longer for things. He even opened the closet door and saw her dresses hanging there, the gay, the elegant dresses that were so a part of her. There was a yellow wool that he remembered. He put out a hand and touched it in a foolish, sentimental way, unlike him. The dress of someone dead. Clean towels hung in the bathroom. "I'm competent," she said. And in the living room the blank space over the mantel. . . . It was all the same, except for the geraniums, the empty shelves, the dust, the blank space. And yet it seemed incredible that they had ever laughed so here, talked with such brilliance, put wood on the fire, walked out in the snow or into the summer night, heard John playing. The house said not only that it was all gone, but that it had never been. He saw Elspeth's skates hanging in the corner of the kitchen where were brooms and mops. He took them down, then took John's skates too.

And that was all he took away from the house, all that seemed still to have meaning. He locked the door, hung the key up, and went back to the inn.

"Find everything all right?" Miss Halsey said from the small sitting-room lounge where he had first found her paring potatoes.

"Yes, everything seems to be in order. It's rather comforting to find a place where you can hang the key in plain sight and no one uses it."

"Well, by and large, we mind our own business around here," Miss Halsey said. "Sit down. Have an apple."

He took an apple, sat down in an old-fashioned rocker.

"I see you got the car back all right. Got a few crotchets, but you must have made friends right off."

"Odd, that," Sebastian admitted. "I'm no mechanic, but I have a knack with cars."

She laughed, just a short chuckle of laughter. " 'Tisn't much like that fancy one of Mr. Doorn's you had down here."

"It's all right. It goes. I never stopped to think—I suppose John's car is right there in the barn. I could use that. But I'd rather use yours, if you don't mind."

"Just help yourself," she said. "I more or less dig in in the winter—don't drive unless I have to. Mrs. Esker all right?"

She hadn't even asked him yesterday, and he had been grateful. And even now she didn't demand any real answer.

"No," he said.

She hesitated before she said, "Well, it takes time."

When he did not speak she said, "Wish we'd get some snow. Used to be more snow when I was young. Came and stayed on. Or seems that way, looking back."

"It isn't even Christmas yet," he said. "I always settle for snow for Christmas."

"Getting close."

"Yes. I haven't bought any presents," he said. Such an ordinary conversation, but somehow comforting.

"I knit mine," she said. "I knit mittens and socks. I can turn a corner in my sleep."

"You wouldn't knit me some socks, would you? I'd get the wool."

"Why, if you want some. I'd be pleased to."

"Not for me—some skating socks for Mrs. Esker."

She gave him a quick look, then said, "I'd be pleased. Does she skate in town?"

"Yes."

"What size?"

"Oh, nine, I think. Wait." He went out to the car and brought the shoes in. "Five A," he said.

It puzzled her, he saw, thinking of Elspeth, not all right but still skating; but he didn't feel able to explain. He almost said, I wish you'd never told me of your sister Dodie, but he didn't. He sat there and finished his apple and said, yes, he thought white with red bands at the top would be all right.

Miss Halsey got up, said, "Well, for goodness' sake, if I don't get dinner started there won't be any. There'll be a couple truckers today too."

He wasn't used to hearty meals at midday, and he couldn't finish his pork chops with dressing, though they were good. Miss Halsey eyed him sharply as he put down his fork, but she didn't urge him to eat. He had eaten all his breakfast, and perhaps he would have been hungry now if he had not gone up to the house. It had depressed him terribly.

After dinner he walked up to the old cemetery and found John's grave. There was a stone there, but a small, plain one, with just John's name and the dates, nothing else at all. There were pines behind the cemetery, and perhaps in summer it would be peaceful and cool there, but now it looked forlorn and gloomy. And most of the stones bore witness to very long lives. John did not belong here with the old. There was a small, lonely wind, and Sebastian stood there, tall and austere against the pines, and the wind entered into his heart, into his bones, and chilled him through. He had the look of one listening. But there was nothing but the wind.

After supper he sat in the lounge with Miss Halsey. "I found I did have some white wool," she said, her needles clicking away. "Got it for a blanket for the Simpson baby, but it won't even be here till March so I might as well use the wool and get some more. How come you're not teaching?"

"I'm taking a year off, studying in Paris," he said.

He watched her big hands, skillful and quick with the wool.

She didn't make any remarks about how upsetting it must be for him to have had to cut into his year like this. She just went on knitting.

He had offered, after supper, to help her with the dishes, and she had let him. "Paying for your board," she'd demurred, but she'd handed him a dish towel and let him help. He'd been the only outsider for supper, and only the truckers had been added at noon.

"Did you see John often?" he asked.

"No, can't say I did—or not to talk to. Knew him, though. You know somebody quite well when they're young, it hangs over, you might say. Used to wave to me when he went past. First time, I met him coming out of Goudge's, and he said, 'Well, I'm back, Miss Halsey,' as if it had been just the other day he'd been here and stayed in your room up there. Never brought his wife to see me, though. Met her just over in the village—just chanced to."

There seemed some question in her mind, and he said, "That wasn't like John, not bringing her to see you."

She stopped knitting for an instant and said, "Oh, well, I was just his landlady. No reason."

"No reason except for the kind of person he was," Sebastian said. "He always remembered everything and everybody."

She gave a little frown and began to count stitches.

"Is it true that he used to call for square dances at the hall?"

"Guess 'tis. So they said. My dancing days are over—never started, as a matter of fact. Last winter that was—never had much to do with the people around here before that. Oh, friendly, but didn't do anything with us."

"I keep wondering about it," Sebastian said. "Did Elspeth go too?"

"So they say."

"But they never mentioned it when I saw them in the spring —nor in letters. I'm sorry, Miss Halsey. I shouldn't burden you with my worries. And yet you're my one connection with the town."

She put the knitting down on the table, folded her hands in her lap, said, "And what *is* your worry, Mr. Esker?"

"If I could name it, it wouldn't be a worry," he said. "It's only that something seems wrong—not seems, *is*. I was very close to my brother. I thought I was. I suppose we're never so close to anyone as we think we are. I never knew he had been here before, and I don't think Elspeth did. Why? I suppose you think that's a very small thing to worry about. And the dances—that seems odd. Not so much that he did it—he was preoccupied with rhythm—but why did he never mention it to the family? Why didn't Elspeth?"

"I guess I can't help you there," Miss Halsey said.

"No, of course you can't. But you are easy to talk to. They

loved each other very much. Then why did she burn his picture?"

"Burn his picture? But then, she maybe couldn't stand it to look at it."

"It was a very fine portrait that her sister and brother paid a good deal for. I suppose it's true, she couldn't bear it. I suppose that's all there is to it."

"But you think otherwise," Miss Halsey said.

"Yes, I think otherwise. I don't know why I'm here, Miss Halsey, except that I have to know the why of things. But if you never saw John much, I don't suppose you can help me. Did he see anyone around here?"

"Not so many. There's a sculptor up the Hollow used to go there. Some of the outsiders. But not so much. They didn't go back and forth all the time, if you know what I mean. Maybe met for cocktails once in two or three months. But Mr. Esker, if I were you I'd let it all go. Your brother's dead. His wife is something else again. I expect she needs help. But let your brother lie."

Sebastian stood up. "I can't," he said. "And it's all one thing. I think I'll say good night now."

"Good night," Miss Halsey said.

He'd met the sculptor, a man with a sharp beard and a fine head that looked like one of his own modelings. Tomorrow he'd go and see him. What was his name—Dudevant? Something like that.

And downstairs Miss Halsey sat idle, her hands still clasped, staring straight ahead of her. At last she said, with a shake of her head, "No. Let him lie," and got up, made everything snug for the night, and went to bed.

The next day Sebastian went to see Dudevant. At the opening of the door Dudevant was distant, impatient at being intruded upon, but then he said, "Oh, yes, yes. Met you at Esker's. Come in. Caught me at a bad moment. My wife's away, and I'm being housekeeper and, as it turns out, a nurse. Felice has a very bad cold, and I kept her home. Sit down, if you can find a spot."

Felice, flushed but happy, was lying—or sitting—against pillows on an old couch, cutting out animals from some magazine pictures.

"Hello, Felice," Sebastian said. He remembered her in a yellow frock at John's, running down the little slope at the back, collapsing in a small heap of happiness under the pear tree. "Remember me?"

"You said you'd tell me another story next time you came," Felice said. "You can do it now if you want to."

Dudevant said, "Now, now, Mr. Esker came to see me, Felice."

Sebastian smiled at her. He could never resist children. He said, "Maybe I could—a very short one." And he sat down beside her and then could think of nothing but the story he had told Lexie above the sea near Bandol. He tried to think of another—he knew many—but that one stayed there clear and simple. So he began: "Once in Punaauia there was an old woman . . ."

Dudevant, a little embarrassed at the imposition, sat down nearby, but when Sebastian finished he said, "Very nice. Very nice. Now suppose you let Mr. Esker come out to the studio and tell me a story."

Felice giggled and began to cut out pictures. "I liked that," she said simply.

"Good. Next time I'll think of another." And he went with Dudevant out to the studio, which was an old barn hitched onto the back of the house, big and high and not very artistic, filled with the stuff of Dudevant's profession. There were two barrel-shaped wicker chairs, and they sat in them.

"Shocked about your brother," Dudevant said. "Difficult to believe, even yet. How is Elspeth? We went up, but no one seemed to be there. My wife's been worried about her."

"She's in town with her sister," Sebastian said noncommittally. "But I think she'll be back after a little. She always loved it here."

"It bothered Marie that she didn't want to see her—good friends, she thought. Marie took some of her French bread—she makes good bread—left it inside the door. Not that Marie wanted thanks, but it wasn't like Elspeth not to phone her."

"It's a bad time for her," Sebastian said.

"Of course. Naturally. Is there anything I can do for you?" It was a natural question. Sebastian had never called there before. He must want something.

"Thanks, no. I just had this impulse to talk with people who had known John. But the truth is, now I'm here I'd rather not talk of him. I remember that he thought very highly of your work. Isn't there a little figurine of a unicorn you did, at the house?"

"Yes. Birthday present for Elspeth. He was kind about my things. He got me the Woodville Memorial to do, which made all the difference last year. Sculptors don't live too high—musicians either, in the ordinary run of events. Esker was lucky."

"I suppose so. Not only lucky, however."

"Sorry. Didn't mean to sound sour-grapish. I feel nothing of the kind. I meant only that talent rarely gets paid for. He was never blown up by his success. Very modest man—but sure of himself. Knew what his powers were. Odd, your telling that story. I'd heard it before."

"Oh, had you?"

"Believe you sent it to Esker a year or more ago. Didn't he make music for some of it? Happened to drop in just at mailtime, and he had this letter from you. 'Listen,' he said. 'This is something extraordinarily nice. Sebastian always knows the exact thing I need.' And he read the story. Seemed strange, hearing it again."

"I don't know why it came to mind just then," Sebastian said. Then he could talk no more of John. He asked to see some of Dudevant's things and spent an hour looking, admiring, asking technical questions.

When he went away Dudevant said, "Give our love to Elspeth. And come again, any time."

Sebastian smiled and did not answer more than a murmur of thanks.

He got into the car and drove back to the inn. A decent man, Dudevant. Enchanting little girl. And now he remembered Marie, a handsome, peasantish-looking woman who could make good bread. He wished Marie had been there. He hadn't probed enough, and yet it did seem that there was nothing probing would uncover. They had known each other only in the way of neighbor artists—not intimately, but respectfully. Only Marie had taken bread over—there was some real friendship implied. Yet Elspeth had never phoned her or thanked her. If there had been real feeling Dudevant could not have been diverted so easily to discussing his own work But Sebastian was glad John had said that of the story.

He left the car behind the inn, under the open shed, said "And what now?" before he went in.

He went to his room after dinner, sat there for a long time doing nothing. Then he wrote two letters, just to evade doing anything else.

About three he went downstairs, took his letters across to the post office. The children were just coming from school, laughing, shouting. He saw the red-headed boy John had taught to whistle. The boy was whistling now, tossing a book in the air at the same time, as he came down the street. Sebastian caught up with him, said, "Hello there. What's your name? Wish I could whistle like that."

The boy grinned and said, "Peter Wiggins."

"My name's Sebastian Esker. I heard my brother taught you how to whistle."

The boy was embarrassed. His freckled face reddened, and he dug his toe in a patch of grass by the sidewalk, tossed his book in the air again, caught it expertly. "Yeah," he said. "Gee, I wish he wasn't dead."

"So do I. Well, so long, Peter."

"So long," Peter said and ran away swiftly, as if escaping his own embarrassment.

Miss Hattie Halsey stood by the desk near the door and watched them through the window. She frowned, tapped her pencil nervously on the desk. But when Sebastian came in she was busily working on accounts.

"Think we're going to get our snow," she said, not looking up. "Graying off for it."

"I hope so," he said. She seemed disinclined to talk, and he went slowly back to his room. After a half-hour he came down again and asked to use the phone. She nodded to it beside her on the desk, rose, and went out to the kitchen.

He called Marcy's office. "Hello, Marcy? Sebastian," he said.

"Oh, Sebastian! You've been gone an eternity!" she said. "How is everything?"

"No good—or no change. I wish you'd come back."

"I suppose I might as well—but not quite yet, Marcy. I'll call again."

"Oh, don't hang up!"

He hesitated. "There isn't so much to say, Marcy," he said. "I am in the plight of the man in the picture. There seems no way out."

"What man? In what picture?"

"Why, David's. Take care of her—and yourself. Good-by, Marcy."

She hung up very slowly. It wasn't much, after all the hours of waiting, not very much.

But she went around to David's after work. David was just going out.

"I wanted to see your picture," she said.

"Well, you can't. Not now. It's not on exhibit, anyway."

"You let Sebastian see it."

"Oh, well, Sebastian," he said. "Look, girl, I have to go, really. I have a date that won't wait."

She came unwillingly out into the street with him. "I thought you always made them wait," she said.

"This one's a member of the Working Classes. After the shop closes she goes home."

"Oh? Alice doesn't mind?"

"She never has," he said lightly enough, but Marcy looked up at that instant, and his fair, bright face was troubled.

"Oh, run along," she said. Well, she thought wryly, that's a new one—a girl in a shop. He's never gone in for shopgirls before.

She would have been amused had she seen him fifteen minutes later.

"Oh, she's been gone quite a while. Looked like snow, and

I told her to go. Nothing going on here anyway the last hour. Did she know you were coming?" Miss Mack said.

"No. Just passing by," David said airily.

"Well, now you're here I think I'll get it off my chest and say next time you're passing by, just you pass by on the other side of the street. Fanny's too nice for your shenanigans, Mr. Doorn."

"Why, Miss Mack! How you malign me!" David said.

"Couldn't, could I? You know very well you're just out for a bit of fun. Well, you have your fun at Twenty-One or somewhere—not with my Fanny Drake, who's going to work into as good an assistant as I ever had. You leave Fanny alone."

"Don't you think that's up to Fanny?" he asked.

"She hasn't had much experience with wolves like you."

"How would you know? I do think she's quite able to look out for herself. She has actual tiger's claws," he said.

"H'm," Miss Mack said skeptically. "Trouble with you is you think you have only to smile at a tiger and the claws go under."

"A very nice compliment, Miss Mack. Well, I'll drop in again."

"Don't bother," Miss Mack said crossly.

"No bother at all," David said and went away.

And back in the inn the early winter night settled down, and the world was black and still beyond the inn windows. A few flakes came lazily down into the blackness, but you could not see them from inside.

"Mind if I sit here and watch you knit?" Sebastian said.

"Not a bit. Like to have company."

At first they said little; then she asked him what it was he taught, and presently he was telling her some of his theories about linguistics, about the special project on which he had embarked in Paris—about Beth and Greg and Lexie, about his colleagues at college. And all the time she led him on, being interested.

"I'm talking too much," he said at last.

"Like to hear you," she said. "Never had too much schooling myself. Got through high school, that's all."

"I discovered one thing. I came away from Dudevant's with the idea that if he'd been a real friend of John's he couldn't have talked so much about himself. That is false, I see. I don't know when I've talked so much about myself. You're a very good listener."

"Get considerable practice," she said. "Mrs. Dudevant used to go shopping with John's wife. See them going into Goudge's together every little while."

"She was away. I didn't see her."

"She'll be back tomorrow," Miss Halsey said.

His eyes crinkled at the corners. "Is there anything you don't know about your fellow townsmen?" he asked.

"I saw her on the street, and she told me," she said. "There's a lot I don't know—don't even want to know. Though I must say I like quirkiness—always interested in people's quirks."

It was pleasant to talk with someone who did not use the elliptical approach, someone who said what she meant so that you weren't forever having to hunt for meanings behind words.

"Then," he said, "it must have seemed strange to you—it must have—that John never brought his wife to see you."

"No," she answered as soberly. "No, it didn't seem strange. I didn't expect him to."

"Why not? If you like quirkiness, there's a quirk for you.

For he was not like that. I told you that. He was very proud of Elspeth, and if he knew you well enough to say, 'Well, I'm back,' admitting he remembered you well, that his coming back meant something— He was always loyal. Did he ask you not to tell Elspeth he'd been here before?"

"No." The needles were idle in her fingers. "Mr. Esker, unless you think there was something wrong about your brother's death—you don't, do you?"

"Oh, no. He's always had a bad heart."

"Well, then, I wouldn't try so hard to get all his past back. It isn't healthy, and neither is it right. We've all got some things we don't talk about, thank goodness. I suppose your brother had—and you. If he didn't tell them to you when he was living, why now? I know all about obsessions. I don't like them."

He thought of Dodie. "I suppose you're right. I just imagine he wants me to, that he's asking me to do this. I wonder how much the expectation of greatness has to do with greatness? I've always thought the expectation was demanded, that that was all you could do for another in the long run, to expect the most the other was capable of performing. But perhaps we haven't the right to demand so much."

"Guess I'll go along with the first, Mr. Esker. I get disappointed lots of times, but I always expect the best."

"But suppose—suppose in the effort not to disappoint the expectations, you found you were carrying just too heavy a burden?"

"Nonsense. Don't think trying ever hurt anybody."

"I don't know," Sebastian said tiredly. "I just don't know. And it isn't only my brother. I loved his wife before he ever saw her. I don't mean I coveted her after she was his wife. I didn't—I don't think I did. But I can't help her either unless

I know. For something strange has happened, of that I'm sure —something that has changed Elspeth into a different person."

"I see," Miss Halsey said. She put her knitting into the old cheesebox stand beside her, rose. "I see too that you're so tired you can hardly sit up. I'll get you a glass of milk, and then you go to bed."

She spoke firmly, like a mother, like a schoolteacher. She brought a small tray with milk and a piece of apple pie on it. "Take it up with you," she commanded. "And then get some sleep."

"It's not much after eight!" he protested, but he obeyed.

16

BUT AT nine Miss Halsey rapped on his door. "Mr. Esker?" she said.

He came to the door.

"Mrs. Dudevant's here. She wants to see you. Shall I send her up? There's a salesman in the lounge."

"Yes, do, if it won't give the inn a bad name," Sebastian said.

Miss Halsey smiled and went away, and almost at once Marie Dudevant, big, handsome, earthy, was in the room, holding out her hand. "Came as quick as I could get Felice to bed," she said. "Hattie's treating you right; isn't this the bridal suite?"

"Not that I know of. It's very comfortable. It was kind of you to come. Sit down."

"Well, I had to know first hand how Elspeth was. How is she? Can't get her out of my mind. Jean told me not to be a fool and come pestering you, but I had to. I guess you never know what you'll be like when your turn comes to lose someone. Might sometime, for Jean's twenty years older than I am, and none of us lives forever—I might know. But the truth is I can't feel right about the way Elspeth took John's going. I've got a kind of a haunt about it."

"Yes. I know," he said. "But why? Your husband said you took bread over—and she didn't come to the door."

"That's right, I did. But that's all right. I could understand that. It's just that she wasn't that kind of a person. You know, it's not easy, if you're raised in the city, to take on country life. Lots of little inconveniences, snow and garbage to cope with—all that. But it never bothered her a bit—not a bit. She could do anything any other woman could, she said, and she could. Beat me at keeping house. Of course she didn't have any children to mess things up and pick up after, but she took everything in her stride. Had a real vegetable garden and did all the work herself. Made jelly this summer. And kept looking like something out of a story. Jean fell dead in love with her—oh, in a nice way, you know. I didn't mind. Loved her myself—that keeping looking the way she did, out here on a back road, that was something of what I mean. Me, I wear slacks from morning to night, or jeans and an old sweater—get to doing the easiest, the most practical thing. But she never did. Even in the garden she looked clean and all right—you know, as if she only had to wash her hands to serve tea—and always funny, always making a joke out of everything. Me, now, when I'm funny I get a little rough, but Elspeth was just funny naturally, the way she breathed. Don't know how we got to be friends—not a bit alike. But we were friends, Mr. Esker. We were friends."

"Yes, I know. She has changed," Sebastian said gently. "But I don't know why either, Mrs. Dudevant."

"We're outsiders, you know—will be if we live here forever. But folks liked her, let her in more than some of us. Everybody liked her—you couldn't help it. John, too, though he was more standoffish."

"But I hear he went to their dances, things like that," Sebastian said.

"Yes, he did. I was the one got him started at that—kind of kidded them into going one night. Kind of thing I like—lots of gusto to country dances. Well, we went all winter, and we had fun too—or nights we could get a sitter for Felice we went. We had fun. Can't seem to get out the thing that's really bothered me. Day after he died, it was. Haven't even told Jean this. Don't ask me why not. Scared me too much, I guess."

"Yes?" Sebastian said patiently.

"This was before I took the bread over. I didn't hear till the next morning, and I got out the car and drove right over. Nobody came to the door, and I thought maybe she'd gone in to the undertaker's or something. So I started home, and then I saw her. She was up in that pasture lot across from the house—just standing there among the rocks and bushes, standing still as a rock herself, looking off toward town. I stopped the car and got out and climbed up there. She never moved a hair while I was coming, never said a word. It scared me; but we were friends, as I said, and friends can't be scared when you're in trouble. So I went right up to her and put my arms around her, and I said something, I don't know what—just 'Oh, honey, I'm sorry!' Something like that. Wasn't much, but what is there to say? And she—well, she just drew away from me as if she didn't like me to touch her, almost as if she didn't see me. She said, 'Sorry for what?' Sorry, I can't help crying, thinking about it. We were *friends*—I can't help crying. We were, no matter what. We went shopping together and traded cakes and bread, and twice she's kept Felice when I had to go see my mother, who's sick most of the time. I tried to say something about John, and she didn't even listen, just stood there, staring off. I had to go away and leave her like that. I'm sensible. I can bring folks back to earth pretty fast if I have to. But I just had to go away and leave her there. When I took the bread I don't know why I hoped anything would happen, for nothing did. When Jean asked me I just said Elspeth didn't feel like talking—but it was so awful. And when Jean said you were here I had to come and see—"

"Don't cry," Sebastian said. "Please don't cry—though God knows I often want to myself. I can't tell you she's all right, for she isn't. I can't even say to myself any more that it's just grief. Marcy says that isn't what grief is like, and she's right. I can't help you at all. But you will be friends again —I hope. It was kind of you to come."

"No. I just had to, for my own sake," she said. "I didn't mean to ever tell anyone that. I shouldn't have, I guess."

"But I thank you. You see, Mrs. Dudevant—"

"Oh, everyone calls me Marie," she said impatiently.

"You see, Marie, she won't let any of us touch her any more. It isn't just you."

She gave him a sudden smile, like a mother's. She was one given to comforting. "How terrible for you," she said. She got up. "I'll go now," she said. She gave another rub at her eyes, shoved her handkerchief into the pocket of her leather jacket. "And of course you can't know—you just can't know —what it would do to you in her place," she said.

The trouble was that he did know, as Marie herself had known. They knew that the old Elspeth would have taken even death in her stride, that she would not have stopped being Elspeth. Marie knew she had a right to be scared—and hurt. From some people Elspeth's actions would have been acceptable. Just so might death affect some people—this withdrawal, this apathy. But not Elspeth; that was the rub—not Elspeth. She had more courage than that.

The next day he went to Dr. Ventry's office, waited his turn in the small waiting room which seemed to be filled today.

"Yes?" Dr. Ventry said. "What's troubling you?"

"Well, sir, a good deal," Sebastian said. "But nothing you can mend. I didn't come to see you professionally, though I consider this a call and will pay for it. I am here clearing up my brother John Esker's affairs, and I wanted to know if anything was owed you."

"Could have written," Dr. Ventry said impatiently. "No, Mrs. Esker paid what little there was. Far as I know Mrs. Esker's never had a sick day—or if she has she didn't call me in. Saw your brother some three or four times—twice for flu, twice for his heart. And then after he was dead. Expected he might go suddenly one of these days, and he did. Worked too hard, played too hard. You a musician?"

"No, a teacher."

"Oh. Have all your brother's records. Playing 'em just last night. Sonata Number Two's my favorite."

"He has a new one called 'Snow,' " Sebastian said.

"Lots of artists, one kind or another, in these hills," the doctor said shortly, as if waiting to call his next patient in. "He was the best of the lot. Sorry I didn't know him better. Doctor here doesn't have time to get clubby with anybody. Your heart all right? Not trying to drum up trade, but you have a look—"

"My heart's fine," Sebastian said. "I had the flu not long ago, and maybe I look a little ragged, but I'm fine. Well, thank you, doctor. What do I owe you?"

"Nothing. Haven't done anything."

"You've spent your time."

"Oh, that's all right, quite all right. 'Snow,' you said?"

"Yes. It's not published yet. I think it will be—and a recording made. I'll send it if it is."

"Why, thank you, sir. Thank you very much indeed," Dr. Ventry said. "That I would appreciate."

So Sebastian went away from there, liking the doctor, wishing him well, making a mental note about the record, if record there ever was.

"I ought to call Marcy. I ought to go back," he said to himself. Yet he did neither. And that night as he sat in the little room that had begun to seem like home to him, and watched the socks for Elspeth growing, he said suddenly, "Why did you remember John so well from that time so long ago?"

"He's just one you remember," Miss Halsey said sensibly.

"Yes, I suppose he is. But he was young then."

"He was grown up enough," Miss Halsey said. "Place was full, or there were a good many here—always is, time of the festival. That's when I have to make hay. It's twelve miles over there, but no distance with a car. I said to him, 'How you going to get back and forth?' and he said he'd hitch a ride. I remember that because he didn't look the sort to be hitching rides—you know, very much the gentleman, the way he was at the end. Showed him that room you're in, and he said, 'It looks peaceful, but haven't you anything smaller, not so expensive? I'm a very poor young man.' Shows you—I let him have it very cheap, right when I could have rented it three times over. When you do things out of character you remember it."

"But there must have been places nearer," Sebastian said. "That's why I keep wondering why he came here."

"Maybe not. We do a land-office business around here, festival time. I asked him if he was a musician, and he said no, he was a composer. Remember that because he was young, young to be a composer. But he said it sure as gospel, and you couldn't doubt it was true, young or not."

"He was sure very young," Sebastian said. "You make me see him so clearly."

"Don't suppose, all told, I talked to him much, being so busy. But some people make themselves felt. You know how it is. Then one day he wanted to know if he could have a box lunch put up. People did that some, but Clara Young was helping in the kitchen and didn't have time for that sort of thing, and I said, sorry, I couldn't. He looked disappointed, and I said, well, I'd put him up a couple of sandwiches. And I did—well, I made up a good big box, because he was so thin. And I said, 'You have to like music a lot to sit all day on the hard ground, eat box lunches, and all that.' And he smiled at me and said, 'But I'm not going to listen to music. This is a day off, a whole day off.' Now you tell me why I remember that? You know how 'tis Christmas morning before it gets light, and you think: This is it. This is Christmas day, and it's all ahead—hours of it? Well, he had a look of Christmas—know what I mean?"

"I know what you mean. I wonder what he did with the day."

"Can't say. Just wandered around, I expect. Went off with his box and didn't come in till late that night. Went on foot, anyway."

17

THAT afternoon David Doorn waited outside Miss Mack's shop, and when Fanny Drake came out he said, "Hello, Fanny." And though ordinarily he would have said something light and witty, now that was all he said.

"Oh, hello," Fanny said with a little frown. "What do you want?"

"How without finesse!" David said. "Can't I lead up to it? I thought we might have dinner together. Is Miss Mack watching us?"

"And if she is?"

"I hope so. I want to show her you don't mind walking down the street with me. Where shall we go?"

"Nowhere. My mother expects me home for dinner."

"She could set another place, couldn't she? Or won't there be enough pork chops to go around?"

She laughed, but unwillingly. "What a man to push himself in where he isn't wanted!" she said. "Oh, do come along,

Mr. Doorn. Mother'll be delighted—much more delighted than I will, I assure you. She thinks it shows something if there are enough young men hanging around. She thinks that's the way a girl's life should be—young men calling up, coming for dinner, all that. Do come!"

"Thanks. I'd love it," he said promptly. "Where?"

"In the Bronx."

He winced but said, "Lead on, Fanny."

On the subway he read all the signs and talked a great deal of nonsense.

Fanny's house couldn't have been more ordinary—a two-family place, with the Drakes on the first floor, decent, neat, uninteresting.

"Is that you, Fanny?" a woman called.

"Who else?" Fanny said. "Set another plate on, Mama."

So then her mother came, a worried, half-pretty, small woman, with an apron over a print dress.

"This is Mr. Doorn, Mama—for supper, if there's enough."

"Why, Fanny, what a thing to say! As if we'd got to the point where there wasn't always enough for one more! If you can't have friends drop in, I always say—"

"And don't bother to get out the good china," Fanny said.

Her mother had been smiling a nervous welcome at David, trying at the same time to take her apron off.

"I resent that," David said.

"Oh, you don't want to be 'just one of the family'?"

"That remains to be seen. But our family always put its best foot foremost for company. I think you ought to put the best china on, Mrs. Drake."

Mrs. Drake hardly knew how to take this, but she laughed and said she would—it wouldn't take a minute to change—and did he want to wash up or anything?

"Bathroom's at the end of the hall," Fanny said.

There were clean but much-washed towels hanging in the small bathroom. David washed up, grinning as he did so. He was enjoying himself hugely. "Have to tell Miss Hodge about the decor," he said to himself. He was wont to describe rooms to Miss Hodge and got great fun out of imagining zany rooms for her. It was a game they had played for two or three years now. The Drake living room was ordinary to the point of symbolism. It had an oak bookcase full of books, and a copy of *Life* lay on a mahogany—or mahogany-dyed birch—oval table below a lamp with cutouts of flowers on the shade. The rug was an imitation oriental that would never, by any stretch of the imagination, fool anyone into believing it authentic. There was a little stand with a stiff jade tree growing from a bright blue pot. He would say, "And in the bookcase were Zane Grey and Temple Bailey and such . . ."

He went back to the living room, and it was just as his imaginings had proclaimed it in the bathroom—or just as his memory had stored it up in one quick, flicking glance. He picked up *Life* and started to turn the pages, for Fanny was in the kitchen with her mother and he had the room to himself. Then he looked toward the books to make sure, and the first book that caught his eye was *Four Quartets* by T. S. Eliot.

"You don't say!" he murmured.

The front door opened, closed, and a thin man in an overcoat came into the room, looked surprised, turned to go.

"How do you do?" David said politely. "I'm David Doorn. I suppose you are Mr. Drake?"

Mr. Drake turned back, put out a hand, and shook hands with David. "Glad to see you," he said. He had a thin, tired voice.

Then Fanny came and said, "Hi, Pop. Mr. Doorn introduce himself? Supper's all ready, so hurry."

She took his coat and hung it away in some closet off the tiny hall. There was something not mocking about the way she did this, though she spoke to her father impatiently enough.

They came without any formality into the miniature, crowded dining room. On the sideboard was a silver teapot covered with cellophane wrapping. David stored that up for Miss Hodge. The dishes were of very white china with small pink rosebuds round the edges—everything to match, even the pickle dish. David had the feeling of swimming through rosebuds to food.

"Now it's just pot roast," Mrs. Drake said. "If Fanny'd let me know, we might have had a rib roast."

"There's nothing better than your pot roast," Mr. Drake said in his thin voice. "No need for apology, Mary."

"And if people drop in they can take what they get," Fanny said.

Mr. Drake served everybody skillfully enough, and Mrs. Drake jumped up once, murmuring that she'd forgotten the jelly.

"It's jolly good," David said.

Mr. Drake lifted tired blue eyes and eyed David an instant before he said, "Oxford?"

David was startled, then laughed. "No," he said. "Certainly not. That's a silly habit, I grant you."

"Are you in the shop?" Mrs. Drake asked then.

"Oh, Mother, what do you think we'd use him for? Decoration?" Fanny asked.

"Why, Fanny! Don't be so rude!" her mother said. "I was just being civil. What *do* you do, Mr. Doorn?"

"I'm an artist," David said.

Again the tired blue eyes took David in. "Is that so?" said Mr. Drake.

"Now that's wonderful," Mrs. Drake said. "All the boys Fanny brings home—she's never had any artists. Me, I couldn't draw a straight line. Fanny, she's always been artistic, and Papa, he can draw anything; but it always seems wonderful to me, being an artist."

Fanny frowned, and her pony tail bobbed. "I don't believe he's that wonderful, Mama," she said.

"You do have a rude daughter, Mrs. Drake," David said. "Extr'ordinarily rude. It is about as wonderful as anything is these days, being an artist. And Fanny ought to know that."

"Oh, I think plenty of things are wonderful," Fanny said. "I don't limit wonder. I don't think you have to belong to a club."

"Papa, fill Mr. Doorn's plate again," Mrs. Drake said. "Just you have some more of everything, Mr. Doorn. It's a plain supper, but there's plenty of it."

"Thank you. I will," David said, though he didn't want more.

"We've just got plain apple pie for dessert, nothing fancy," Mrs. Drake said.

"That's quite fancy enough," David said. "And what do you find so wonderful, Fanny?"

"Oh, just about everything," Fanny said. "And Pop, don't look at me like that. That's the way he talks—that's the way he likes to talk. I'm not being rude."

"Was I looking at you, Fanny?" Mr. Drake said, smiling at her. "I didn't realize it. I wasn't being critical, my dear. I know how the young talk. I was just wishing you'd all keep still a minute or so, so Mr. Doorn could maybe say something about being an artist. I like to think about such things, and if he had a chance he might talk about it a little—though I suppose he can't just turn on a speech when there's a little quiet."

David laughed. Fanny was quite like this thin man, he thought, only not so gentle. But maybe that was just because she was younger. "Well, no, I couldn't," he said. "Though I presume if all I had ever said about art were written down in one long line it would stretch around the world and back. Talking about it and producing it are two different things."

"*Papa!*" Mrs. Drake said in a small warning voice.

Mr. Drake had taken his knife and was drawing imaginary lines on the white cloth. He put the knife down with a reassuring smile toward her. "Didn't cut it," he said. "Failing of mine," he explained to David. "I'm a draftsman, not an artist, but I draw lines all day long. Sometimes I get to thinking that if color were washed in I'd sometimes have something very like what you see in the gallery windows all the time these days. Only they are getting away from that a little, aren't they, not bothering with design? All right, Mama. I'm sorry." For he had taken his knife again and was making long creases in the cloth.

"I suppose there's no real design for confusion, and our world seems confused," David said.

"Don't know. You couldn't run a machine that's just made up of all the pieces thrown in a heap. World wouldn't run either without some design. Now could it? Places where it doesn't run right, but it runs."

Mrs. Drake frowned a little. She didn't like abstract discussions. They confused and worried her. She felt they were not hospitable, somehow. She got up and made a fuss over carrying the dishes out. She brought in the pie and a small dish of cheese. "Fanny's the one can really make pie. You ought to have some of her lemon pie! It melts in your mouth! She doesn't get so much time for baking nowadays, but on her day off sometimes she makes something for a treat for us, and to give me a rest from the kitchen."

"Trying to build me up, Mama? I don't believe Mr. Doorn's looking for a cook."

"I guess even artists have to eat, Fanny," Mrs. Drake said.

"How right you are!" David said, his blue eyes mocking Fanny.

Then the dinner was done, even to the good coffee, and Fanny began to clear the table.

"You don't have to," Mrs. Drake said. "You run along, Fanny. I'll take care of the kitchen. If you're going out to a show or anything, you'd better put on something else."

"We're not," Fanny said. "Mr. Doorn can talk to Papa." And she went on with her task. Nor did she hurry, but stayed in the kitchen till the last dish was on the shelf.

David, because he was seldom bored, was not bored with Mr. Drake. He found something gay and funny in almost every situation, and his whole face was bright with enjoyment and mischief as he took the copy of *Four Quartets* idly from the bookcase and said, "Who reads Eliot around here?"

"Well, I suppose everybody reads Eliot one time or another," Mr. Drake said.

"Everybody?" David said. "Oh, I don't think so."

"If you're interested in that sort of thing," Mr. Drake amended. "Used to be, but I don't read poetry much, the older I get. Fanny treated her mother and me to *The Cocktail Party*, but I guess it just wasn't my kind of play. Fanny's got *The Waste Land* on a record somewhere, and I like that all right. But *The Cocktail Party*, now—seemed awfully flimsy people to mean so much. I heard Mr. Eliot'd gone religious, but somehow he seemed to be mixing up his psychiatrist with God."

A flash of wicked laughter went through David's head as he thought of Mrs. Drake at *The Cocktail Party*.

"What kind of an artist are you, Mr. Doorn?" Mr. Drake asked then.

"What kind? Well, just an artist. I don't know that you could classify me," David said. "I sell an occasional picture, but not enough to live on. I design stage sets to make money."

"Still," Mr. Drake said, lighting a battered old pipe slowly, "still, I don't know as I'd want the state to support artists. Don't know as I'd want that."

"Good Lord, no!" David said.

"Maybe if artists painted better pictures, that folks could understand, they'd sell more," Mr. Drake said.

"You may have something there." David put the book back in its place, sat down, and lit a cigarette. "Yes, you may have something there," he said again. "It could be that we like being the class no one understands—makes us special to ourselves."

Mr. Drake gave a gentle but quick smile. "Once a year I go to the Metropolitan. I have ever since I was a boy," he said. "I'll say this, the bright new things make the old ones seem kind of old-fashioned. But some things you always like to look at all the same."

"What, for instance?" David asked.

"Well, there's a picture of a woman—"

But then Fanny and her mother came in, and Mr. Drake never finished his sentence. David stood up and said, "Get your coat, Fanny. We're going to a movie."

A kind of stubbornness settled over her face, but her mother said, "Yes, you run along, Fanny. I was afraid you were going out. There wasn't any need for you to do the dishes."

Mr. Drake picked up the evening paper and seemed to have forgotten them.

"Oh, all right," Fanny said.

David shook hands gracefully with the Drakes, said he'd liked the dinner and hoped he'd be invited again—he hoped he could talk with Mr. Drake again—and so on to the closing of the door and the stepping out into the cold, dark winter's night.

"What a hopeless little snob you are, Fanny," David said.

"*I?*" Fanny said.

"Yes, you. You thought I'd be bored. You were trying to punish me. I liked it."

"How big of you! No, that isn't true. I did think you'd be bored, but I wasn't trying to punish you. Why should I? It's just—well, this is my world, that's all. It amuses you, one glimpse of it. But it wouldn't amuse you long. I never meant I was ashamed of it, though."

"Didn't you? Didn't you, Fanny? There seemed a certain amount of bravado in your taking me home. As if you were saying, 'All right. So we live on the other side of the tracks. So we live in the Bronx. So what?' But I never supposed you lived in a penthouse. Can you really make lemon pie?"

"I can. It's not one of my favorite amusements, however. There's a movie just around the next corner, if you really want to go to a movie."

"Well, it's cold to walk the streets. Yes, let's go in. It looks very gory."

Fanny couldn't help giggling now and then when it was just too gory, when the guns went off too fast. They stayed clear to the end, then came out again and walked homeward. At the door Fanny said, "Can you find your way home?"

"Honey, I was born and raised in d' briar patch!" David said. "You aren't going to ask me in for coffee or anything?"

"Not tonight. I have to be up at six-thirty."

"It was fun while it lasted," David said. "We'll have to do it again sometime."

"Yes, let's," Fanny said, but her voice still mocked him.

"You're very like your father, aren't you? Except that he doesn't kick against the pricks any more. I find that singularly refreshing. Good night, Fanny."

"Good night," Fanny said.

The Drakes were still up when Fanny went in. Mrs. Drake looked up expectantly. "What a nice young man!" she said. "I don't know when I've met such a nice young man! He's got such good manners!"

"Yes, jolly charming," Fanny said.

"I don't know what you'd ask for any nicer than him," her mother said reprovingly.

Mr. Drake put his paper down and smiled at Fanny, his faded eyes almost disappearing in a mesh of wrinkles. But he didn't say anything except, "Well, Mama, isn't it time to turn in?"

In their bedroom Mrs. Drake said, "Sometimes I think Fanny'll never marry. She treated that boy like dirt. They don't like you making fun of them all the time."

"Maybe they do. Maybe that's the new way," Mr. Drake said. "Anyway, Mama, just because she brings a boy home to dinner is no sign she wants to marry him."

"Well, when I was young it was," Mrs. Drake said. "I remember as if it was yesterday worrying about asking you to supper—if you'd like my folks, and if they'd like you. I didn't see how they could help it, but I worried. It seemed something big, asking you to supper."

"And so it was," he said. "But the things that seem big to us might not to young folks now."

"I guess people don't change much," Mrs. Drake said stubbornly, and curled her feet into her flannel nightgown.

18

MARCY was supposed to be working at home, but she sat at the phone, asking people to drop in on Christmas afternoon. "Quiet," she kept saying. "We don't really feel we want a lot of excitement. But we don't want Christmas just passed over, either. Good. See you." Over and over she said this or something like it, being just a little different to each one, for she had a sure feeling for personality. But the substance was the same. "Oh, yes, she's here," she said to one. "But I think she'd like her friends about her." She didn't think any such thing—but she thought Elspeth ought to want her friends around her.

At the moment Elspeth was out. She had gone out soon after breakfast and hadn't come back yet. Toward noon David dropped in. He met Miss Hodge in the hall downstairs, and they exchanged gay greetings. Then he gave a quick laugh and said, "Oh, I've got such a room for you! Such a house! Pure railroad architecture, the house—" Then he hesitated. "Well, not now. Another time," he said and ran up the stairs.

Miss Hodge, after letting Soutan in, went back to Bessie. "David's in a great hurry this morning," she said. She liked to talk with David and was disappointed.

"I wish Elspeth would go back to the farm. She gives me the creeps."

"Nonsense, Bessie."

"She does. I've talked to her; you haven't. You ought to see her when she goes out. Shouldn't think they'd let her out alone. She just wanders off like she was in a dream, not knowing where she was going. She does give me the creeps."

"She's just lost her husband. I expect she feels as if she were in a dream, or a nightmare or something," Miss Hodge said.

"You haven't talked to her," Bessie insisted.

"I've seen her. She's the most beautiful girl I've ever seen."

"Oh, I don't know. What's so beautiful about her? When she had some life in her she was attractive enough, but beautiful is something else again."

"I said beautiful and I meant beautiful," Miss Hodge said.

"You always were romantic," Bessie said.

Upstairs David threw his coat off, sat down near the desk where Marcy was still engaged in her inviting. "What's up?" he asked, when she put the reciever down. "Where's Elspeth?"

"Out. And I'm asking people for Christmas."

"Oh. Think you should? It won't be expected."

"Yes, I think I should. Don't ask me why. Partly to wake Elspeth up, partly for my own sake. We've always had open house, or spent the day with Elspeth and John. Partly out of pride, I expect—or anger or something."

"It might be disastrous," he said. "Really, Marcy, I wouldn't. I'd call it off."

"No."

"Sebastian—he'll be back, won't he?"

"Oh, yes. Or I count on it," she said.

"What do you want for Christmas? What can I get for Elspeth?"

"I don't want anything. I mean that. I can't think of anything I want. Something very good for Elspeth, something gay and expensive."

"I saw a gem of an old map on parchment, very ancient-looking, perfect for the dining room at the farm. But then I thought it wouldn't do."

"No, that's the very thing. Something that doesn't break off all the past as if it were nothing. Something that says we expect her to go on. No, that's it. Bless you, darling. Get it. Much?"

"Sixty dollars, I think. A lot."

"I'll go half, if you like."

"All right. Mind if I bring a new girl?"

She gave him a quick glance. "Your shopgirl?" she asked.

"Well, yes, my shopgirl. She sells flowers for Miss Mack."

She remembered how he had taken the pitcher, which she'd thought so odd at the time, but now saw was reasonable. "Oh. Bring anyone you like—except Isobelle. I don't want Isobelle."

"I couldn't agree more."

There was a little silence, then Marcy said, "What's happened to Alice? Anything?"

"Well, yes. We seem to be finished. Something of a wrench, but such wrenches aren't so intense as once. I had a letter from her today making it quite definitely off. It was a grand passion while it lasted."

"Maybe we aren't very faithful, we Doorns," Marcy said slowly.

"Oh, but we are. I think we are. I'd have married her in a minute if she'd ever had what it takes to leave Henry."

"Would you? I wonder. What's her name, this new passion?"

"We haven't got to the passion yet. Her name's Fanny Drake. She's just your cup of tea. But you needn't worry. I couldn't go a-courting her. She lives in the Bronx, and there's no place for Papa and Mama to go to, except maybe to bed, while we court. So you needn't worry."

"I'm not worried, knowing you. I feel a little worry for her. Well, bring her. Miss Hodge and Bessie?"

"Couldn't we bypass Bessie? Impossible, I suppose. Oh, well, Miss Hodge always makes a nice macabre touch. There's a fantastic artificial tree in one of the windows—stunning effect. Want me to do one? I could."

Marcy looked out of the window, down into the street. Elspeth was not in sight anywhere. "No, I think we'll have a real tree," she said slowly.

Then she saw Elspeth coming. Elspeth walked erect, as she always had, and yet Bessie had been right—she walked as one in a dream. Hurry! Marcy wanted to cry out. Get inside, before something happens to you!

Then Elspeth was there with them in the room. She said, "Hello," but so gently, sat down. "It was so quiet," she said. "There wasn't anyone else there. Out of all New York, there was no one else there. And I knelt there, and the quiet spread out and out—hush. I shouldn't break it, should I?"

"Knelt where?" David demanded.

"In the church, down the street. I know it doesn't need to be in a church, but it was so quiet. You can't always make the quiet come, can you?"

"You've been kneeling all morning?" David said sharply. "You'll get housemaid's knees, my sweet."

"Hush," Elspeth said again. She leaned her head back and closed her eyes.

David got up, reached for his coat. Marcy went out into the hall with him. His face was not so youthful as it had been a few weeks ago. He said, "You know, you ought to call it off. You really ought."

"No," Marcy said. "No, David." And she went back to Elspeth.

"He said his name was Father Duquesne. Are not names beautiful? Father Duquesne; and David Doorn, and Sean O'Faolain—how beautiful names are. And I said, 'Thank you for the peace, Father Duquesne.' And he said, 'Do not thank me, my child. The peace is in you, and is a gift from God.' His face was so pure and so remote. I was just a child strayed in from the street—so remote. How beautiful upon the mountains are the faces of them—"

"The feet," Marcy corrected her dryly. Queer, how so many phrases from the Bible she never read were there in her head, familiar as her own skin.

"Faces too," Elspeth said. "They say you never see faces in dreams. But in the night—whether in dreams or not I can't say just now—I see the faces, all the beautiful faces: Miss Evangeline Snow, with her wispy hair, such beautiful eyes, so anxious, so intelligent, so—so dedicated; and Isobelle with her crooked tooth; and Marie, mother of all the world—Marie Dudevant, with the loaf of bread in her arms; and Miss Hodge. They come like a pageant and keep going before my eyes—all the beautiful ones. Where's Sebastian?"

"Sebastian? He went away on business. He'll be back. Don't

you see Sebastian among the beautiful ones? Or—or John?"

"No," Elspeth said, but more slowly. "No, I never do."

Then Marcy got up and took Elspeth's coat away to hang up. Not Sebastian's face? Not John's? Isobelle's, and not Sebastian's? Not John's?

She went back to Elspeth and said sharply, "Why Isobelle?"

"Why not? When loneliness is so pure, so deep, it is beautiful, isn't it?"

"Is it? But her loneliness is all of her own choosing. It doesn't make her beautiful to me."

"To me."

Marcy leaned against the edge of the doorway, her shoulder hunched a little as if she were hurt in body somewhere. "Well, we're all lonely enough, God knows. The whole human race ought to look beautiful to you, darling, if that's what makes beauty."

"But there's an end loneliness," Elspeth said, "when that is all there is."

"I thought you were against ends and beginnings and lines that went somewhere. I thought everything was all one thing. I'm trying to understand, Elspeth. You ought to see I'm trying to understand. If it's all one thing, then loneliness or beauty or anything ought not to stand out special, had it? I'm just trying to understand, darling."

Elspeth sat silent, her eyes half closed, her hands clasped as they would have been in the church.

"David's right. We shouldn't have the party," Marcy said to herself in the kitchen. But she knew they were going to have the party.

In the afternoon of that day Sebastian stood out by Miss Halsey's desk—just stood there, talking of this and that, not wanting to go out again into the town, hear the same words over and over, come up again against the same wall. And yet nothing changed in his mind. He knew that over the wall, if he could just get over the wall, he would there find some truth, something not seen now, never seen before.

"I think I'll go back to town," he said suddenly.

"Yes," she said, "I think you ought to, I think you're tormenting yourself for no good reason, Mr. Esker."

She was doing accounts, which were simple enough this time of year. But she was very exact about accounts and kept a big brown ledger under the shelf of the desk, with everything in it—everything. The ledger was now open on the desk, and she was making entries in a square black handwriting.

"No," he said. "There's a reason, Miss Halsey. I will never rest till I know the answer. I went into this bookstore in town where John often went and talked to the old man who runs it. John talked about conscience to that old man. The old man asked what conscience had to do with music. Well, of course it has everything to do with it. It carries over into everything if it means anything at all, doesn't it? You can't be absolutely honest in just one department of your being, can you?"

Miss Halsey put her pen down. "Well, I don't know. Yes, I guess you could be," she said. "I guess it does happen."

"Does it? Can it? Oh, well, it's not your problem, Miss Halsey. I mustn't burden you with it. It can't matter to you, but it still matters to me, and I can't let it go. I want to go back for Christmas. I feel I must, and yet—yet I feel close to the edge of something that I must know before I go. Who is that, in that little car?"

For at that moment the rattling old Ford went rushing up the street, the old car he had seen twice that day at the farm.

Miss Halsey picked up her pen, said matter-of-factly, "That's

Jennie Wiggins—teaches school out over Derby way." She made an entry, and there was a sudden blob of ink on the page. She reached for a blotter.

"Oh. Any connection of Peter's? The boy who whistles?"

"His mother."

"Friend of Elspeth's?"

"Not that I know of. No, I guess not. The mail ought to be sorted now. You wouldn't want to go over and see if there is any, would you?"

"All right."

After he had gone out Miss Halsey sat there, doing nothing, staring after him. She held the pen in her hand but made no more entries.

"So," she said at last tiredly. "So."

And that night, after dinner was done and all was in order for the night, Miss Halsey said, "You want to take over the inn for an hour or so? Won't anybody be in, or not likely. I've got an errand that won't wait. If you could bring your book down here I'd take it kindly."

"Glad to," Sebastian said.

In her plain black coat, with a scarf tied over her dark hair, making her long face longer still, Miss Halsey stepped out of the inn, made her way along the street past the church and the Community Hall, past the old white houses, to the end of town. Just after the sidewalks stopped there was a small Cape Cod house, set back on a little slope. Up the path to this neat house she went. It was dark, and the gravity of her face could not be seen, but the gravity was deep. She went around to the back and rapped on the door. Mrs. Webster came to the door, startled at a caller this late.

"Why, it's Hat Halsey!" she said in surprise. "Come in."

"No, I can't. Is Jennie here?"

"Yes, she's here. What's the matter, Hat? Don't tell me Peter's got into some mischief. He's so lively, but he's a good boy."

"No, Peter's a fine boy. No, I just wanted to see Jennie a minute, Mrs. Webster. I'll just step in out of the cold."

She could see Mr. Webster out in the kitchen, playing solitaire at the old deal table. Mrs. Webster called, "Jennie!" at the stair door, and Jennie came running down the stairs. She had on slacks and an old sweater, her Saturday uniform, and she looked young to be the mother of Peter. Or did she? Miss Halsey revised that in her mind. No, there was something old about that face, something very old indeed.

"Why, hello!" Jennie said in surprise.

"Jennie," Miss Halsey said without preamble, "would you get your coat and come out with me a few minutes? There's something I want to talk over with you."

"Why, yes. But come in. We can talk here, can't we?"

"No," Miss Halsey said gravely. "If you don't mind, Jennie."

Jennie looked suddenly troubled, anxious, but she went and got her things, came out almost at once with Miss Halsey into the night.

"Let's walk this way. It's dark, but we can make out the road, I guess," Miss Halsey said, heading toward the country.

"What is it?" Jennie asked. "Has Peter—?"

"No, Peter hasn't. I don't know why you expect Peter to do something he shouldn't. Peter's a good boy."

"Yes, he is. It was just—well, I couldn't think what could be wrong."

"You wouldn't consider me a meddler, would you, Jennie?" Miss Halsey asked after a brief pause.

"That's the last thing I'd call you," Jennie said.

"Good. I just don't want you thinking I am. I think if I were you I'd take Peter and go somewhere for the Christmas holidays. Is there someone you could go to see easily? I mean at once—tomorrow, let's say."

Jennie stopped still in the road. "What for? What do you mean, Miss Halsey?"

At that moment the moon came from under a heavy cloud, and Miss Halsey could see Jennie's face. Her dark auburn hair was black in the night, combed back smoothly. She wore a small black knitted cap with a green tassel, like a child's skating cap. Her face was thin, unbeautiful, but strong and pared down to a purity that moved Miss Halsey.

"I mean this—it's hard to say, Jennie. But I've thought about it all day, and I must say it, I find. John Esker's brother is here, and he knows there was something about John's life that is unknown to him and all of them. He knows that, and he can't rest till he finds out what it is. He's got an obsession about it. I think he is getting close to it. He asked today, when you drove by, who you were. So far as I can remember he hasn't asked about anyone else in town. But there was something in the way he asked that made me know he was getting close. If you were gone for a couple weeks it would be a good thing. Then he might go back to town for Christmas, and stay."

She paused and saw Jennie standing there helplessly in the moonlight. She wanted to take her in her arms and comfort her but was not given to softnesses of that kind.

"Far as I know," Miss Halsey went on to Jennie's stillness,

"no one in town knows anything about it but me. No one. I've never so much as heard it whispered. But that day—the day he didn't go to the festival—I knew he spent with you. I happened to know that, don't ask me how now. And after that you went away and came back with a baby, a new name, and no husband. So far as I know, even with this town what it is, I haven't heard anyone doubt that there was a husband, which speaks well for you and your father and mother. Nor did I know, not really know, till one day I was talking with Peter in the street. He's got eyes exactly like John's—exactly. It's troubled me, but I've never mentioned it to anyone. You don't forget eyes like John Esker's."

"Miss Halsey—oh, *Miss Halsey!*" Jennie said in a small but agonized voice.

"I'm sorry, Jennie. I never would have mentioned it if it weren't for this Sebastian Esker, who is bound to know the truth, whatever it is. I haven't any idea how he's connected you with it, but connected you he certainly has. He is in love with John's wife—a very nice man, too, very nice indeed. I thought, if you weren't here for the next couple weeks, if there was nothing to work *on,* he might go away and stay away. He's talked with Peter in the street—because John taught Peter to whistle. But if he ever really looks at him— I'm sorry, Jennie. I felt I had to come. John should never have come back here."

"No," Jennie said dully, "he shouldn't have. But he didn't know about Peter—not when he came."

"He did know—afterward?"

"Yes."

Such desolation in that one quiet word on the cold night air. For a moment Miss Halsey couldn't go on. Then she said,

"He shouldn't have come here. He shouldn't have brought his wife here. I don't see why he did—unless he was pulled here, in spite of himself. He must have cared for his wife. How could one help it? Then why did he try to mix his two lives? I cannot understand it."

"I suppose," Jennie said tiredly, "I meant something special to him. He loved her, all right—but I meant something special. And then when he knew about Peter it all changed. I can't tell you, Miss Halsey."

"No need to. I don't want to pry. I just didn't want anything sprung on you without any warning, that's all. Did his wife know?"

"I don't know. I don't think so—not at first, anyway. I don't know."

"Mr. Sebastian Esker, he knows there was something on John's *conscience*. I think John's wife knew. I think, at the end, she knew. Well, I've told you, Jennie. I guess that's all. I didn't want to upset you, but I felt I had to come."

She turned and began to walk back along the way they had come, and Jennie kept at her side. At last Jennie said—but oh, with such pain under the dignity of her voice—"I don't see how I can go away, Miss Halsey. There's nowhere I could go, nowhere that would seem natural. My folks are looking forward to Peter's Christmas. They've got a tree all picked out to cut, and Peter's going to help cut it. My father's bought new skates for Peter. Could you just tell him and ask him to leave us alone? We've managed so far. If we're let alone we shall manage forever."

"Yes, I could. I doubt if it would satisfy him. I'll try if you want me to. He has an obsession, as I said. He can't let it go. Looks to me as if he can't bear it that he didn't know his brother better. And he doesn't know how to help John's wife unless he knows the truth. A great one for the truth, he is."

"Life's queer, isn't it, Miss Halsey?" Jennie's voice trailed off into the night. It made Miss Halsey think of the night whistle of a train, receding in melancholy.

"Queer enough," she conceded. "But, like you say, you've managed it so far, Jennie. Done a good job of it, by and large, I'd say. I guess you'll go on managing. Maybe I shouldn't have come. Maybe I should have just let things take their course."

"No. Thank you for coming. Thank you very much, Miss Halsey. But still, I don't know anything to do but wait."

"All right. I'll try to steer him off, but I'm not sure I can. I'll get back now. Bless you, child."

Jennie stood still, and Miss Halsey took a step homeward, then stopped. "You know," she said in a troubled but kind voice, "in a way I think you've got a right to be proud, that you meant something special to him."

"Yes," Jennie said at last, "I am proud."

And all the way home her voice stayed there in Miss Halsey's head. "I am proud. I am proud." In spite of all, in spite of Peter and the loneliness of her life, her struggles to support Peter and all, she was *proud*. Life was queer; it certainly was.

Miss Halsey came in, and Sebastian sat there with his book. How like and how unlike he was to John! He didn't look like him, but he had such an intelligent, good face—and there was something like, all the same, some dedication of spirit, some intensity of vision. Miss Halsey tried to keep busy, tried not to brood, get philosophical, analytical, but she had the feeling, seeing Sebastian sitting there in her little room with his book, that these brothers had changed her life in some fashion, and how strange it was that they could do so, when they had really touched her life so little. But one way and another they had given her a lot to think about—loyalty and conscience and talent, all that.

"Well, thanks for keeping the inn going," she said in her brisk, dry way. "Would a piece of apple pie and some milk be the thing to finish off the evening with, would you say?"

"Yes, I'd like that," he said.

But when she had brought the pie she could not begin to tell him. She let the moments slip past. The pie was finished, the milk gone. She carried the dishes away, wished him good night. Her heart was too full for telling him tonight. Jennie's voice, the way she had taken it, standing there in the dark, then with the moonlight on her face—Miss Halsey's heart was too full of the queerness, the sadness of life.

19

IN TOWN, away from Sebastian's insistent, impatient search for a brother who seemed lost, Marcy sat at her desk and made herself one with that search. A girl, eager, collegiate, had come for an article on design, and the interview had ended with Marcy's saying she would write out her own ideas on design and give them to the girl.

"Design?" she said now angrily, put her pencil down with a click upon the desk. "Where is it? What is it? How do I know?"

She stopped at Miss Mack's on the way home, but all the way there the word "design" rang in her head.

"And the end of the week will you send a lot of holly and pine branches up to the house—mistletoe and such? And could you get me a tree?"

"Yes, I could do that. Don't display them here—no room. But I have a source. How big?"

"Oh, eight feet—no, seven and a half; got to have room

for the star. Fat, with cones on. Could you? I want it old-fashioned."

Miss Mack gave a little grunt. Anything less old-fashioned than the Doorns she had never known. But she said, "I'll fix you up," then, one big hand clutching her pad, "Oh, Fanny, come here a minute. Want you to meet Miss Doorn. Miss Doorn's one of our regulars—always pays her bills on time, and always knows what she wants. This is Fanny Drake, Miss Doorn."

Fanny said, "How do you do," gravely, formally.

"Hello," Marcy said. "I think I know you already, don't I? Aren't you the one my brother is going to bring to our party Saturday?"

"No, I'm afraid not," Fanny said.

"Perhaps he hasn't asked you yet. He will—and so do I," she said with a smile of such friendliness as only she could give.

"Thank you, but I always spend Christmas at home," Fanny said.

"Oh, but for an hour or so? Just an open-house sort of thing," Marcy said easily. "Do try. I know David is counting on it!"

"That's kind of you, but I couldn't, not possibly," said Fanny.

"You weren't very civil," Miss Mack said as soon as the door closed after Marcy. "It's the brother you ought to be cool to. Nice girl, Marcy Doorn. No side to her. Means what she says."

"Yes, she looked nice," Fanny said. "But I always spend Christmas at home, Miss Mack. I never go to parties on Christmas Day. And I shouldn't think they'd be having a party, anyway—not so soon after Mr. Esker's dying."

Miss Mack gave her a quick glance. "Well, that's life for you," she said. "Folks don't stop much for dying any more. Day of crepe veils is over. Might be you tomorrow—snatch what you can get while there's time. That's how they think nowadays. Maybe more sensible than the old way, at that. Widow couldn't lift her eyes to a man for a year. Nonsense!"

And Marcy went homeward, even this meeting with the girl David liked mixed in with her thoughts of design.

She didn't like me! she thought once in surprise.

Then her heart cried out: And what design makes me faithful to Sebastian and Sebastian faithful to Elspeth and David faithful to—to *us,* yes, he is—as if we had no choice. But I do have a choice. I made it once when I said I would not love John. I stopped. I had a choice then. Suppose I said right now, "I will not love Sebastian any more. It is futile. I will stop. I will change the design of my life." How can I say it? The design is set, it's all made. Oh, Sebastian, why don't you phone? Why don't you come? And suppose this is to be the design for Elspeth forever? I couldn't bear that. He couldn't bear it. He's trying to find some way to help her, but I wish he would come back. . . .

But he did not come. On Sunday morning he said to Miss Halsey, "Have you finished the socks?"

"Almost," Miss Halsey said. "Three or four more rows will do it."

"Are you going to church?" For the first bell of the Congregational church was ringing.

"No. I'm out of the habit of church, tied down to the inn as I am. I used to go—just put a sign on the door and went. But I'm out of the habit."

"I haven't been since I was a child," Sebastian said. "Yet

I think I worship, in my way—man, or life, something—life, I suppose you would say."

"Are you in a hurry for the socks?" Miss Halsey asked.

"Yes, rather."

She rose from the desk, went past him into the lounge, picked up her knitting. She sat down, and her needles flashed. Then she asked—casually, it seemed—"Why did you ask who Jennie Wiggins was?"

"Why? Well, I wondered, that was all."

"But why? Why did you wonder?"

He lit a cigarette slowly. "Why did you make a blot when I asked you?" he asked then.

Her long face reddened. "Well, you interrupted me," she said with sensible irritation.

"I don't see what she would have to do with John and Elspeth, do you?" he asked then. And then more insistently: "Do *you?*"

She frowned, said, "I was the one who asked."

"It was at the farm," he said. "Twice she went by. Twice Elspeth saw her and was frightened. It was seeing the car the second time that made her come back to town with me. You can say I imagine that if you like—perhaps I do. Yet, without a word being said, I knew that car was what frightened her. Why?"

"You're just like a terrier with a rat. You never let go, do you?" she said.

"No. I can't. It's the nature of terriers that they can't let go."

She let the socks lie idle in her lap, looked at him gravely, sorrowfully.

"I have her leave to tell you," she said at last. "Yet it seems wrong. Some secrets are better buried."

"Her leave?"

"That's right, her leave. And then she hopes you will go away and leave her be and let the secret lie. It's only this—when they were young they loved, or I suppose they loved. And Peter, the red-headed boy who whistles, is their son. That's all there is to it. But no one knows—and I would know if anyone did. No one here dreams the truth. She's a fine girl, Jennie Wiggins, brave and good. She earns a living and brings up her boy in a good fashion. She never let your brother know about Peter. And I think, after all these years and the way she's lived, she has a right to be left alone. I think you haven't any right to pry. Those are the facts, and she gave me leave to tell you."

And Sebastian sat there looking at her, and was washed over and over with such a wave of sorrow, of grief, for John, for Elspeth, for himself, for Jennie Wiggins. The inn faded away, and there was only the sorrow. These were the facts—but what were facts?

"And how did you know?" His voice was far off to himself. He did not know whether he had spoken aloud or not.

"Let's say I didn't know for sure till one day Peter came in with some tickets to sell for school. His eyes are John's eyes. He looks like Jennie with her red hair and all, but his eyes are that dark hazel, with little lights in them—exactly like—"

"You wouldn't have known from that," he said.

"That and other things I knew before. I was sure then."

"No," he said with sudden sharpness. "No. John wouldn't be cruel enough to do that, to bring Elspeth here. He was not cruel, Miss Halsey."

"He didn't seem so. I wouldn't have said so. He didn't know about Peter."

"And then, I suppose, he knew, and then the guilt began—and all of it."

"I suppose so. As Jennie says, life is queer. But I don't see the use now, not after all this time, of torturing Jennie, when she's come to some kind of terms with living and makes out so well. I don't see any use of adding cruelty to what trouble there is. So I ask you to leave her alone, Mr. Esker—just to leave her alone."

"You went to her last night."

"Yes. It wasn't easy, but I had to warn her. I thought if she went away for the Christmas holidays, just went somewhere with Peter, out of town—but she had no place to go. She's taken her stand here; she can't go anywhere. I'd never spoken of it to her or any living being before. And since your brother never told you, doesn't it seem maybe it was because he didn't want you to know?"

"No," he said heavily, "it doesn't, Miss Halsey. It doesn't. It seems as if it killed him, no one knowing. But Elspeth knows. At the end she knew."

"Yes, I think she did. But that is between her and John, isn't it? It's not your business."

"I'm sorry—no, it's my business too. Because it's killing her as well."

He looked away from her, toward the window through which he could see a few last stragglers winding toward the church. "I'm sorry," he said again, "but I have to see her, Miss Halsey. I'll try not to hurt anyone. But I must see her."

Miss Halsey put her knitting down in her lap, looked at him sternly. "I will arrange it," she said with stiffness.

"I'm sorry," he said for the third time, but there was no giving up in his voice. He was one who had to know.

The phone was ringing, and Miss Halsey moved toward the desk.

"It's for you. It's long distance," she said.

"You were awfully slow," Marcy said. "I'm at the drugstore, and I have to keep putting money in. Sebastian, aren't you coming for Christmas?"

"Yes. I will try to."

"You sound strange. Are you all right?"

"Yes, I'm all right. Is anything wrong?"

"Everything's wrong. You'll surely come?"

"Yes, I'll come."

He did not eat any lunch. He wasn't hungry, he told Miss Halsey. He went out and walked for a long time in the snow, not knowing where he went, what houses he passed. He had been given an incredible fact, and it explained nothing. He had been searching for what seemed a long, long time for something to give to Elspeth—and to himself as well—some sure thing that would not cancel out love or faith, that would give John back to her whole, so that she could weep. He had been so sure the thing was there somewhere, that there could not possibly have been in that life he so admired, that brother he so loved, anything that could cause withdrawal like this withdrawal of Elspeth's. He had been so sure. And this was the gift he had to bring back to Elspeth. This.

He sat in the dining room when night came and heard dimly the chatter of a nice family on its way to the grandparents for Christmas. The family went away, and Miss Halsey came and stood by his table.

"You know where my sitting room is, at the back, don't you?" she said.

"I think so."

"If you'll come down at eight and come back to the sitting room—Jennie will come."

"Thank you," he said.

Up in his room he arranged his few things in the drawers of the bureau. The room was more truly his own than many rooms he had lived in. He had only a little time, yet the moments were like eternities.

He came down the stairs, and he was the little man walking in the tunnel of light. Everything reached out for him, but he was safe so long as he kept in the light. Miss Halsey was in the front. She did not even speak to him, and he went directly back along the long hall to the little room he had often seen her enter but never as yet entered himself.

The room, intimate, small, was too small to contain him, wound tight like this. He saw a rose chenille rug on the floor, and that was all, because then he saw Jennie Wiggins turn from beside a table and stand there, waiting.

"I'm Jennie Wiggins. You wanted to see me?" she said clearly.

He shook his head a little, to shake her away and bring into his focus someone else—he didn't know who else, but just someone else. She was a young woman without glamour, a rather plain, straightforward young woman with dark auburn hair, pulled back straight to a knot at her neck, rather high cheekbones, and an honest mouth. Miss Halsey had said she was a schoolteacher. She looked as if she might be a very good one, firm and sure and intelligent. He was confused, not being able to let his imagination picture John taking this woman out of wedlock, giving her a child, who was that sturdy, red-headed whistling boy.

"Yes. Thank you for coming. Shall we sit down?"

The room was too small, they were too close. She clasped

her hands in her lap, and she clasped them too tightly. It released something in him, that she was frightened too. Yet her eyes were candid and unfrightened.

"I don't want to hurt you in any way," he said. "So far as I am concerned, no one will ever know I have talked with you. This is a personal, a private, thing. You are not what I expected."

"No? Just what is it you want, Mr. Esker? Miss Halsey has told you the facts. What else is there?"

"It begins to seem unpardonable," he said. "I think I didn't expect to be talking to another teacher, like myself, though I knew you were a teacher. Yes, I know the facts. They don't explain anything, just the facts. They don't explain what's happened to Elspeth, nor why John needed you, why he came back *here*—nothing seems clear."

"I don't know why he came back," she said. "I think his wife found the place, the farm—and it had all been so long ago. But he hadn't forgotten and he tried not to come. It was she who—who found it, the one place in the world— But he remembered. He felt, he said, when the deed was signed, doomed. Yet he knew nothing of Peter."

"He *said?* Then you knew him here too—this time, I mean?"

"Yes."

"But why didn't you tell him of Peter?"

She hesitated. "What I would say now has nothing to do with then," she said at last. "Then it was just an instinct, a blind instinct, not to. Now—now I feel that I knew he belonged to a world I could never belong to. But then—I don't know. I only knew I couldn't. I told my people it was a boy in town, but I never told what boy, and they didn't make me. They never even knew I knew John Esker. Nor did I, except for that one night and that day. My people have been kind, but this has made them older than they should be. Still, they love Peter very much."

"You must have been very young, " he said awkwardly.

"Not that young," she said. Her voice had some of the dryness of Miss Halsey's voice. "The doctor had a season ticket for the festival, and one night he let me use it, because I could play a little and he thought I loved music. You sit on the grass or on little folding stools you bring. I sat on the grass, and your brother came and sat beside me. And I said, 'It's beautiful, isn't it?' It was all romantic, and the stars were out. But he didn't say, yes, it was beautiful. He had his knees hunched up, and he folded his arms on them and put his head down and didn't answer me at all. And that upset me, not being answered. I'd never been to the festival before, or heard good music except on records or the radio, and it all seemed new and exciting, and I hated it not to have the feeling shared. I suppose I hated it not to have him share it, for he seemed part of it—beautiful, you know."

"I know," he said more gently, less tightly wound, though he could not have said why.

"I tried to think of something sharp to say, but I couldn't think of anything, and then—"

"And then?"

"Then he said, as if he had seen me, as if he had heard me all the time, 'Would you like to go on a picnic with me tomorrow—away from all this? Where do you live?' I said, 'Old Quagatuck,' and he said, 'I'm staying there. Meet me at the bridge below town at ten.' It— I don't know how to say it. It wasn't like any pick-up. It was as if he needed me and I had to come. 'All right,' I said. And that was all. He got up and went to sit somewhere else. That's the way it happened. It sounds queer, doesn't it? But that's the way it happened."

"Yes. It sounds like him. And so you went on the picnic."

"Yes. I couldn't dress up because my folks would have thought it odd, a morning like that. The girls were wearing dirndls then, and I had a very full one in different shades of brown. I wore that and a blouse with a round neck. I wore my hair in braids around my head then. But those were my ordinary clothes. I just walked out of the house without saying a word about where I was going, and I walked to the bridge, and he was standing there with a box of lunch. Just past there is a woods road that leads to an old lumbering camp, or where one used to be. We walked up this road into the woods. And all day long, all day long—"

"Never mind," he said. "You needn't. I see it."

"I tried to talk about the concert, but he wouldn't. 'Oh, time enough for music,' he said. 'A whole lifetime long for that.' Once in a while, once in a great while, something happens that's cut off from ordinary living, if you know what I mean—something apart that doesn't have anything to do with going to school or getting meals or—or anything."

"I know," he said.

"I've never said it before, but that was a day like that—cut off, with nothing before or after. We were very happy."

"Yes, I know. He had a gift for being happy, on occasion—rarely."

"It wasn't like a pick-up," she said again, with a sudden doubt, as if she couldn't possibly make anyone see what the day had been like.

"You needn't keep saying that," Sebastian said. "I know quite well that John was never promiscuous. And I know that days like that can be— Go on."

"It's hard to say. I've never tried to say it before. And I didn't think it out then. I wasn't too young to know the difference between right and wrong, but still I was too young to think much. I just felt things. My mother was never angry with me, but she did think I should marry the boy, whoever he was. I never thought of marrying him. Never. Keeping the day apart, special, was somehow more important than having the baby. That sounds stupid."

"No, it doesn't sound stupid at all. So then you went away and came back after a bit with another name and the baby. That I know. And no one questioned the name."

"That's the way it was. You see, we were 'good people'—I'd never played around, been wild, like some. No one expected me to be wild. My people are poor, but no poorer than many others around here. We were respected. And at first I was frightened all the time and expected the whole thing to be known. But no one seemed changed toward me in the slightest—no one. And after a while I almost believed myself that I was a widow with a little boy, come home to live with her folks. I finished at the normal school where I'd started, and got a job teaching school. It's one of the last one-room schools in these parts. My folks took care of Peter while I was in school. It would have been easier if it had not been so easy, if someone had reproached me. No one did. But I was brought up with a conscience."

Her voice had grown quicker and harsher. Then she stopped dead still.

"John too. He had a conscience too. And then he came back."

"Then he came back." Now her voice was quiet again.

"I heard it in the post office," she said after a moment. "Fellow named John Esker had bought the Wheaton farm. Another house to 'do over,' they said—they laugh at some of the outsiders that come, but they do over the old farms for them, all the same. There are three or four who make their living that way around here. But no one was asked to do over that place.

"It was a cold autumn night when I heard that. I walked out of the store, and the stars were whirling around, and I felt sick all over. I walked for a long time, and when I went in my mother said, 'Why, Jennie, what's the matter? You look like a ghost!' I said I thought I was getting the flu and would she make me some hot lemonade and I thought I'd go to bed. And after I was in bed I was suddenly sensible again, and I said to myself that if he even so much as remembered he wouldn't have come here, that he couldn't possibly know about Peter, because Peter looks like me, not him, with his red hair and all—and that I was being sick over nothing, that all I had to do was to go on as I had always done. It had nothing to do with me at all. For I was more grown up by then and I knew that just the fact that that day had been important to me didn't mean that it had been so to him. And he hadn't had to bring up Peter or change his name or anything."

She was quiet for a moment, and then she said, "Was this the way you wanted it? Is this what you wanted to know?"

"Exactly," he said.

"I knew very soon that he had become famous. We hear a lot about music around here, because of the festival and all. No one is truly musical, though. But we hear about it. We heard there was going to be a movie over in the next village, and that this Esker had written the music for it. So everyone who was curious—and most of us are that curious—went. I went. And then I knew I needn't worry any more, not any more; for I knew he wouldn't remember me, that he had had too much else to think of through the years. One day I saw his wife in the street. It was like the night the stars went around

—I'm not poetic, Mr. Esker. This—this that I am telling you is all the poetry I have ever known, or ever will. I wasn't jealous. She seemed exactly what he deserved. But I felt sad, seeing her, and knew I was plain and sensible. I felt safe, too, for I knew that no one who had her for a wife would even remotely remember me. Yes, I felt safe."

"But you weren't?" Sebastian asked after a long silence.

"Yes, for a while. It was like after I'd brought the baby home—frightening for a while, always expecting something to happen, then nothing happening, and then feeling safe. And then—then one day I met him face to face in the street, by the Congregational church. It was spring by then, soon after Easter. He looked just the same—no, older, but just the same. I had some of Peter's papers in my hand that he had thrust at me, passing in the street. I looked down at them, pretending to be examining them, and I was almost by him when he said, 'Hello, Jennie.' It was a shock, because his voice said that he remembered everything. It didn't pretend I was half a stranger, that he was having any difficulty remembering my name. It said he remembered *everything*. You'll think I imagined that."

"I think nothing of the sort."

"He turned and walked with me a little way, not far, and he said, 'I hope you don't mind that I live nearby. My wife fell in love with a house, and we had to buy that house, no other. Has life been good to you?' And I said, 'Very good.' He said, 'You're married too?' and I said, 'Yes. My name is Wiggins now. And I have a little boy.' He said, 'Good. I haven't any little boy.' Then he just smiled and went back, and I didn't see him again for a long time. But it upset me, talking with him. He seemed to say I had a right to mind his being there. It was upsetting."

"And then he found out about Peter."

"Oh, no, not then—not for a long time. In three years I only saw him once more, to talk to. That was on a winter night. I was at school, cleaning up after the children had all gone home. It was late, beginning to be dusky. But I had looked over papers, and then I'd begun to sweep the floor. And the door opened, and snow blew in, and I went to shut it, and there he stood in the hallway. 'Hello, Jennie,' he said, just like he had that other time. And I said, 'Hello,' and something about the storm. He came in and said, "So this is where you teach. My brother is a teacher. I've always envied him.' He sat on a desk near the stove. The fire was dying down now in the stove. We used wood then, though we have oil now. He sat there and looked around. I finished sweeping and put the broom away. 'I heard your husband had died. I'm sorry. Were you happy?' he said. And I said, 'Yes, very happy while it lasted.' 'Good,' he said. And then he said, 'I like this little schoolroom. I like it very much. I've had it in my mind to say something to you but haven't had the courage till today. Today I just forgot courage and came.'

"I was sitting down at the desk, trying to look like a teacher, nothing else. He said, 'I love my wife more than life. I must say that. And yet I've had this feeling that I must say to you that the happiest day in all my life to date I spent with you. Perhaps I don't need to say that, but I've felt the necessity. I have never before or since been so free or so happy.' Then he smiled at me. It was true, you know—he did love his wife more than life. He did. And I knew it. I said, 'Thank you. I was happy too.' So he smiled again, got up, and went out into the snow. You can't help feeling something for a man as honest as that. He wasn't philandering, not anything like that. It was just something he owed me—admitting at the same time that he had a good life, a life he didn't want to change, that he knew people did go on that way, not stop dead still because of a day's happiness, and yet—yet he had to tell me. It made me feel good all through. I've never talked to anyone this much in all my life."

"We're both teachers," he said.

"Maybe that's it! It was queer. I felt proud of him, as if I'd married him, and at the same time I wasn't jealous. I never tried to change anything. You must believe that."

"I do believe it," Sebastian said.

"And nothing did change. I heard about him. I saw the movies with his music in. I never mentioned him to anyone—not to my folks, not to Peter or anyone. And the months, the years went by, and nothing happened at all. Till—"

"Till when? Till the square dances," Sebastian said.

She gave him a slow, wondering look. "Yes, till the square dances," she said. "I used to go sometimes. Everybody around here goes. And then this night he came in with the Dudevants—Mrs. Dudevant loves square dances. This night they came with them. Some of the outsiders do come, just for a lark, showing they know they're out of their own circle. But Mrs. Dudevant always seemed to have fun, and people like her. But they—John and his wife—had never come before, and at first people were a little shy of them. But after they danced no one was so shy, for they could dance as if they meant it, as if they'd done it all their lives. And I met John in the changing of partners in a dance, and he said, 'Hello, Jennie,' and that was all. Perhaps I was wrong to go again—perhaps that was wrong. I don't know. We have the dances every two weeks in the winter, in the Community Hall. The next time he asked Fred Weller if he could call for the dances just once. He wanted to try it, he said. He was so nice about it—so eager and yet not showing off—Fred said, sure, try it if he wanted to, but it was hard work. And so he did, and he was good at it. Of course his voice isn't that hearty, earthy kind, like Fred's, but he felt the rhythm just as much, and so, all winter long, people wanted him to, and he did. He called for the dances. I suppose it was exciting to some, because he was famous and all, but he didn't act above us or anything. He was very good. And it was exciting watching his wife dance. We aren't used to people like her—as beautiful or even as gay. I think we aren't really ever gay around here. We laugh sometimes, but—"

"I know."

"He didn't dance any more, because he did the calling. And I thought that was good because then I didn't need to think about dancing with him. But I think it may have been wrong to go at all. I did go. And nothing happened—just a smile when we met, that was all. Except once, when his wife was close by, he said to me, 'Good night, Jennie,' and she turned and looked at me in the strangest way. Yes, that was important. She *saw* me. But the dances stopped around Easter, and that was all of that. Yet—yet somehow I thought more about him. I couldn't help it, seeing him so often, seeing her. But it was over. And then—then it was near the end of school, the last part of May; it was Peter's birthday . . ."

"It was his birthday," Sebastian prompted gently after a silence.

"My folks and I had got a bicycle for him. He'd had a second-hand one before, but this was new. He was riding it all around, showing off, I suppose. He went into Goudge's, and John was there after the mail. And Peter was all full of the importance of his birthday and his bicycle and told everyone about it. And he was trying to whistle, and John said,

'Here, now, you're old enough to whistle if you're old enough to have a bike—to whistle properly,' and he began to explain to Peter how to whistle, and I think they laughed a lot, and then Peter asked John if he didn't want to see his bike—it happened something like that. And John went out and admired the bicycle, and then he said, 'How old are you today?' 'Twelve,' Peter said. My folks had always told people that Peter was premature, all that, but we'd never denied when his birthday was. It's strange, people never raising their brows and saying, 'Oh, premature, eh?' the way they do. But I don't believe they did. You'd know if they had."

"Yes, I think you would," Sebastian said gravely.

"Peter looked up at him and grinned, and then jumped on his bike and rode away. John said—he said he recognized himself in that look. I don't know. They're not alike—not at all, except for the eyes sometimes. But he said so. Or maybe he knew suddenly, because of the time and all—just realized it all of a sudden. Anyway, he came straight to the school. I was locking the door when he drove up. He looked strange, frightening. He took my wrist and said, 'Sit down,' and we sat on the steps, which I didn't want to do, thinking someone might be going by and see us. But I sat down, and I said, 'What is it? What's the matter?' And he said—he said, 'Peter's our son, isn't he? Isn't he?' I should have lied. I know now I should have lied. I'd done it so many years; I shouldn't have stopped then. I know now. But he was so honest, I couldn't lie to him. I said, 'Yes, he is. But that's nothing that need trouble you. No one knows it.' 'I know it,' he said. '*I* know it.'

"I was sensible. I was. I was matter-of-fact and sensible. But all the time he looked as if he'd had a terrible shock, one he'd never get over. I made light of it all. I truly did. I said no one had ever known; that I'd never thought of marrying him or wanted to; that I'd got along and would, if let alone; that it was nothing that needed to be on his conscience; that I'd never asked anything of him because I wanted nothing. I'd made my life as he had made his, and I didn't want it changed or interfered with in any way. Oh, I was very cool and very sensible. I truly was, Mr. Esker."

"I believe you," Sebastian said.

"But it did no good. He jumped up suddenly—you know how tall he was; he looked very tall, and somehow I was frightened. 'I knew it. I knew when I signed the deed I was doomed,' he said. That's when he said that. And then he said, 'You hadn't any right—how dared you not tell me? He's my son too. *He's my son too!*' We've said so little together, I remember every word. And it was then I began to really know I'd done wrong—that I hadn't had any right not to tell him. But I went on pretending I had been right. I said, 'That's nonsense. Because you wouldn't be what you are today if you'd had me and Peter to worry about. You wouldn't have had Elspeth for a wife—or anything.' But he said, 'You hadn't any right to decide for me.' Then he got quieter and said, 'I'm sorry. I didn't mean to make a scene.' I was afraid it was a scene, and I didn't want anyone going by to see him. So I stood up too, as if it were over and I had to go. But I was trembling, and it seemed as if I couldn't stand up. 'It's all all right,' I said. 'Please don't trouble yourself about it any more. It's done now. Wrong or right, it's done. Nothing is changed, and nothing can be changed. So please just leave us alone. And we'll leave you alone.' He just looked at me, and then he said, 'What do you think I am, Jennie?' And then he went, striding over to his car and driving off."

For all she was telling all the poetry of her life in an hour, telling of years in minutes, Sebastian Esker saw it all with an intolerable vividness. Even the gestures of John came back as if he were there in the room. And he saw John in the bookshop talking of conscience to the old man. And he saw him on that long-ago day, standing under a tree in the woods and smiling down at a girl in a brown dirndl and white blouse, auburn hair in braids around her head—or lying on the grass, his head against the brown skirt, forgetting music, forgetting it and living. He saw John going back home after that moment at the schoolhouse, beginning a symphony for his son. But he never finished the symphony. He never finished it.

He thought she wasn't going to say any more, but she did.

"And then I didn't see him any more, not all summer long. Peter was invited to go to Vermont with the doctor's boy, who goes to his grandmother's up there every year. And I let him go, though he'd never been away from home before. And things went on as they always had—except that everything seemed changed. And I knew I shouldn't have told John.

"It wasn't till after school opened that I saw him again. He came to the schoolhouse one night, came in, and put a little book on the desk. He looked sick. But he said without any fuss, 'That's a bank book for an account in the Chase National. I thought it might save some talk if I made it a New York bank. I am not a rich man, though I have made a lot of money the last few years. We spend a good deal. This is not for "services rendered." It's not that kind of money. It's meant for Peter's college. It might not be enough. I will add to it when I can. He's not musical, is he?' And I said, 'No. Right now he wants to be a naturalist, but next year it might be something else.' 'Thank God it's not music,' he said. I picked up the book and opened it, and it was made out for me, and there was an entry for ten thousand dollars. I said, 'But I cannot. I don't want it. I'll see that Peter gets to college somehow. I don't want it.' And he said, 'It's not for you. It's for our son.' And I put my head down on the desk and cried. I haven't cried much in many years, Mr. Esker. But I couldn't stop. I don't know what came over me. It was partly that, in spite of everything, it was wonderful to have someone share Peter and all the years that were so hard with me. It was partly that. I was tireder than I knew. But it was partly that I couldn't bear it to have it all opened up again, my life changed around, his life hurt. And there was his beautiful Elspeth, that he loved better than life—for he did, oh, he did. But he put his hand on my hair, and he said, 'Where have the braids gone to? Don't cry. I'll work it out somehow—if the Hound of Heaven would only let me go. Don't cry, Jennie.' But I cried for a long time. I couldn't stop. But at last I did. It was all over. I said, 'All right. I'll save it for him. Now go away.' And he did. He just walked out and went away.

"And maybe that would have been all if Peter hadn't fallen out of a tree the week after Halloween and broken his arm. Some boy came running and said Peter was killed, and it was awful for a little while, and a lot of people gathered around when the word got out that it was worse than it was—for he had a broken arm only, and it's all right already. But at the time—thinking it was worse till I got there—it was bad. But somehow the word got to John. He heard it somewhere. He came right to the house, as if he didn't care who saw him or anything, and my father went to the door and John said, 'Is he all right? I heard Peter—' And my father thought it was just someone who was kind, and he said, 'He's all right. Broken arm, and they've taken him over to the hospital. But he's a tough boy; he'll be all right. Let's see, I guess I don't know you.' And John saw me and came to his senses in a way, and he said, 'I'm just a neighbor—I was worried about the boy. I'm John Esker.' But he looked awful. And I think he went home and told his wife—right then. And that afternoon he died."

He couldn't speak. She leaned back in the chair in exhaustion, her face white and utterly weary. "And that afternoon he died." The words stayed there in the room. How did she know he had gone and told his wife? Of course he had. Why else was Sebastian here? Why else could he have demanded this painful telling from her? "And that afternoon he died."

She opened her eyes, said, "May I go now?"

"I'll walk home with you," he said.

"Thanks, no. I'd rather go by myself."

She stood up and took a coat from over a chair arm, slid into it, pulled a cap from the pocket of the coat, but did not put it on. Then she looked straight at him and said, "And you can't ever have a day apart, can you? Not ever. It always hitches onto life. I thought I might go to her and tell her. But I couldn't. For she ought to know, hadn't she, if she loves him, how good he was, how honest, and how kind? And if he loved her, shouldn't she have known it? I know all that, and I was never married to him. I'm glad he's Peter's father, in spite of everything. I'm glad."

Sebastian said, "Yes, I'm glad too. Let me walk home with you."

"No. I'm used to walking alone," she said and went out the door and down the hall. She'd said that not with self-pity, but with a kind of dry mockery at herself.

Sebastian was still sitting there a half-hour later when Miss Halsey came in. "Is everything all right?" she asked with some trouble in her brusque voice.

"Yes," he said. "Yes, thank you."

"Good. You look tuckered out."

"That's the first thing you said to me," he said. "No, I'm quite all right. I have to go out now for a little while. I'll let myself in."

"At this hour?"

"At this hour," he said.

Early the next morning Sebastian packed his few belongings. He picked up the ashtray, not wondering why he had brought it, for he knew. He had been touched by the warmth of Marcy's giving, and that warmth had been something he was sadly in need of. He packed it, put in the tissue-wrapped parcel with the skating socks inside.

"You've been very kind to me," he said to Miss Halsey. "I wish you weren't angry with me now."

"I'm not angry."

"Yes, you are. I couldn't help myself."

"I guess you have to work things out your own way. I can't help thinking it was a pity, all the same."

"Yes. But Miss Halsey, you said it yourself—her eyes look like Dodie's, like your sister's. You couldn't bear that, either. I'm sure you couldn't. If anything in the world could change that, you'd try to find it—wouldn't you?"

"I guess I would," Miss Halsey conceded. "But if you want the truth, Mr. Esker, I don't see but what you're just making it worse, with your poking and prying."

He knew a moment of shame, seeing himself with those shrewd eyes, then he remembered Jennie Wiggins sitting there in the light, and the shame went away. "But I loved my brother, Miss Halsey—I'm only now beginning to know how much. I never understood him, but I loved him. I am very grateful to you—to you and Jennie."

The shrewd eyes softened. "Have a good Christmas," Hat Halsey said.

"Thank you. And you."

She put out a strong hand abruptly, shook hands with him. "It'll come right," she said firmly.

He picked up his bag, the two bags with the skates, which he hung over his shoulder, went out of the inn and across the road to the store where the bus stopped.

When he got on the bus, dropped into a seat, he had a distinct sense of loss, the loss of leaving home, a place of no ambiguity, a place of warmth and love. In that small back room he had looked deep into a human heart and been shaken by the vision. He did not feel that because one did not show the heart there was none. He had always felt that Elspeth, Marcy, and even David had hearts, no matter how brittle and surface-like their speech. He had never desired to revert to the primitive. Yet the simple, completely honest voice of Jennie went on and on in his head, and he knew it had been like a draft of pure spring water, hearing her. And the voice of Miss Halsey went with the other, shrewd, yet never begging the question. Then he thought of Elspeth—or let her come out fully into his consciousness, for she was always there in his mind and heart somewhere. It wasn't the Bible, for one could find true comfort there. It wasn't that she did not weep, for one can keep tears in from pride, even in grief. It was that she was dwelling in some place where there were no tears, where warmth was folly, where love was discounted. "Strange beyond grief" were the true words for Elspeth. It was this fact of Jennie, that he knew. Somehow she had known it. It was as Jennie had said, John had gone home and told her, and his heart had stopped of the telling. *But because he loved Elspeth so.* Not from guilt, not from present passion deflected, but *because he loved her so.* Somehow she must be made to say those words, "I know he loved me," or she was finished. She would never be Elspeth again. And Marcy and David depended on him to make her say them. They knew, because they did have hearts, that this was something on which life itself depended. "We are frightened," Marcy had said.

The fields and houses dropped behind him—sometimes a snowy field, sometimes a field swept bare, with only snow in fence corners, sometimes a lone shaggy horse standing forlornly in a scrubby pasture—all dropping away, while the bus went on its lumbering way to the city, to Elspeth. Once a boy got on, a boy Sebastian had known in class. For once Sebastian did not welcome an old student, did not give of himself in his usual generous way. He kept his glance on the fields and did not welcome the boy.

He did not ask himself how he should do it, how he should break through this awful shell in which Elspeth was encased. He knew only that it must be done and that he must do it.

He had a key, and he let himself in and went up the familiar stairs. He went in, and Elspeth looked up from a book and smiled at him, not eagerly, more as if he had been away but a half-hour on some easy errand. Over and through him went the knowledge of how much he loved her, of how desperately he wanted to keep pain from her, of how little he had had from her and yet how much, of how little it mattered in what mood she was, or whether she were ill or melancholy or gay—he loved her with all his self and always would. If that was a weakness, so be it. But he felt old and tired and burdened with his knowledge.

"I've missed you," Elspeth said.

"Not much, I expect. Here are your skates. I've been up to the farm, and I picked them up."

"The farm?" Her eyes grew still.

"Yes. I wanted to see if everything was all right there. And I wanted to see where John was buried. Everything is all right. There was a lot of mail piled up. I just left it there."

He could see her pulling her mind away from the farm. She said, ignoring his words, "You mustn't mind about the party, Sebastian. They think we want our friends around. They think that life is what we need. Don't mind."

"I didn't know there was to be a party."

"On Christmas."

"Oh, well, it doesn't matter. I have a present for you." If, he thought oddly, he could only give her Miss Halsey's kind hands that had worked so steadily with the white wool.

"I don't want anything—no presents any more."

"You're going to have this present whether you want it or not. And use it too. Shall we go shopping tomorrow and get things for the rest?"

"Let's not. Let's just feel Christmas." She folded her hands in her lap in a childish way.

"But giving's part of the feeling, isn't it?"

"Not things out of stores. I feel safer when you're here."

And perhaps this was the moment, when she was grateful for his return, when it should be said. He simply smiled at her, gravely, lovingly, and said, "Good."

Then Marcy was there, holding out both hands. "Oh, Sebastian, bless you!" she cried. "I was afraid you'd ditched us for Christmas! And I have a million errands for you to do, and an article you've got to help me write. And—"

"Hold it!" Sebastian said. "I'll run errands, but leave the article out of it."

"I can't. I've said I'd do it, an article on design. I was out of my head, but I said I'd do it by next Wednesday. Don't laugh, it isn't funny. It goes round and round in my head, and no sense comes. You've got to help me."

"We'll have a good heart-to-heart on it," he promised.

"You will? You really will? You won't have to give me any other Christmas present, if you'll just do that. Elspeth could, if she would. She's the writer of the family—but you'd just say, 'Let there *be* design, don't write about it!' Now wouldn't you, darling?"

"Yes, I would," Elspeth said, "if you're just trying to pin it down on paper, to show what a good mind you have."

"But it isn't that!" Marcy protested. "It isn't that at all!" Her voice was passionate, but then she grinned and said, "Or is it?"

So they let it go and talked of other things. Marcy told them about David's girl in the flower shop. "She *snubbed* me!" she said, in half mock, half real amazement. "She really snubbed me. I asked her to the party, and she wouldn't come. Just said no politely, but oh, so firmly! And I liked her too, right off. I liked her a lot. What's this picture of David's you were talking about? He hasn't let me see it."

"He hasn't? Perhaps he doesn't want it talked about, then. He didn't say so."

"Oh, he always talks about his pictures."

"It is a terrible picture—a little modern man, a very little man, with the world, the universe, all nature, or what have you, crowding in on him. He walks in light, and perhaps that's some sort of affirmation, I don't know. But the beasts and the dark that beset him are horrifying. You will never forget it, once you have seen it. Perhaps it means that it is ridiculous that all the ages have culminated in this feeble little creature —or perhaps it means that, in spite of all, man does survive, that he does walk in some tunnel of light and survives thereby. I don't really know what it meant."

"That doesn't sound like David."

"No. Or maybe we've never heard David," he said.

"And the Tahiti picture opens Friday. Oh, so much to do! That's Christmas Eve, and the tree to trim and all—"

"Elspeth and I can trim the tree. We're lilies of the field," Sebastian said.

So they managed, so they talked, so they got over the moments.

And the next day Sebastian walked with Elspeth in the streets, not buying presents, just walking, and sometimes Elspeth talked a little in a sweet, vague way. And at last she said, "I stop here a little while. Come with me, Sebastian." And they went into the church, and Elspeth knelt, but Sebastian sat erect, watching her bent head, so fair, so beautiful, so loved. They walked out into sunlight and said not a word till they reached home.

And all the time the sorrow deepened, the necessity to speak, and the silence became more difficult to break. Now was the moment and yet when he heard her voice, so remote, saw her bent head in the church, he could not speak.

"All right," Marcy said at night, "you promised. Not here. Let's go somewhere, because I have to concentrate no end. David's coming around here tonight, so we could go to his place."

"If you like."

But when they sat in that charming, civilized, but not especially comfortable room, Marcy said, "This isn't the place, is it?"

"It will do."

"Shall I go see the picture?"

"No, I wouldn't. Wait till he asks you."

"It's odd, you know. David always has previews before the first drawing's on the canvas—and then, step by step, previews day by day. It's odd."

"This must have called for a special bout of concentration," Sebastian said.

"Odd, all the same. Not like David. But then, I am behaving in an odd fashion myself these days. And I wish David would really forget Alice and Isobelle and all the rest and cleave to this girl in Miss Mack's shop. I don't know what there is about her, but there's something. She's not even awfully pretty. But he wouldn't have that much sense."

Sebastian smiled. "Let him work it out," he said. "He might have that much sense. This design business—what about it?"

"I know. I'm talking of other things out of nervousness. I don't want to get to it. And yet, you know, I think of it all day and all night too. But the truth is I've always designed by some sort of instinct, not by reasoning about design. Very vague have been my connections with real design. I've just had a sure feeling that such and such was right, and that's been *it*."

"Let's say you're a genius," he said, only teasing her a little.

"Let's not."

"To that extent," he insisted. "You know, without analysis, what the right thing is. But the fact remains that when the right thing has been decided upon its rightness depends on its having followed certain laws that others have formed on design."

"But I can't talk about the laws, for I don't know the laws," she said. "I lie in bed thinking about seeds and snowflakes and stars—and I get so astonished. It's incredible that just by chance, just by scientific chance, a snowflake is always a snowflake or the stars don't go running berserk—well, life, you might say. Just life. But there's no life in a snowflake, is there? And still it has order, order as old as time, as the first snowflake."

"Yes," he said, "it's incredible—incredible and terrifying and beautiful."

"And then I get to thinking about people—up to a point being so and so, physically alike. Distance from nose to chin same as distance from end of nose to brow socket—same as distance to top of forehead. David told me that. It's almost always the same—almost always. And then why is anyone different from anyone else? They can make statistics from now to doomsday on sex and character and those things, and yet people are different. You can't put them in files and say they will always be so and so because their parents are so and so, because they've been brought up here or there. Or can you? When I think that maybe you can, it terrifies me. But the one thing they announced, as if it were a discovery, in that Kinsey report, seemed to be that there were as many attitudes toward sex as there were women. But *do* we have any choice at all? I shiver when I ask it. *Do* we?"

"I think so, within limits. But some, I think."

"Bless you, for sounding so sure. It might be true that, given a certain stage in physical and emotional development, you love, are ready for love. But whom? You have a choice there, don't you? I mean it might be by chance that it was this one or that one, but still, there's nothing that says it *has* to be this one or that. There's no God that preordained that you see Elspeth at the Gowans and say, 'She's the one. Now you are free to love.' "

She paused, wishing the words back, then rushed on, trying to make this too personal utterance part of her article, putting her heart back where it belonged, "No, I won't have it that way. Life's not that unchancy. Even if a tree can grow out of a little winged green thing that you can hold by the hundred in the palm of your hand—I won't have it that way!"

"It's strange, though," Sebastian said quietly. "It seemed as definite as that. As if something, someone, said, 'She's the one.' "

"Well, no one did. Otherwise, why do people shift and change in their loves? They do, you know. You say, 'Well, life, or God, or what will you? You were wrong that time.' "

He was silent for some time, and then he said, "Was this article to be on love, or design?"

"I don't know. It seems all one thing. I can't separate it."

"Perhaps you're right."

"You aren't helping me. You're just letting me talk on and on. But sometimes I get to thinking you were *doomed* to love Elspeth. It seems like doom—that I'm doomed to love you and never be loved as you are never to be loved, as if we can't help ourselves, and that terrifies me. It does, Sebastian. If that's design, it's from hell."

Now the silence was too long. "Why, Marcy," he said at last. "You must have thought me very stupid. I never knew that."

"Well, I hope I don't wear my heart on my sleeve," she said angrily. "I don't know why I said that. It was just said, as if you weren't here. It needn't trouble you."

"But it does. It troubles me very much."

"It's just that I get afraid the pattern is fixed, that all this pain people feel is ordered for them. Yet I don't really believe that. I said once, of John, 'No, I will not love John. He is for Elspeth, and that is that.' And I did not. But perhaps I didn't really love him at all. Oh, I know it's useless, Sebastian. I know. And part of me says it's right, that I want you to go on being faithful, no matter what, that if you could shift and change I wouldn't love you. You might not be you if you were faithless. I wouldn't so much as put out a hand to take you if I could—and I know I couldn't—but if I could I wouldn't. And yet, if that is the design that has to be I want to scream out that I won't have it that way. I'm sorry, Sebastian. I didn't mean to go into these paths. I'm sorry."

"Come here," he said.

She stopped talking, looked at him, her dark eyes wide.

"Come here," he said again.

She got up and came to him, and he drew her down into his arms, where she lay against his heart, with his arms tight around her.

"Hush now," he said. "I wish I loved you, I wish I did. It would be better, wouldn't it? I feel such warmth for you—I do love you, in a way, but not that way. For you are right, Marcy. I cannot help loving Elspeth. That's the way I have to go, having, as you say, a faithful heart. It is a bitter way, with no end to it. Be still. You comfort me. Let us comfort each other the best we can."

Her face was wet against his coat. "Oh, Sebastian! *Sebastian!*" she whispered.

"If I could change, I would," he said.

"I know."

And no matter what came after, she had this. His arms were about her, so firm, so warm, so loving. She was in his arms, and they were strong and comforting. She had this moment, no matter what. But there would never be another, and that she knew too. This was it. This was all of it.

They sat there quietly for a long time. It was still in the room, but neither was conscious of the bizarre pictures on the wall, of the exotic hangings at the window, the thin, good rugs on the parquet floor.

When at last he spoke, it was not of the moment at all. He kept his arms about her, but he said, "I think you could begin with the stars, Marcy. I think you could walk out at night, on the farm, down to the pond, and there the stars were, thick, fixed, the pattern brilliant and clear. And you could think on pattern, the unchangeable. And then there is the snow all about you, and you could talk of snowflakes—and then imagine the place in spring, with snowflakes gone and the other order, that of seed and leaf and flower taking over. I mean, go from inanimate to animate. Then man, if you wanted to—and then the dress, the dress that came out of all these thoughts. Not insisting that the dress came out of them, but showing it, and letting the reader see how the pattern was insisted on. Could you do that? Difficult, but I think it could be done—and full of poetry and passion too. Can you see it that way?"

"Yes. Yes, I can see it. Thank you, Sebastian." Her voice was quiet.

Then the silence fell again. A car went past, honking nervously in the night. Silence.

It was she who said, "We must go back."

"Yes," he said. Then he lifted her face and kissed her. And

all her life she would know how sad a kiss could be, saying so much and so little—a kind kiss, even a loving kiss, but so sad.

She got up and picked up her coat, pulled on her purple beret, and said, "Let's go."

And he came with her. And that was that.

20

It is too much to ask of any man that he should go through Christmas with such knowledge in his heart as Sebastian Esker possessed. Yet he went through the hours of preparation. He went through that sad night in David's rooms with Marcy. And his knowledge was unshared; the hour had not yet struck when he could say to Elspeth, "I know." For it might be, he thought, that Christmas itself would do for Elspeth more than he could. He half knew that for an evasion, conscious all the time that somewhere there waited for him this final responsibility.

The tree came, and Sebastian set it up in front of the windows, and Miss Hodge came up and helped him and Elspeth trim it. Miss Hodge said, "I have a box—we don't use it now, because of the cat and no children and—oh, plenty of reasons. Wait, I'll get it."

And she came with a box of old German ornaments, a bird of paradise with a beautiful tail, an angel that looked the way an angel should look on a tree, a violin with strings that even gave out a tiny sound, a little donkey that shone like a holy donkey. And Elspeth even handed the ornaments to them, but not with eagerness, not with sorrow for Christmases like the ones at the farm that would never come again.

Miss Hodge kissed Elspeth, said, "Good for you, Elspeth, not giving up the tree!" She went down the stairs, proud to be the friend of these young people, yet with tears on her ugly face. She said to Bessie, "You've been talking nonsense! She's sad, but she's right as a trivet!" But she could not quite shut off the angry tears nor Bessie's skeptical "H'mph!"

And David waited outside Miss Mack's, then fell into step with Fanny as she came out to lunch, and said, "You know, since it's near Christmas, and good will flows freely, don't you think we could go somewhere else for lunch besides that place where they rush you through as if you were on an assembly line?"

"I can't take more than an hour. It's that or the drugstore," Fanny said.

"Then *that*," David said.

There was a new girl who wasn't in such a hurry. They sat in a back booth, and he said, "I'm going to take you to a party, come Christmas."

"I've already been invited," she said, "and refused."

"Been invited? Not to my party."

"Yes. Your sister was in, your sister Marcy. She invited me."

"Why, the sly one! Behind my back! You see I've talked of you. Why can't you come?"

"I'd rather spend the day with my folks."

"Oh, now! Than with *me?*"

The waitress came then, and Fanny did not answer. After the girl had gone David said, "Just for a couple hours you could, couldn't you? It won't be anything riotous."

"I should hope not, with John Esker just dead."

"Oh. Are you reproving us for having a party? You think we ought to preserve the three-minute silence indefinitely?"

"Oh, it's none of my business. Have all the parties you want to. Just don't ask me, that's all. I couldn't come, and I don't want to come."

"That's polite, and very commendable of you—so much family feeling."

"Sorry," Fanny said. "Something about you makes me ruder than necessary."

"I wonder what," David said. "Look, Fanny, if I went to your folks—Lord, what am I saying? I don't hanker after a trip to the Bronx—but if I should go and ask your folks if it would be all right, if they could spare you from the home festivities for a couple hours—make it three, coming and going takes so long—would you come?"

"No," she said. "Of course they'd say to go—Mother thinks you're so handsome, such a gentleman! She'd insist that I go. But Christmas is Christmas, and I spend it at home. I've managed to get a set of paints and an easel for Dad. He draws all day, with T-square and such, but he's always wanted, just for fun, to try to paint without rulers. Well, now he can and maybe—I don't know, but maybe he'll be eager to begin right off. And he may want to talk about it. And I want to be there."

"All right. All right. I suppose you think I couldn't possibly understand that."

"No, you couldn't, or you wouldn't be having a party."

"I have a family too. Elspeth and Marcy are my family,"

he said. "I have a father, but he's never here. He counts only by mail. We've always had a party for Christmas, an open-house kind of thing. And sometimes we've spent it with Elspeth at the farm, and sometimes here, at Marcy's or my place. We've always managed to be very gay. Well, though you think us so heartless, we don't feel so gay this year. Not only because of John, but because Elspeth, who has always been the gayest of the gay, has gone into a—a silence. But Marcy and I, we have this feeling that if we go into this silence with her we'll *all* be finished—that we have to at least pretend that Christmas matters, that we're all still alive and have to act alive. I think it will be our great fiasco, because Elspeth just doesn't care any more, and she won't catch on to life in a crowd any more than she does alone. But that's neither here nor there. We are going to have a party because we *do* know what being a family means. And I do see why you'd want to be at home. It was purely selfish asking you, because I thought you a very steady sort of person I could lean on through all the emotion. And I did think you might interest Elspeth. That's a revolting sandwich. Are you sure you ought to eat it?"

She lifted the sandwich, put it down. She reached for a paper napkin, dabbed angrily at her eyes.

"For heaven's sake!" David said.

She tried to grin. "Miss Mack said it was part of your stock in trade, making girls cry," she said. "All the same, I'm sorry, about your sister, and the party—and everything. You *really* love each other, don't you?"

He looked around, his blue eyes surprised to find himself here, in this hot, crowded, noisy little restaurant, with this girl. "Yes," he said. "We do."

"I'll come—for an hour. You needn't get me. I'll come by myself."

"Why, bless you!" he said. "But I'll get you."

When they had come near the shop again he said, "Why did you change your mind? You were so infernally firm."

"Because—because I know what it feels like not to be able to catch onto life. I know just what it's like. No, don't come in and loiter. We're very busy. See you." And she was gone.

Marcy sat at the desk all night, working on her lyric on design, let dawn, gray above city roofs, find her there. And it was the day before Christmas.

And still Sebastian Esker waited, remembered Jennie Wiggins' face under the dark red hair, remembered her voice saying, "This is all the poetry I have ever known," remembered John, looked at the Doorns, so a part of him, all the family he had, loved them and willed this Christmas to be good for them, yet wept inside at all their gallant efforts. Into these efforts could he walk with his knowledge, face Elspeth and say, "This is it, my darling; this you must see"? Could he?

It was abruptly Christmas Eve, with the tree all trimmed and the lights turned on. Marcy said, "There's David. Are you ready to go, everybody?"

"Go?" Elspeth said.

"Come along," Sebastian said, and he took Elspeth's hand and pulled her to her feet. "Come along. And no questions asked," he said. "It's Christmas Eve, and we're all going out together—*all* of us."

Elspeth made no resistance. She came. And when they came

to the great movie house and saw the glittering sign, *The Island*, she made no sign that the word meant anything to her at all. Then, with no breath left in the rest of them, who had feared this would not happen, that at the end she would not come with them, they were inside, they were sitting side by side. They were here.

The Island. It wasn't one of those glamorous South Sea tales at all. It wasn't full of sarongs and beautiful brown girls and scenery. It was just the story of a young man who chanced to go to Tahiti on a job and took his children with him, because his wife was dead and he always kept his children with him. And with his own hands he built himself a house such as the natives lived in. And all the time he was trying to keep his little family a family. He kept them at their lessons, and he kept on making their home America, keeping their roots there, no matter how enchanted the children were with this strange place. Yet he took them on little expeditions and he told them stories of the island, and somewhere along the way he told them the story of "The Blink-eyed Pig," and there was the little song the old woman in the story sang:

* * *

It's the little wee fish,
In the bunched coral,
In the branched coral . . .

And there was even a Christmas in it, and the man trying to make an American Christmas in a house on stilts. And the man did not fall in love with a woman on the island, either. It was all about this small family. And there was joy in it and sorrow too. The Christmas, with only palm branches for the tree, was one of the saddest scenes ever put on a screen.

Yet it was beautiful. And the music was right, just right. And they thought of John, and it seemed unbearable and at the same time comforting, and right for Christmas Eve.

They came out into the brightly lighted street, and the spell still hung over them, so that they were halfway home before they even spoke. Even then they did not speak of *The Island*, but of other things, and in quiet voices. Only Elspeth said never a word. And when they came to their own street and to the church, she put her hand on Sebastian's arm, and, with nothing said, he turned and went with her into the church, which had people in it now for the midnight service. And this time he knelt with Elspeth, even though the only prayer he said was, "He loved you, Elspeth. He loved you more than life."

David and Marcy went alone into the apartment, and David turned on the tree lights, and they sat down together quietly.

"Well, that was Christmas," Marcy said at last. "Christmas —and it's all over." Then she rose and went to the phone.

"You can't call anyone at this hour," David said.

But she dialed and said, "Hello, Isobelle? . . . Marcy. . . . Could you come to our party tomorrow—five or so?"

"I'm afraid I'm all tied up," Isobelle said.

"Yes, I know I'm late. I meant not to call at all. But try to come, Isobelle," Marcy said.

For a long instant there was no sound at all, then Isobelle said, "I'll try, Marcy," and hung up.

David just gave her a small smile. He didn't say anything about Christmas spirit oozing out of her, nothing caustic at all—just the small and loving smile.

"We might as well have some of the cake Miss Hodge brought up tonight," he said. "Hadn't we?"

Neither was hungry, yet they sat and ate the cake, and still did not speak of *The Island.* They piled presents under the tree, said good night.

In the morning they said, "Merry Christmas!"—trying to make it sound right, trying to take in grief and joy in the same breath. Elspeth said it too, though oh, so gently and quietly. She even seemed to like the skating socks and the map, though she did say, "But where can I put the map?"

"On the dining-room wall with the rest," David said.

She sat looking at its blue seas, its fabulous shores, the lovely creamy brown of the parchment. "You look as if you'd like to go there," Sebastian said.

"Yes," she said. "I'd like to go there."

It wasn't too bad. It was just quiet, the most quiet Christmas morning they had ever had. There was one bad moment. There was a package which Miss Hodge had delivered last night, tied with a big red satin bow above a spray of mistletoe. It contained the pictures Eddie had taken at the farm, carefully finished, big, too sad.

And then Mrs. Parley, who did for them on occasion, came to clean up and make food ready for the party. There were the tissue to discard, the evergreens to arrange in the best places, the best dishes to get out, and the glasses and trays.

"Go get your girl, David," Marcy said.

"Shall we go skating while they get ready for the party?" Sebastian asked Elspeth.

"Good idea," Marcy said. "You're underfoot." She couldn't bear to be getting ready for a party with Elspeth's eyes upon her, with Sebastian's eyes upon Elspeth, guarding her so.

And Elspeth wore the socks and even asked for an old skating skirt of Marcy's quite normally.

"Last Christmas you wore the red dress, with a white ribbon round your hair," Sebastian said. They moved up and down, in slow, graceful strokes. "And John lighted the Christmas pudding. We looked beautiful about the table, didn't we?"

"We are a beautiful family," she said.

"You are indeed."

"Sebastian—"

"Yes, Elspeth?"

"I don't know—I don't know whether I can get through this day or not."

"We just have to try," he said.

"I'm so tired, Sebastian."

"I know. We're all tired. Would you like to bypass the party? I will if you want that."

"No, we can't. Only all the faces—I don't want all those faces crowding in on me. You don't mind what I say—I don't have to explain, do I?"

"No."

"In the church it seems easy, or even walking alone in the streets—even here with you. But when the faces come crowding at me it all goes away, and there isn't any peace or anything."

"I'll stick close by," he said. "How would you like to go back to the farm, Elspeth? It's no good here, after all, is it? How would you like to go back? You can be alone as much as you like there. Only would you mind if I got you a cat, or a dog? There *isn't* any place like on the map, you know. There just isn't any place like that. But the farm is very still, and it seems to miss you."

"Oh, if I could!" she said. And for an instant her heart seemed to beat again, to be laid bare. "If I could shut the door and hear no sound and see no face and think and think. I can't get there, Sebastian. To myself—I can't get there!"

"I'll take you back," he said.

Why not now? Why not say: I know. I know all about Jennie and Peter. I know, but it doesn't matter, Elspeth. I know what you are pushing away. I know what you are refusing to see. Yet he loved you. He loved you more than life.

He could not. After the party he would take her away, take her back to the farm. He would take her back to the source place of her grief.

They turned toward home. And the rest converged upon the Doorn's party also—Freddy and Isobelle and Sam and all the rest of the people they had known so long.

David heard Mrs. Drake say anxiously, lovingly, "Now drive carefully," and, with his hand on Fanny's arm, went down the Drake steps to his car.

"You look mighty elegant," he said.

"This is my best coat," Fanny said. "It looks *almost* like beaver, doesn't it?"

"There you go again, trying to establish yourself from across the tracks. Don't you know that's snobbery? I said you look elegant, and you do look elegant, except maybe for that hair-do. Even that looks all right on you."

"Oh, I just do that because it feels neat and I hate bothering with curls. I know it's silly and too young. I didn't really expect you. I didn't think you'd ever find the place."

"Why, I came straight as a homing pigeon. You knew very well I'd come."

"No, I didn't. I think if you wanted to you'd evade an engagement. You'd manage somehow, wouldn't you?"

"How you do fancy yourself as a reader of character, Fanny! I do like your father!"

"How generous of you!"

"Oh, stop it. I'm not being condescending, and you needn't

be either. It's easy to see you haven't much Christmas spirit in you. I said I liked your father. Is there anything wrong in that? And I don't suppose it matters a damn that he's sitting there in the worst possible light, painting away. I wanted to turn on a light somewhere, but he didn't care whether he had a light or not. He was completely happy. It's wonderful."

"Yes, he's wonderful," Fanny said more quietly.

And then they talked of other things. He found out that she had gone to Barnard, just like any girl; that she didn't want to work in a bookstore or teach or be a stenographer; that she liked working in the flower shop, though she didn't make much money. He found out that her two brothers had been killed in the war, and that she was all that was left to her folks, and that somehow she had to make it up to them a little. There was no self-pity in her voice. She'd had a lot, she conveyed, considering what her folks had to manage on. She and the boys had always had a lot.

For a little space they stopped being impertinent to each other. Then David said soberly, "This is important, this party. Think so or not, Fanny, I know what families are. If it hadn't been important I wouldn't have made you come away from your family. I don't even know what I expect of it. We've always stuck together, we Doorns, come hell or high water. When you said you knew the feeling about having to catch on to life again—of course you didn't know Elspeth before all this, you can't know what she was like, and yet I had to have you there. I don't know how you can help, at a party, and yet I had to have you there. It's important."

"Yes, I know," she said.

They walked up the stairs, Fanny's silly hair-do making a shadow on the wall, went into the party.

The party was in full swing. There were laughter and noise;

glasses being raised; talk, talk, talk. It was the noise of party that was to cover up a sorrow. Everyone was feeling he must do extra talking, extra laughing, extra drinking.

Sebastian saw David and Fanny come in, even saw Fanny very clearly with a sudden sense of protection, of approval. He was waiting for Elspeth to come back, but he saw Fanny. In fact he rose from the window seat and went to her and said, "Hello, I'm Sebastian Esker. Just go down the hall and leave your coat there. You must be Fanny."

"My girl Fanny," David said.

For an instant the impertinent small face turned shy; then Fanny went off down the hall.

Sebastian waited. Suppose Elspeth didn't just put away her skates, change her dress? Suppose she wouldn't even come out to the party? The crescendo of voices struck against Sebastian's ears with sudden stridency. They ought never to have asked this of Elspeth. Why didn't she come?"

In the bedroom Elspeth stood before the mirror and fastened the bright pin at the throat of a clean blouse. Her fingers moved like a robot's, and she was not even seeing her own face in the mirror. Then another face was beside her own in the glass, a young face with an impudent nose and eyes of strange honesty, eyes that were recognizing her but that she had never seen before.

"You're David's girl," she said, not even turning away from the eyes in the mirror.

"He brought me," Fanny admitted.

"He's hurt you already. It shows in your eyes," Elspeth said.

"No, that's another hurt," Fanny said. It was such a strange moment, saying such a thing to a stranger. "I suppose it always shows, no matter how you try to cover it up—like it shows in you. I was so sorry, I was so terribly sorry—"

"But there isn't any hurt in me," Elspeth said, and Fanny was in an instant one of the Doorns, knowing that cold fear that comes when the heart is denied. She turned away, walked slowly out of the room. She had come, believing David, feeling some bond between herself and this unknown Elspeth. Now she felt the bond cut, felt only a curious anger.

She was caught up into the party. She saw Elspeth come out, saw the tremendous relief in Sebastian Esker's eyes when he saw her. She saw Marcy talking, laughing, passing food, filling glasses, saw her look just once toward Sebastian, his gaze protecting Elspeth.

And then the party rushed toward Elspeth, and Freddy's high voice said, "Oh, Elspeth, my lovely one! We thought you'd deserted us entirely!"

Elspeth had let him take her hands in his, but then she drew her hands away, looked down at them oddly, said, "I have."

A silence fell. Bessie Hamlin's triumphant glance swept toward Miss Hodge, but Miss Hodge said sensibly, "Leave Elspeth alone, why don't you?"

They began to talk again, but on a still higher pitch. Nor could they leave Elspeth Esker alone. Too long now had she been the center of their parties. They could not believe in a world where Elspeth was not conscious of her own drama. Not only that—Elspeth was the one who made them feel they were *at* a party, who drew them out into greater brilliance than they knew they possessed, the one who set the key for the excitement, the nonsense. It was, "Oh, Elspeth, darling! Bless you for letting us come!" Or: "We've missed you so, Elspeth! Nothing's any good without you!"—trying to be warm, trying to comfort, meeting only that remote, blank look. David watched her with an angry pain, tried to steer people away from Elspeth. Marcy watched with a sinking sensation, aware always of Sebastian standing so close to Elspeth, but aware too of averted glances, of fright, of embarrassment.

"Is there anything I can do?" Sebastian asked her.

"You can call it all off," Marcy said. "It's horrible, isn't it?"

It was horrible enough. Marcy moved away, talking to this one and that, willed time to pass. Once she did come out of misery for a moment. She saw Isobelle standing by the tree, looking at the decorations. She had an impulse to go to her and say: It is Christmas. She says you are pure loneliness—and last night we saw *The Island.* Oh, let us be friends after all, for you were right, Isobelle, and her mind is changed!

She did not, but she went to Isobelle and said, "Miss Hodge brought us the angel and the bird of paradise and all those odd, old ones. Aren't they lovely?"

"Enchanting," Isobelle said.

Sebastian saw no one but Elspeth. He was not conscious of any particular person there, only that there were too many people, and all pushing at Elspeth. He ought never to have let her suffer this. She looked completely lost, a lost soul, unable to be one of the crowd. He kept near her, answered people when he could.

And they might have got through it but that someone said, "Couldn't we drink a toast to John? May we, Elspeth?"

Elspeth turned and looked into the mirror back of her. They all saw her do it, saw her stand there, not as if looking at her own face but at all their faces blurred together. She turned back very slowly, and Sebastian knew that this was too much, that she could bear no more. He hardly heard her say,

"What are you all doing here?" He was walking swiftly down the hall, opening the closet door, taking out Elspeth's fur coat. He went back to a room where no one was speaking and where Elspeth stood alone, at bay, with back to the mirror. He went straight to her, put the coat around her shoulders, said, "Come on!" in a sharp voice of command. She didn't move, and he said again, "Come!"—drew her away through the crowd, past all the faces. When he came to David he said, "Your car keys, please"—again sharply. David took them out and handed them to him.

And Elspeth came with him, blindly, past all the curious eyes, the hands that held glasses waiting for the unsaid toast, the girl with the honest eyes, down the stairs, beside Sebastian, and out into the cold dusk.

"Get in," Sebastian said angrily. "We're going home."

21

It was strange how quiet came to the party with the going of Sebastian and Elspeth, how no one had to laugh any more, how difficult it became to say anything at all. Almost all together they went away. "Lovely party." "Good night." "Good night."

"I'll come along with you, Isobelle," Freddy said.

"Of course I can't afford a taxi," David said, "but I'm going to. Be back, Marcy."

"I thought you were off Marcy," Freddy said.

"I was," Isobelle said.

"Ghastly about Elspeth," Freddy said.

"She'll come out of it." Isobelle's voice sounded thin to herself on the night air.

"I doubt it."

She did not answer. Freddy went on talking, but she did not even hear him. Had it been only yesterday that she had stood there in her best finery in the snow, waiting for the

Sedgwick Day School children to come out, fearing she had come too soon, too late? Only yesterday? And why had she gone? All the children, so plainly, so fashionably-plainly dressed, coming in pairs, getting into cars, getting into the chartered bus . . . Frank had called Frances "doll"—she'd always hated that so, in spite of that fair hair, that exquisite face. Had she really called it aloud—"There she is!"? No, she'd been quiet as stone. Frances had been all alone. Her hair was still just as fair, almost white in its blondness—plain little blue military coat, a beret. Like the rest, yet all alone, proud and lonely. Frances had everything in the world a child could need or want. Everyone was free, and it was better so. No one could have borne life with Frank without losing her mind. Isobelle had stood there in the snow long after the bus had gone, saying over and over—she was saying it still—"But why was she walking all alone?" She had been saying it when Marcy called and asked her to the party.

"We might go on to the Kendricks'," Freddy said.

"No," Isobelle said. "One party is enough." Then she said, more gently than he had ever heard her speak, "But come in, Freddy. We'll drink one more toast for Christmas. Come in."

And Father Duquesne looked down the dim aisle, thought of the bent fair head he had seen so often of late. It was a pity, he thought, that she was not of the faith. But, in or out of it, he should have helped her more. It was plain enough that she was desperately in need of help. He prayed. If she comes tomorrow I shall say something to her, he vowed.

"I'm sorry it turned out all wrong," David said.

"Yes," Fanny said.

How could she say to him: It isn't the way you think. She

isn't sick. She's afraid. And how did she know that, anyway? How could she know it with just those few words spoken between them? How was it that she was suddenly so sure that it was better to hurt and know it than hurt and pretend you didn't? Yet, she thought, he really loves her. He isn't pretending about that. He's really sad. She wished she had never gone to the party, wished she had never stepped out of her world into that world of the brittle, the beautiful, the glamorous, the *dead*. No, she took that back. It wasn't so simple as that. It wasn't simple at all.

"Do you have to be so quiet?" David said.

She thought of those eyes in the mirror and shivered. "I seem to," she said.

David did not even ask to come in. "I'll see you," he said.

Her mother said, "Why, Fanny, where's Mr. Doorn? You didn't stay very long. I didn't hear the car."

"I stayed long enough," Fanny said.

Mr. Drake frowned, held his brush away from the picture. He was conscious of the trouble in Fanny's voice. Maybe they'd snubbed her, those people. But he asked no questions and went on painting. "I got the sky all wrong at first," he said ruefully. "Now I'm afraid I'll run into the bridge."

"You're getting it now, though," Fanny said. "That's exactly the right gray. And what if you do have to do the bridge over? You can. That's the kind of thing you can do."

"Right, I could. Don't know why I was so afraid to try." And he brought the gray down across the span so carefully drawn.

Fanny's eyes filled with tears. She thought of Elspeth Esker and would like to have cried out to her: Don't you see? Oh, don't you see? That's what it is to be *brave!*

Marcy sat alone with the tree, all the sound gone, everything gone but the tree. She went over, looked slowly at Eddie's pictures, put them down, and then sat crosslegged on the floor beside the tree, lifted the big book Sebastian had given her to her lap. It was an elaborate and beautiful book, about clothes in medieval times. On the flyleaf it said, "With love, Sebastian." She could see as if she had been there his careful effort to rub off that "with love"—out of kindness, out of a heart with no cruelty. It had resisted elimination, and he had written it over again, boldly, blackly.

When David came in much later she still sat there, alone, quiet.

"They didn't come back?" David asked.

"No. He's taken her home, I think."

David sat down with his coat still on. "Christmas," he said flatly.

"I don't know what we expected of it," Marcy said.

"I know. But it didn't happen. We ought never to have brought her from the farm."

"No, I suppose not. I like Fanny."

"Do you? Elspeth didn't so much as see her."

"No, I don't believe she even spoke to her. She didn't take any clothes—nothing. But where else could they go?"

"I expect you're right. We'll have to wait and see. But waiting is hell."

Then he said, unless she wanted him, he thought he'd go home. She wanted him, but she told him to go. He kissed her good night, said, "Call me if you hear anything. I'll be up." And at the door he turned and said, "The tree's nice, you know."

Something in his voice touched her. She said, "Yes, in spite of everything, the tree is nice. And I like Fanny awfully much."

He made no answer to that, just smiled and went away.

So, on Christmas night, the Doorns were separate.

"I'm not taking you home to find peace," Sebastian said. They were far out on the parkway now, rushing through the night. They had hardly spoken.

Nor did she speak now. "I don't believe in paying such a high price for peace," Sebastian went on. "I'm not going to let you pay it, either. You can come to terms with grief, but not by death, Elspeth. You're willing yourself to death, but I won't let you, because I love you and I love John."

"But, darling—"

"And never say 'darling' to me like that again. I might strike you. I won't have it. I'm a human being—as John was a human being, as you used to be but are no longer. You can't say John was a leaf, because he wasn't. He was a man, and he loved you. And once, for a day, he gave all of himself, his manhood, all of him, to a girl in Quagatuck—Jennie Wiggins. And conceived a child, who is Peter Wiggins, a nice boy with red hair. Because he wasn't only a vehicle for music. He was a man like me, with a man's desires, needs. And he loved you as a man loves, too. And I know why you try to block it all off, refuse to admit that love. Because you went away and left him when he tried to tell you—and came back and found him dead. It's enough to break anyone's heart—and it ought to break yours. If you ever loved him— I'm sorry. You did love him, I know that."

He felt he was saying it all wrong. He was shocking her in the way of Marcy and David, when all he wanted to do was take her in his arms and feel her, warm and loving, against his heart. And, he thought with despair, even this was not getting through. He had told her he knew, and yet there was no sign of listening. Or had she moved a little away from him?

"Don't be like them," she said suddenly, but not vehemently. The words were only a sigh of protest.

He came to where a parking place made a semicircle beside the parkway, turned into it, stopped the car.

"Why are you stopping? Are we there?" Elspeth said.

"No, we're not there. I'm stopping because I am too tired to drive. I get tired too." He was, indeed, too tired to hold the wheel. If, even now, nothing happened, he felt he would never be rid of the tiredness. So there they sat for a moment in stillness. Cars went by, bright twin lights approaching, smaller red lights vanishing. But it was still in the car, too still. Sebastian pulled himself together. "Surely," he said, "you are as strong as Jennie?"

"It isn't being strong you need, it's giving up being strong," Elspeth said. She wasn't even hearing the name of Jennie.

He reached over and took her hand, held it tightly. "Listen to me, Elspeth. *Listen to me*," he said. "There's an old saying that there are things harder to bear than death. Trite or not, that's true. It won't be the same world without John, that's true enough too. I miss him every moment. Nevertheless, I've had him and so have you. He's made life immensely richer than it would have been without him. And why? Being a genius was only a small part of it. He was so alive. There was nothing that did not matter to him. He could concentrate, true—but I can see him so plainly, taking your hand and saying, 'Come!' and you going with him, hand in hand, down the road. Even when he was so deep in creation that we couldn't so much as approach him, he came out always to us, to *you*—"

"Don't," the sigh said.

"But I must. For weeks now I've been searching for the thing that made you like this, the thing in my brother John that hurt you so that you died. For this is death that you are in, Elspeth—*death*. And wherever I went, there was the John I knew, brilliant, but loving and kind. I didn't ever find a John who could have hurt you. But at last I found Jennie. I've used those words before—that John loved you more than life. He did. But Jennie used those words to me first. She had John once for one day when they were very young. One day. He shed the burden of his talent for one day and was simply young. Peter Wiggins is the result. Jennie never tried to take John from you. She didn't even tell him about Peter. She went on, though she must have known what death was like too. She knew he loved you, and she wanted nothing changed. But he found out about Peter and felt responsible—it is hard to tell you, but it was only that John was a man of honor that made him ever see Jennie again, ever speak to her. He put money in the bank for Peter. But he is the one who told Jennie that he loved you more than life. How would you like to have been Jennie all these years? How would you have liked that?"

Did her hand tremble in his? "Take me home, Sebastian," she said in a whisper. "Take me home."

He took his hand away, started the car. "At least she's proud," he said. "Jennie's proud that she had one day of John—even if she has learned that you can't take any day out of a life and leave it set apart. And did *you* marry John just for the glory? Or because he was a human being who could love and take love? Answer me."

"But I told you!" And now there was something of real protest in her voice. "I told you—you have to get past the human. *You have to!*"

"Why do you have to?"

"You have to," she said again.

"You were human enough to shiver when you saw Jennie's car," he said.

But it was no use. She would not respond. All this awful effort, for this! And presently, she put her head against his shoulder and slept. He drove steadily on through the night, aware of her head there against him, aware of her slight body so close, aware of his own failure, of helplessness. If, from all he had said, there came nothing, then she was gone too far away from them ever to come back. And yet his heart kept yearning over her, trying to find words that would get to her. He kept seeing her face at the party, millions of miles away from the people around her, lost, damned. It had been real love that Marcy and David gave her, and she had rejected it. Peace was something that came after pain, it wasn't a denial of pain. But what was there now to say? He had given her the gift of his knowledge, and she had rejected that too.

At a few minutes after nine he stopped the car at the side of the house, dark and lonely in the night. "We're here, Elspeth," he said gently.

She lifted her head, said only, "Oh," and got out of the car and moved toward the door.

But it was Sebastian who took the key down, opened the door, turned on the light. Elspeth stood there, a stranger in her own house, though it was here she had wanted to be. Sebastian put his hands to the shoulders of her fur coat, drew it off quietly. "Go up and put on something else," he said. "I'm tired of seeing you in that skirt and blouse. I'll try to find something for supper, though I don't suppose there's much here. And I'll get a fire going in the fireplace."

With the same still face she moved away from him and up the stairs. He turned up the thermostat, went to the kitchen, and looked at the shelves. There were spaghetti and meatballs in a can. He lifted the can down slowly. It didn't seem the right food for Christmas night. He put the coffee on. He opened the can and found a pan to put the contents into. The thought of food sickened him, and he felt his preparations useless. *Come back, oh, come back, Elspeth!*

He turned the fire low under the spaghetti and went down the cellar stairs after wood. In the dim, old-fashioned cellar with the dirt floor he stood still, staring at the woodpile. He thought oddly of Marcy and her talk of design. And this was the design of his life, that he should be standing here in this cellar, thousands of miles from his job, and waiting for Elspeth? Yes, this was the design. This was it. Because he was human, not an intellectual machine. He was human, like John. And, standing there in the cellar, he was suddenly sure as he had never been before that he *knew* his brother John.

He filled his arms with wood and started up the stairs. He was passing through the kitchen when he heard the crash, fearful, crazy loud in the stillness, the sound of glass breaking and blows sounding. He dropped the wood and almost fell over a chunk as he ran toward the living room. And there was Elspeth, tongs in hand, striking at the Florentine mirror that had always hung there between the windows. She had taken off the skirt and blouse, as ordered, and put on a red housecoat with a wide, swirling, quilted skirt—a fantastic costume for death. The hanger gave way, and the mirror fell, and the glass sparkled against the carpet, and Sebastian called out, "Elspeth! Elspeth! In God's name, what are you doing?"

And she dropped the tongs and turned and held out her hand, from which blood dripped. She looked at her hand and said, "Get me a towel."

He ran for a towel, water, bound up her hand, all the time aware with something of a fierce gladness under his fright, of the voice in which she had said, "Get me a towel." Such an ordinary thing to say, so sane! She held her hand still while he bound it up, but as soon as he had finished she dropped down on the stool in front of the hearth, put her head down, and began to cry. He sat beside her, his heart pounding with his fright, pulled her against him, and she wept and wept, without talking, such sobs as he had never known were in her. Nor did he tell her not to grieve this time. He simply held her, let her weep, and, for all he was not a religious man, saying "Thank God! Thank God!" over and over. He thought he smelled the spaghetti burning, but he did not move.

At last she lay still in his arms. She put up a hand to his face, drew it away, said, "Oh, John, John!"

He did not make her explain her act. He only knew that this was Elspeth in his arms, no stranger, a woman grieving for her husband. It was Elspeth, whom he too loved more than life.

They were still sitting there when the door opened and someone called out, "Anyone home? Are you here, Elspeth?" And Marie Dudevant appeared in the doorway, a scarf tied bunchily around her head, snow on her shoulders, her face red, in her arm a loaf of bread wrapped in a towel. "Saw the light," she began, then took in the glass, the wood, Elspeth's tearstained face. "What's happened? Oh, honey, you're not hurt?"

Elspeth got up, not even wiping her face, went toward Marie, saying, "Not a bit. Oh, *Marie!*" She kissed her and said again, "Oh, Marie! How good of you to come! I just broke a mirror, that's all. And you've brought bread, bless you! It's so awful, right at first. Take that dreadful scarf off—I'll get you a new one—and we'll have some toast and coffee. Watch where you step."

"You scared the living daylights out of me," Marie said. "Sit down. I'll put the toast in." She pulled the pan off the stove.

"Wait," Elspeth said. "Wait till I call Marcy."

Sebastian got the number for her, went out to the kitchen with Marie. Marie gave him a warm smile and went on making toast. They could hear Elspeth's voice clearly: "Hello, Marcy. Just wanted to say good night. . . . You hadn't gone to bed, had you? . . . Yes, where else? It's snowing here. Lovely. . . . Yes, he's here—Marie too. We're just going to have coffee. I wish you were here too. . . . Come for New Year's if you can. . . . Good night, darling."

So usual, so loving, the voice she always had for them, wanting to hear their voices for good night or good morning; a brave voice like—like Jennie's, able for life. So *usual!*

Then Elspeth was walking to the sill, picking up a pot of geraniums with her good hand. "How wicked! I forgot the geraniums," she said.

"I've got a lot of slips I can give you," Marie said.

On New Year's they walked home across the snowy meadow from the pond. It was night, but there was a bright moon, and the snow was very white.

"You know," Fanny Drake said to Marcy, her voice rough with embarrassment, "I didn't think you were like this."

"Like what?"

"Like a *family*. David told me, but I suppose I didn't believe him. You seemed so awfully *worldly* to me."

"We are worldly. But we're a family too—of course we are."

"Yes, I see you are. The other Mr. Esker loves your sister too, doesn't he?"

"Yes." The voice was quite calm and friendly. "I expect someday he'll marry her—someday."

Then David called out from behind them, "You might carry a shovel, Fanny!" She paused, took a shovel obediently. "I wouldn't want you to think I was going to carry all the luggage," David said.

"You should bring a porter along, or train a dog team," she told him.

"I like that last one. That sounds right to me. Need a flashlight, Marcy?"

"No," Marcy called back. "I've got cat's eyes."

So Marcy walked alone, ahead of the rest of them. Elspeth and Sebastian walked more slowly.

"In spite of everything, it's been a good day," Sebastian said.

She turned to him in sudden concern. "Are you getting rested?" she asked.

"Yes."

"John always said we put all our troubles on you. We do, don't we? I'm glad he didn't hear you say, 'I get tired too.' I'll never forget that. Have you got money enough to get you back to Paris?"

"By skimping—I think so."

"Then go, darling, and soon. We can stand on our own feet now."

He gave her a quick smile, but she was not looking at him. "I didn't know you even heard me say I got tired too," he said.

"Well, I did. It was the first thing I'd heard, with all of me, for a long, long time. There's nothing I could do for Peter, is there?"

"No, he has all he needs."

"Do you think John would want me to know him? Do you think John would have wanted me to try?"

"I don't know."

"If I could only ask him!"

His hand tightened on her arm, but he made no reply.

"It was right here I walked," she said with sudden passion. "Right here. 'Then it's all been a lie!' I said, and I walked out here and down to the pond through the leaves. That was the last thing I ever said to John. Oh, Sebastian, how can I ever live with that? How can I?"

"You can because you have to," he said.

"Yes, because I have to. You must all forgive me because I haven't been able to these last weeks. But I can't ask John to forgive me. I can't tell him how much I love him—nor that I know he loved me. You'll write to me, won't you?"

"Of course."

"And you'll come back in the summer?"

"Yes, I'll come back."

"You're so different—and yet it's almost like talking to John when I talk with you. You help me over the rough spots, as he always did. He used to say, 'The Doorns and the Eskers—we aren't the whole world.' It's taken me a long time to find out he was right. When I think of the things I can't ever tell him! I want to tell him that about hope for a tree, that it will sprout again even if cut down. You see, even if

I was truly mad, I've learned something. It hasn't all been a dream."

"I never thought it was."

"And another thing, Marcy and David—they've done better without me, haven't they? But let's not be solemn. Fanny's perfect, isn't she?"

"Perfect? That's a big word."

"Perfect," she repeated firmly. "John would have said she was exactly what the Doorns needed. She's got such honest eyes."

They had come near the house now and paused to look toward the pasture, where, in a strip of moonlight, one tree stood out, every twig and thorn touched with snow and light.

"How beautiful the thorn tree is in the moonlight!" Elspeth said.

"Incredibly beautiful," Sebastian said.

Elspeth said nothing about the tree's coming out of barren ground. She didn't even know it.

So they walked, so they talked, the five of them, came trooping into the kitchen, where the little new slips of geraniums stood in their pots on the sill, where the kettle simmered on the back of the stove. They were not wildly gay, because their human hearts cried out for John in his brown jacket; but still they talked, they even laughed, and they ate bread together. And Sebastian looked up at Marcy, with the bread knife in her hand, and thought: How lovely she is. I don't know why I don't love her. I cannot, and that is that.

And Marcy, cutting the bread, thought: It's all over. I never thought I'd be a spinster. I thought some miracle would happen. It's just not going to happen. But she thought too, with a faint surprise: Well, so be it. I feel quite strong, as if I could stand it.

And Elspeth, behind Fanny's chair, suddenly lifted the pony tail of dark hair, twisted it swiftly into a little knot, pinned it down on top of Fanny's head. "There," she said. "I've been wanting to do that for hours!"

Fanny laughed, helped herself to jam from Marie Dudevant's supplies, and looked up to David's thoughtful glance at her, the thoughtfulness quickly turned to mockery as he said, "About time. Fanny's a big girl now!" And she thought: I feel frightened. But I *feel*—that's something.

Nothing in their faces showed that they knew they could not be a family apart, any more than Jennie could have a day apart. Nothing showed that they were wiser or kinder or more humble than they had been a few weeks ago. They looked, as always, one, a family held together in all ways, self-sufficient, proud, and beautiful.